Rufus puts his hands on his hips. "See, this is what I'm talking about. . . . If Lord Harrowmage wants you to guard his fortress, he should at least give you something in return. It's only fair."

There's a low muttering as the gargoyles converse together. Finally, the swamp gargoyle turns back to Rufus and asks, "What kind of thing should he give us?"

"I don't know. What do you want?"

"Mud," says the swamp gargoyle.

"A name," rasps the beaky gargoyle.

"Freedom," brays a gargoyle with huge, curly horns and pig tusks. . . .

Watching the gargoyles from his salt-dusted hollow, Noble wonders if Rufus really wants to see hundreds of gargoyles let loose upon the land. Noble doesn't trust those gargoyles. They're dumb beasts with big fangs and razor-sharp claws. Yet Rufus seems to think they won't run amok.

Unless, of course, he's lying.

SAVING
THANEHAVEN

CATHERINE JINKS

EGMONT

USA

New York

EGMONT
We bring stories to life

First published by Egmont USA, 2012
This paperback edition published by Egmont USA, 2014
443 Park Avenue South, Suite 806
New York, NY 10016

Copyright © Catherine Jinks, 2012
All rights reserved

1 3 5 7 9 8 6 4 2

www.egmontusa.com
www.catherinejinks.com

THE LIBRARY OF CONGRESS HAS CATALOGED THE HARDCOVER EDITION AS FOLLOWS:
Library of Congress Cataloging-in-Publication Data

Jinks, Catherine.
Saving Thanehaven / by Catherine Jinks.
pages cm
Summary: Set in a computer game, a knight is swayed away from the game's
rules by the promise of winning the affections of a princess and ending his life
of torment
ISBN 978-1-60684-274-4 (hardcover) — ISBN 978-1-60684-284-3 (ebook)
[1. Computer games—Fiction. 2. Virtual reality—Fiction. 3. Knights and
knighthood—Fiction. 4. Science fiction.] I. Title.
PZ7.J5754Sav 2013
[Fic]—dc23
2012046190

Paperback ISBN 978-1-60684-546-2

Printed in the United States of America

To Richard Buckland,
who really knows his way around the inside
of a computer

CHAPTER ONE

Noble stands on the fringes of Morwood, assessing the terrain. Spread out before him is a forest of dead trees. They look like antlers, ivory pale and twisted, their barbed limbs clawing at the sky. Beneath them the ground is as slick as a bog. It's a strange color—the color of raw flesh—with clumps of coarse, snarled hair clogging up its clefts and hollows. There are fragments of armor strewn about.

The silence is eerie. No birds are twittering. No wind is blowing. Flashes of blue sheet lightning flicker across the lowering storm clouds, but there's no thunder. The very shadows seem to throb with menace.

Smite squirms impatiently. She's caught in Noble's iron grasp, her shaft changing from gray to silver to a molten, eye-searing white as she slowly and irritably begins to shape-shift. Her mace-head flattens and unfurls into an ax blade. Then it sprouts a spike to become a halberd. When he sees the spike widening into a double-edged sword, Noble reluctantly advances.

It's no good trying to reason with Smite. She's a Tritus—a dumb animal—and all the training in the world won't tame her ravenous appetite. If Smite doesn't slake her hunger very soon, she'll start feeding on Noble. She's done it before. He generally keeps his right hand clasped around her neck, so that her small, scaled head is nestled against his palm like a pommel. This means that, if she wants to bite him, he can only stop her by disarming himself.

And *that's* not going to happen. Not until he's conquered the fortress.

Though large and muscle-bound, Noble treads lightly. His hauberk is made of leather, not chain mail. His head is bare and he carries no shield. From his belt hang only a flask, a purse, and a knife. Even so, the land yields to his weight like blubber; his boots leave a faint depression with every step. They also shed the salt that he's collected on his long and dangerous trek across the dried-up sea that rings Morwood. During this journey, he managed to fight his way through a crystalline labyrinth full of salt devils—leathery creatures that were frantic to suck every drop of moisture from his body. Now, as he moves from hummock to hummock, he scatters so much salt in his wake that the ground sizzles like fat on a fire. He doesn't like that. He doesn't like anything about Morwood. There's no shelter here, and his path oozes a reddish liquid whenever Noble applies any pressure to it. Once or twice, he slips and loses his footing.

That's why he heads for the nearest crop of hair. Before he reaches it, however, a low rumble stops him in his tracks. He can feel the ground shake. As the vibration intensifies, the noise becomes louder.

Then—*whoomp!* Something is blown out of a distant trench on a jet of air and fluid. It's like the eruption of a blowhole. The objects being expelled are silhouetted against the sky for an instant; they're pieces of armor and fragments of bone. A human skull ricochets off a tree trunk.

Noble retreats a step. He does it instinctively, without checking behind him, and pays dearly for his error. Because there's nothing solid back there to support his right foot. A hole opens up beneath it. And when he tries to fling himself forward again, he overbalances.

"*Yaah!*" he bellows, swinging his weapon. Smite responds, morphing into a halberd, her ax blade biting deeply into the rim of the yawning mouth that's trying to consume Noble.

Bloody water gushes from the wound that she's inflicted.

Luckily, she's made the right choice. A sword blade wouldn't have worked—not from that angle. With a sword in his hand, Noble would have found himself sliding down a wet, pulsing gullet toward a double set of subterranean teeth.

But he's been saved, thanks to Smite. He's hanging off her shaft, scrabbling for a foothold as she works her ax head more and more deeply into the lip of the hole. There's a tuft of hair not far away, and Noble makes a desperate grab for it. He misses. When he tries again, stretching every ligament to snapping point, his fingers close around a mangy, fibrous clump that's as strong as braided leather.

Miraculously, he doesn't uproot the hair. Instead, he manages to shift his weight, hauling himself slowly out of the hole with one hand while relaxing his grip on Smite. It's a tricky maneuver. But at last, with his belly braced against the edge of the precipice, he feels safe enough to retrieve his weapon.

He's only just plucked her free when something coils around his ankle.

"Aagh!" He chops wildly at the threat before he even knows what it is. Then he sees that an enormous tongue has shot out of the gaping maw below him. Its barbed surface hooks into his flesh, tugging him toward a ring of teeth and a rippling throat. If he doesn't fight back, he could end up like that bundle of dancing bones he just saw, spat out of a crevice and dispersed across the landscape.

He needs an ax. An ax would do the job, but Smite has failed him. This time, she's made a bad choice, though not a fatal one. She's become a sword when she should have stayed a halberd. So Noble finds himself slashing the tongue to pieces, slice by slice, instead of cutting it in half with a single blow.

The strain on his joints is immense. He's losing his grip on the tuft of hair. As he's dragged lower and lower, he sets his teeth and hacks away until the giant tongue snaps suddenly, like a frayed rope. By now he's barely holding on by his fingernails. And though the severed tip of the tongue is lifeless, he can't seem to kick it off. It's still clinging to his leg with a thousand tiny barbs, weighing him down.

He swings his weapon above his head, hoping that Smite won't make another bad choice. Luckily, she takes on her halberd form again, plunging deep into the side of the hole and giving Noble just enough purchase to climb out of it. He scrambles over the rim, then rolls clear. The hole slaps shut. Next thing he knows, he's staring at Smite's exposed hilt, which is trapped in the ground.

"Smite!" He reaches out and grabs her neck. He strains and heaves and nearly dislocates both arms. Finally, with one huge, muscular contraction, he liberates her.

When he climbs to his feet, he's panting and glad of a break. Smite is no longer hot. She's not even warm.

Her hunger must be satisfied.

"You know what? You don't have to do that," a voice behind him says.

Noble gasps. Then he whirls around, ready to face his next challenge.

He's not expecting it to be a beardless, unarmed youth.

"Hey!" The youth shuffles backward, raising both hands. "Don't point that thing at me. I'm harmless."

"Who are you?" Noble exclaims. "What do you want?"

"I'm Rufus. And I'm here to tell you that you don't have to do this." Rufus peers up at Noble through a thick curtain of hair. "You can stop. Right now."

Noble is highly suspicious. "What do you mean? Stop what?"

"This," Rufus replies. "All this stupid stuff. The fighting. The heroics."

"You want me to surrender? To *you*?" Noble's lip curls as he studies the boy, who's about half his size. Rufus is skinny and pale, with a spot on his chin and a hole in his shoe. His clothes, though exotic, are badly tended. A checked shirt droops from his narrow shoulders, flapping open to reveal a soiled undershirt. His hems are frayed. He slouches. His pants are almost sliding off his narrow hips.

"I'm not asking you to surrender," Rufus says with a sigh. "I'm asking you to think. Just think about what you're doing. Do you *like* doing it? Are you happy?"

Noble frowns. He doesn't understand. Is the boy trying to lure him into an ambush?

"Just look at yourself," Rufus continues. "You look

terrible—like you've crawled out of a goat's stomach."
He jerks his chin at the piece of tongue still wrapped
around Noble's leg. "I mean, is this how you really
want to spend your time? Walking around with a
giant leech hanging off you?"

"It's not a leech." Noble pries the gray, twitch-
ing muscle off his leather boot. A quick scan of his
surroundings tells him there's no sign of imminent
danger. No one's trying to sneak up on him. The coast
is clear.

"See?" Rufus has been watching him closely. "You
can't relax for a second. It's just fight, fight, fight. And
for what? Do you even *know*?"

"Of course I do. But I'm not stupid. What makes
you think that I would discuss my quest with a
stranger?"

Rufus rolls his eyes. His face is extremely mobile
and expressive, though barely visible beneath all his
woolly hair.

"Oh, right. Your quest," he drawls. "You mean the
quest to kill Lord Harrowmage and rescue Princess
Lorellina from the Fortress of Bone?" As Noble gasps,
Rufus shakes his head. "For God's sake, that is *so lame*.
Not to mention pointless."

"How—how . . . ?" Noble is horrified. He's been
betrayed! But by whom?

"Have you actually met this woman?" Rufus
demands. "How do you know she even *wants* to be
rescued?"

Noble can't speak. Instead, he swallows. Smite is twisting with impatience in his grip.

"If I were you, I'd start looking at the bigger picture," says Rufus, folding his arms. "I mean, what's going to happen if you stop fighting? Is anyone going to be worse off? I don't think so."

Noble can't suppress a short, bitter laugh. "*I'll* be worse off," he growls. "If I stop fighting, I'll die." He has no doubts on that score.

Rufus, however, isn't persuaded. "How do you know?" he asks.

"I know."

"How? Who told you?"

"Lord Harrowmage is as pitiless as he is cruel," Noble insists. "He'll not rest until I'm dead."

"How do you know?"

"Because he's trying to kill me!" Noble makes a sweeping gesture with his free hand. "Are you blind? This place is a death trap! The very earth would swallow me up, if it could!"

"So why are you here, then?" When Noble doesn't immediately respond, Rufus adds, "Why don't you just leave?"

"Ah." Noble has a flash of insight. This must be a tactical maneuver. He's familiar with such things. "I understand now," he declares, tightening his grip around Smite's neck. "You serve Lord Harrowmage. You're one of his minions. You want to turn me back."

"Oh, please." Rufus snorts. "Do I *look* like I belong here?"

It's a good question. When Noble stops to reflect on the matter, he realizes that Rufus does seem out of place. There's something about the boy that sets him apart. It's more than just his peculiar clothes, or his odd manner of speaking. Is it the texture of his skin? The density of his color shadings?

"I'm not a part of this program," Rufus reveals. "I'm a visitor, just passing through. And I'm here to set you free."

To Noble, this seems ludicrous. "I'm no captive. The princess is imprisoned, not I."

"Are you sure?"

"Once I release her, Lord Harrowmage will no longer be able to shield himself. Having no hostage in his clutches, he will fall to the remnants of Thanehaven's warrior clans when they join forces to defeat him." With a grim little half smile, Noble concludes gruffly, "Unless, of course, I kill him first."

"So you're planning to kill the guy?" Rufus proceeds without waiting for an answer. "Has it occurred to you that *you* might be the baddie in this scenario? Maybe Lord Harrowmage isn't the problem, here. I bet he's as scared as you are."

Noble blinks. Then he scowls. "No," he says. "You're wrong."

"Maybe. Have you ever talked to him?"

"*Talked* to him?"

"It's worth a try. We can go and knock on his door right now. You can promise not to kill him if he promises not to kill you."

But Noble is shaking his head. "You're mad," he announces.

"No I'm not. I'm a lateral thinker."

"Talk to Lord Harrowmage? I must *get* to Lord Harrowmage first." Noble points at the horizon. "Beyond Morwood lies the Blood River, and beyond that lies the greatest fortress in the world, with walls so high and thick that no one has ever penetrated them."

"Yeah, but there's a road through the woods," Rufus interrupts. "And a drawbridge across the river."

"Both of which are well guarded!" Noble can't believe his ears. "Do you think I'm a fool? If the road was safe, I'd be taking the road!" Suddenly, Smite buries her needle-sharp fangs in his wrist. "Ah!" he groans, conscious that she needs to be fed again.

And Rufus is the closest available meal.

"See—this is exactly what I mean," Rufus says impatiently, nodding at Smite. "Aren't you sick of being bossed around? You can throw that thing away, you know."

Despite his discomfort, which makes it hard to concentrate, Noble doesn't succumb to such a pitiful trick. "You're trying to disarm me," he snarls, shifting Smite from one hand to the other.

Rufus waves this accusation aside. "Actually, I'm

trying to empower you," he explains. "Because guess what? Smite isn't yours. She's taking her orders from somebody else." Before Noble can pour scorn on this idea, Rufus continues. "She fouls things up for a reason, you know. It's not because she's stupid. It's because some idiot you've never met is telling her what to do."

"That's a lie."

"It's not. It's the way the game works. You're not a player here, you're just a puppet. And you don't have to be." Rufus lets his gaze drift down to the writhing weapon in Noble's hand. "Tell the truth, now. Wouldn't *you* like to call the shots, for once?"

Noble hesitates. It occurs to him that Smite is very much a mixed blessing. Every second choice she makes is bad. Whenever he wants to stop and think, she drives him forward.

Right now, she's trying to drink his blood—and he's not enjoying it.

"You've got two options," Rufus argues. "Either you keep fighting until the dingbat in charge gets you killed, or you negotiate a truce with Lord Harrowmage and decide what you want to do with the rest of your life. Because then you'll actually *have* a life." Rufus flashes a sudden, irrepressible grin. "Bit of a no-brainer, really."

Something clicks inside Noble's head. It's an odd feeling, as if a door has swung open. The whole world seems to shift sideways.

He's barely conscious of Smite's gnawing teeth.

11

"Smite speaks to no one," he finally says. "How can she be serving two masters?"

Rufus shrugs. "She's not. She's serving one master. And it isn't you."

Noble can almost believe this. For some deep, unexplored reason, it makes sense to him. "But how?" he asks. "Is it magic? Has someone cast a binding spell?"

"Ummm . . . yeah. Sort of."

"Another mage, perhaps." Noble considers the possibility, which has never before crossed his mind. Suppose he's nothing but a minion? Suppose he's being tracked in the depths of some enchanter's crystal ball?

Suppose his quest isn't really his own?

Suddenly, Smite chomps down hard, derailing this train of thought. "Ouch!" Noble yelps.

"Listen." Rufus's tone becomes more urgent. "We can't just stand around yakking, or that thing will chew your arm off. What if I get you inside the fortress? Will you believe me then?"

Noble's jaw drops.

"I bet I can do it. Infiltration is my speciality," Rufus assures him. "We'll head for that road over there and see what happens. If things don't work out, I'll be your advance guard. Which means I'll cop the worst of it while you're on your way back to wherever."

Noble ponders this strategy. He's sorely tempted.

"Come on," Rufus wheedles. "You're meant to be

a hero, aren't you? Heroes take risks." When Noble doesn't answer, Rufus tries another tack. "Not that it's much of a risk. Your chances are better with me than they are with your friend the carnivorous sidearm. Especially in a marsh full of mouths." He laughs and shakes his head. "I mean, I'd like to know who dreamed this one up. A marsh full of mouths? It's *seriously* sick."

"Why are you doing this?" Noble demands. "Why did you come here?"

Rufus shrugs again. "Let's just say I'm a freedom lover," he replies. "Power to the people, and all that stuff. You're living in a repressive system."

"And you don't like that?"

"Do *you*?"

Noble thinks about it. He realizes that he's never followed his own inclinations. He's rarely *had* an inclination, until now. Sometimes he's wanted a halberd— and has ended up with a mace instead. Sometimes he would have preferred to avoid a dark doorway or a suspicious-looking shadow, but Smite's raging appetite has always impelled him forward.

"No," he confesses at last, "I don't like it much."

"Then let's make peace, not war!" Rufus cries cheerfully. "It'll be heaps of fun! The only thing is, you'll have to get rid of your friend." He cocks his thumb at Smite. "This won't work if you bring her along. And you've still got your knife, remember— which you probably won't need."

Noble looks down at his weapon. She's covered in blood, and white-hot with rage. Her teeth are embedded in his wrist. She's glaring at him with her beady little eyes as she squirms and coils and lashes about like a serpent.

"I'd like you to stop this," he tells her.

But she refuses to stop. So he yanks her free and throws her away.

CHAPTER TWO

The road to the fortress is wide, flat, and dead straight. It's also in excellent shape, with no weeds or potholes. The cobblestones are so white that Noble wonders if they've ever been touched. On each side of the road, bronze gargoyles are perched atop a series of black stone plinths. The plinths are separated by a thick hedge of thornbushes.

Noble doesn't like the look of this hedge. It's clearly been planted to disembowel anyone who tries to push through it. The dazzling white cobblestones also worry him, because they offer no more protection than a salt pan or an ice floe. As for the gargoyles, they seem to be chained to their plinths. And why would Lord Harrowmage do something like that unless they posed some sort of risk?

"It *could* be a security measure, to stop them from being stolen," Rufus says quietly, surveying the creatures from a safe distance. "But if you ask me, it's because they're not statues at all."

Noble grunts. He has a nasty suspicion that Rufus is right. The chains are long enough to allow some freedom of movement—enough, at least, to launch an attack. Noble can see exactly what will happen if he tries to pass between the first pair of gargoyles. One of them will pounce on him, distracting his attention from its partner across the road. Gargoyle number two will then launch itself at his back, propelling him toward the next pair of gargoyles, which will jump off *their* plinths to maul him. . . .

Without a sword or mace, defeating those gargoyles is going to be very, very difficult. Noble finds himself missing Smite. He's been feeling so odd since he threw her away. It's as if he's lost a limb.

"Don't worry," Rufus whispers. "I can deal with these guys, even if they *are* alive."

He and Noble are crouched in a shallow ditch, peering through a screen of thorns. The road begins where the dry sea ends, so there's a lot of windblown salt scattered around. Perhaps that's why all the nearby undergrowth looks so sparse and sickly. Even the ground is more gray than purple, as if the salt is slowly killing it.

Could the giant mouths be staying shut because

they don't like salt? Or is Noble still alive because he's taken off his boots?

According to Rufus, Morwood has been cleverly designed to kill Noble. But there could be a flaw in what Rufus describes as the software. It's possible that the giant mouths haven't been programmed to recognize Noble with bare feet. "In other words," Rufus says as they set off, "you may not trigger the usual subroutines if there's something different about you." It seems to have been good advice, because no holes have appeared since Noble threw his boots away.

Rufus is still wearing shoes, though. "*I'm* not the target, so I don't have to worry about being gobbled up," he tells Noble. "I don't even belong here." It's an argument that he uses again as he prepares to approach the gargoyles. "Chill out," he says. "I'll be fine. They won't know what to do with me. I'm not a part of their program paradigm."

"Maybe I should come with you."

"Nah. Not yet. Just wait," says Rufus. Then he stands up and lopes toward the nearest gargoyle, raising his voice to address it in a friendly, cheerful tone. "Hey! How's it going?" he cries. "My name's Rufus, and I'm here to set you free!"

The gargoyles are all sitting like dogs, with their back legs neatly folded. Even from his sheltered vantage point, Noble can see a variety of tails and crests and ears and snouts. Some of the gargoyles resemble toads, with their wide mouths, bulging eyes, and warty skin. Some have goatish horns and beards. Some are squat and thickly muscled; while others are so skinny that their scales cling like wet fabric to every rib and joint. Yet despite these differences, each gargoyle is exactly the same size and color. Each has four legs, two wings, one head, sharp claws, and many teeth.

They also have yellow eyes. Noble sees this when dozens and dozens of eyelids flick open at the sound of Rufus's greeting. Although there are no other movements, it's as if the gargoyles have snapped to attention.

"You sure look uncomfortable," Rufus continues, gazing down the avenue of gargoyles. "How would you like to get rid of those chains and collars? You must be so sick of them. I bet you'd all be having a *much* better time if you could fly around and do whatever you want."

Noble gasps. He can't believe what he just heard. Is Rufus seriously offering to *release the gargoyles*?

Even the gargoyles seem surprised. Every scaly head within earshot swings toward Rufus.

"If I had a pair of bolt cutters, I'd snip through your chains right now," Rufus adds. "The trouble is, I don't have bolt cutters and I'm not very strong. So I was thinking I might ask Lord Harrowmage to release you. He's probably got a key tucked away somewhere."

The nearest gargoyle opens its mouth and croaks, "Why do you want to set us free?"

Rufus shrugs. "I won't if you'd rather stay chained

up," he says. "But I figure it must be hard having wings when you can't even use them."

A kind of rustle disturbs the ranks of chained gargoyles. Noble senses that a message is quietly passing from plinth to plinth. Then another gargoyle speaks up.

"Lord Harrowmage will never let us go," it declares in a creaky voice. "We're here to guard his fortress."

"Yeah, okay—but do you *want* to guard his fortress? Are you *happy* sitting here like this, day after day, staring at one another?" When there's no reply, Rufus answers his own question. "Of course not. You wouldn't be chained up if you were happy. You'd be off chasing pigeons around a castle roof, or something."

Some of the gargoyles sigh. One gurgles, "Not me. I'm a swamp gargoyle. I like mud, not roofs."

"Oh, yeah? I didn't know there were different gargoyle habitats." Rufus sounds genuinely interested. "So what's your name, then?"

"My name?" says the swamp gargoyle.

"Yeah. You've got a name, haven't you? Mine's Rufus."

The swamp gargoyle looks mystified.

"Come on," Rufus presses. "You *must* have a name. What do your friends call you?" He glances around at the other gargoyles. "What do you guys call him?"

"Nothing," answers a gargoyle with a beaky snout. "We call him nothing."

"Well, he's not nothing. And neither are you."

Rufus puts his hands on his hips. "See, this is what I'm talking about. Everyone deserves to have a name. Everyone's entitled to life, liberty, and the pursuit of happiness. If Lord Harrowmage wants you to guard his fortress, he should at least give you something in return. It's only fair."

There's a low muttering as the gargoyles converse together. Finally, the swamp gargoyle turns back to Rufus and asks, "What kind of thing should he give us?"

"I don't know. What do you want?"

"Mud," says the swamp gargoyle.

"A name," rasps the beaky gargoyle.

"Freedom," brays a gargoyle with huge, curly horns and pig tusks.

"Right on." Rufus lifts his clenched fist in a brief salute. "I hear you. And guess what? Lord Harrowmage can give you all those things. But first, I've got to talk to him."

The gargoyles hesitate. At last one of them says, "Why?"

"So *you* can talk to him." Rufus is obviously hoping that this will satisfy the gargoyles, but they still seem confused. "Okay, look," he argues patiently. "Does Lord Harrowmage often come out here to chat with you?"

"No."

"No."

"He never leaves his fortress," the swamp gargoyle volunteers.

"Exactly! And if he won't come out, you'll have to go in. But you can't go anywhere while you're chained up. Which is why I have to speak to Lord Harrowmage myself." Rufus spreads his hands. "Let me through, and I'll set you free, okay? It's that simple."

Watching the gargoyles from his salt-dusted hollow, Noble wonders if Rufus really wants to see hundreds of gargoyles let loose upon the land. Noble doesn't trust those gargoyles. They're dumb beasts with big fangs and razor-sharp claws. Yet Rufus seems to think they won't run amok.

Unless, of course, he's lying.

"You want us to grant you passage?" the beaky gargoyle asks Rufus. "So you can tell Lord Harrowmage to unchain us?"

"Yes." Rufus nods.

"But why would he do that?" inquires another, cannier gargoyle. "If he's chained us up, why would he want to let us go?"

"Because he won't need guards anymore. Once I've talked to him, the fighting will stop, and everyone can enjoy themselves." Suddenly, Rufus spins around and beckons to Noble. "My friend and I have come here to discuss peace terms. That's why there are going to be so many changes. Hey, Noble! Stand up!"

Slowly, reluctantly, Noble rises to his feet. The instant he reveals himself, the gargoyles unfold their wings as if they're raising their hackles.

"The Slayer!" a gargoyle hisses from somewhere down the line. "The Slayer is our foe!"

"Not anymore, he's not," Rufus promises. "He's sick of fighting. He's come here to surrender."

Noble swallows. But he holds his tongue.

"I mean, just look at the poor guy." Rufus waves a careless hand. "He's lost his boots. He's not even armed."

"He has a knife," the canny gargoyle points out.

"You're right. He does." After a moment's thought, Rufus offers a solution. "What if I ask him to throw it away? Would that make you trust him?"

Noble is becoming more and more disturbed by this ploy—if it *is* a ploy. He realizes, however, that it's too late to back out now. He has no boots, no Smite, no plans for a strategic withdrawal. Following Rufus is his only option.

"It'll be an act of good faith," Rufus is saying. "Come on, guys. I'm not going in without Noble. And if I don't go in, you don't get your freedom. It's that simple." As the gargoyles begin to consult one another in a low, thick, disconcerted buzz, he leans toward Noble and whispers, "You won't need that knife, I guarantee. This is much easier than I expected."

"You're really going to unchain them?"

"Of course! Why not?" Sensing Noble's lack of enthusiasm, Rufus adds quietly, "I'm not making this up, you know. I believe in a better world for everyone. Including the nameless goons doing all the scut work."

Suddenly, a deep, hoarse voice breaks into their conversation. The curly-horned gargoyle at the head of the line has turned to address Noble.

"If you cast off your knife and swear on the Tombs of the Seven Scryers that you won't harm anyone or anything within the bounds of this fiefdom, then we will give you wayleave," the gargoyle solemnly announces.

With a sigh, Noble jerks his knife from its scabbard. He tosses it onto the ground and places his right hand on his breast. "I swear on the Tombs of the Seven Scryers," he intones, "that I will not harm anyone or anything within the bounds of this fiefdom."

"Ditto," says Rufus airily. "I mean—same here."

"Then you may pass." When the curly-horned gargoyle dips its head and folds its wings, every other gargoyle follows suit. A ripple of movement travels down the road.

Rufus and Noble exchange glances.

"I'll go first," Rufus suggests. "Just in case."

"All right."

"Not that I'm worried. This is going to be a cinch."

Together they set off, hurrying between the ranks of silent gargoyles. Noble keeps checking over his shoulder, making sure that no one's about to launch an assault from the rear. The gargoyles, however, don't move a muscle. And there's no one else in sight.

"I'm glad this road is flat," says Rufus. "Since I figure we're in for a long walk."

"Yes," Noble agrees. He doesn't say anything else for a while, because he's concentrating on the gargoyles.

At last, however, Rufus begins to exhibit signs of boredom. First, he whistles a little tune. Then he squints at the road ahead, shading his eyes with both hands. Then he breaks the oppressive silence with a question.

"So what are you planning to do with your life, now that you actually have one? Will you go back home, or marry the princess, or what?"

Noble blinks.

"You'll have to start thinking about the future," Rufus goes on. "You've always lived in the present, and that's no good anymore. The future is where you're heading. It's like that fortress up there—even though you can't see beyond the curtain walls, you have to imagine what's inside."

But Noble isn't ready to tackle the fortress just yet. He's still struggling with an earlier suggestion.

"I can't marry the princess," he splutters. "How can I, when I haven't conquered the fortress?"

"Oh, please." Rufus gives a snort of derision. "Whatever happened to dinner and a movie?"

"What?" Noble is utterly at sea. "What are you talking about?"

"Nothing. It doesn't matter. All I'm saying is, you should consider your options. Do you want to start a family? Or head up the troops? Or keep on drifting?"

Suddenly, Rufus stops in his tracks. "Oh, wow," he mutters. "That's gotta be the fortress. Or is it some kind of cliff?"

Noble can't be certain. Only as they draw closer does it become clear that the pale band stretching across the horizon is a lofty wall. At first, Noble is confused by the glossy, uneven surface of this wall. Soon, however, he realizes that it's made of gigantic teeth—thousands of them—packed together more tightly than his own. Some of the teeth are molars the size of barns. Some are long, pointed fangs bundled up like firewood. The raised drawbridge is studded with razor-sharp incisors. Way up in the sky, the crenellated battlements look like a string of gap-toothed lower jaws.

"Weird," says Rufus. "Mind you, they say that teeth are the hardest part of the human body."

"Yes, but I don't think those are human teeth," Noble rejoins drily. His gaze drops from the gleaming wall down to the crimson river that encircles the island on which the fortress is built. This river is much too deep and tumultuous to ford. "We'll never get a boat across there," he announces, edging toward the sheer drop above the churning rapids. Rufus stares at him.

"A boat?" Rufus echoes. "Who said anything about a boat?"

Noble frowns. The drawbridge is up, and there's no one on the opposite bank to catch a rope. So he can't see any alternative to rowing.

Unless they swim, or fly.

"We can't ride on gargoyles," he points out. "Not until we unchain them."

Rufus grins. "Are you kidding me?" he retorts. "I wouldn't let you sit on a gargoyle, you'd break its back! You're *enormous*!"

"Then how are we going to get in?" Standing on snow-white cobbles at the edge of a precipice makes Noble feel very exposed. He doesn't like it. He wants to move. "Is there a rear entrance?"

"I don't know." Rufus turns to the nearest gargoyle. "Is there a rear entrance?"

The gargoyle nods. "Through the Labyrinth of Lost Hope," it answers.

Rufus laughs. "That would be for door-to-door salesmen," he says. "I think we should avoid that one."

"Then what are we going to do?" Noble demands. He can't understand why Rufus finds their situation so funny. At any moment, someone might open fire on them from the battlements. "We can't swim. We can't fly. We'd be mad to launch a boat and mad to enter the labyrinth."

"Seems simple enough to me," Rufus interrupts. "We'll use the drawbridge." Then he raises his voice to shout across the churning watercourse. "Hey! Hello! Is anyone home?" he bellows. "We've come to visit Lord Harrowmage!"

CHAPTER THREE

There's no response. Silence reigns.

"I'm here to do a survey!" Rufus yells. "I have some questions to ask the householder! I come in peace!"

Still no one replies. After a brief pause, Noble raises his empty hands and clears his throat. "I am unarmed and unshod!" he booms. "I wish to negotiate a truce in good faith and without bias! Not a soul will suffer *any harm* if I am admitted into the presence of Lord Harrowmage!"

"Nice one," Rufus says, grinning. At that very instant, a mighty gust of wind slams into them both. It's come out of nowhere—without warning—pushing them backward as it becomes a minitornado, sucking up a whole column of fluid from the river and sprouting half a dozen watery arms.

Noble retreats a step, because he has no weapon. All he can do is run. But he doesn't get a chance to do so before the column suddenly collapses.

A huge mass of liquid hits the surface of the river. *Crash!* Bloodred geysers shower the landscape in every direction. Noble is spattered with goo. So are the gargoyles at the end of the road. So are the white cobblestones and the leafless treetops and the giant yellow teeth.

Only Rufus emerges unscathed. His jaw drops as the wind and water slowly subside.

"Jeez!" he squawks. "What was *that* all about?"

"It was a trick," Noble informs him. "Doubtless, Lord Harrowmage wished to see if I would fight back."

Rufus blinks. "Oh. Right," he mutters. After a moment's reflection, he adds, "Good call. You're not just a pretty face, are you?"

A sudden clanking sound makes them jump. *Kuh-chang! Kuh-chang! Kuh-chang!* "Watch out!" Noble barks. Two great iron chains are attached to the drawbridge, and as they grow longer, the drawbridge descends, gathering speed. The clanking becomes a whirring noise, then a whizzing noise, then . . . *POW!*

One chain snaps.

Noble ducks to avoid its broken end, which lashes overhead like a whip. The lip of the drawbridge hits the road with such force that the ground shudders. Chips of cobblestone fly everywhere. A gargoyle yelps. Dust settles.

Rufus observes, "That was probably my fault."

Noble straightens. He glares at Rufus in disbelief. "How could that possibly have been your fault?"

With a shrug, Rufus tries to explain. "I'd be surprised if that drawbridge has ever been lowered before. I doubt it was even designed to be used."

Noble shakes his head. "It's a *drawbridge*, Rufus. Drawbridges go up and down. Otherwise they wouldn't be drawbridges."

"Theoretically, yes. But not this one." Before Noble can open his mouth to protest, Rufus continues. "Think about it. Would you ever have come this way without me? You'd have taken a boat or tried the rear entrance. You wouldn't have walked up to the front gate."

Noble can't understand this. It makes no sense to him. "So what?" he growls impatiently. "The fortress wasn't put here for my benefit."

"Yes, it was," Rufus insists but doesn't explain further. Instead he indicates the yawning gateway at the end of the drawbridge. "I'll go first, okay? Seems to me that they're extending an invitation."

Noble is so confused that he doesn't object. He just follows Rufus across the drawbridge, beneath the raised portcullis, and into a vaulted passage that's dense with shadows. Noble can hardly see. Though Rufus is only a couple of paces in front, his slight figure soon grows indistinct. The daylight falling through the arched portal behind them seems pale and weak—no match for the black depths up ahead. Not a single torch or lamp is burning to light their way.

Noble doesn't like the darkness. It unnerves him. *Anything* could jump out of it. He's surrounded by whispers and rustling.

"Can you hear that?" he asks Rufus.

"Yeah." Rufus raises his voice. "Who's there? Hello?"

"Come along . . . come this way . . . come . . ." The words seem to be fluttering around like moths, whisking past Noble's ear before he can catch them.

Rufus stops dead in his tracks.

"No," he says. "We're staying right here until we have a bit of light. Otherwise we're going to break our necks." Abruptly, the whispering stops, and silence descends like a candle snuffer. "Why don't you open a window, or something?"

"Windows . . . no windows . . . no windows here . . ." The air is thick with soft hisses. Then Noble becomes aware of a faint, eerie glow. As he looks around to pinpoint its source, Rufus suddenly cries, *"Eeww!"* and points straight up.

Half a dozen luminous grubs are squirming through cracks in the ceiling. Each grub is about the size of Noble's arm. They're shedding a sickly, greenish light that's barely strong enough to illumine all the insects that cover the walls. Most of these insects are very large and flat, like stink bugs with legs. They have sickle-shaped pincers, clusters of red eyes, and a death's-head pattern on their wing casings.

They whisper and rustle as they scurry out of reach.

"Oh, man." Rufus laughs in an appalled kind of way. "This game is *so sick!*"

Noble sets his jaw. He's noticed that the grubs overhead are inching along the passage in a kind of loose formation. "I think we're supposed to follow the light," he suggests. And the insects back him up.

"Follow the light . . . the light . . . follow . . . ," they confirm, their pincers clicking.

Noble tries to ignore them. He stomps after the gleaming grubs, past a series of alcoves. Each alcove contains a suit of armor, though it's not armor that he could wear himself. The helmets are fitted with strange, curling crests. The greaves come in sets of six. The hauberks are long and scaly, while the plate armor includes wing shields, as if the suits have been designed for a battalion of mutant grasshoppers.

"You know what?" Rufus remarks, from behind Noble. "If you were fighting your way through this tunnel, those things would be attacking you by now."

Noble pauses. "But they're empty suits. Aren't they?" he says, glancing back at Rufus.

"Empty suits or not, I bet they'd still attack you. If there's one thing I can always spot, it's a scoring opportunity." As Noble sets off again, Rufus matches his pace—even though Noble's stride is long and

31

swift, while Rufus merely shuffles. "I mean, what with the bugs and the suits and the twists and the turns, it's a classic obstacle course. There'll be a dragon next, you watch. Or maybe a rope bridge over a lava pit."

Rufus is wrong, though. Because when they round the next corner, they find themselves in front of a stiff, leathery curtain that's hanging from the top of an archway. On closer inspection, the curtain proves to be a giant tongue, dried and cured like leather. The grubs finally come to a standstill in front of it. Even the swarming insects seem reluctant to proceed. Noble soon discovers why; upon lifting the curtain, he's dazzled by a flood of light that pours into the tunnel and scours it clean. The insects scatter. The grubs disappear back into the ceiling.

"Wow," says Rufus. "Now *that's* impressive."

He's referring to the vast hall beyond the threshold, which is lit by a truly monstrous chandelier made of bones. More bones cover the walls in a pretty decorative scheme, like swirls of icing on a cake; there are rosettes of jawbones and knee joints, garlands of ribs and vertebrae, patterns of crossed tibia and finger bones. The ribs of the vaulted ceiling are *real* ribs, bigger than any whale's. The pillars holding them up are femurs.

In the middle of the hall, there's an elevated throne made of skulls. But no one's sitting on it.

"Well, this is weird," Rufus observes. Though he's not shouting, his voice still echoes around the huge space. "It's like *Vogue Living* for the Addams family."

Noble doesn't reply. He's given up trying to understand half of what Rufus says.

"Check out the dead plants," Rufus adds. "Are they supposed to match the decor, or haven't they been watered enough?"

Noble is more interested in some of the other items scattered around the room in forlorn little clusters: the warped embroidery frame, the broken spinning wheel, the dusty musical instruments, the half-finished weaving strung up on a loom. Silks and pins and thimbles spill from an open sewing box inlaid with mother-of-pearl. Brushes stand in pots of dried ink.

"These things must belong to the princess," he murmurs. "They haven't been used for a very long time."

"If she *is* imprisoned, it's certainly a gilded cage," says Rufus.

"I hope they haven't killed her." Noble lifts his gaze to the bones arranged in floral patterns above his head, wondering if the princess's mortal remains might be among them. "I hope we're not too late."

"It seems to me like we're too early." Rufus scans the room with an impatient sigh, before suddenly shouting, "Hello? Is anyone here? We've arrived now, in case you're interested!"

A door bangs somewhere in the distance. Noble tenses. He thinks about picking up the golden sewing scissors—or perhaps ripping a shaft of wood from the loom and using it as a club—but changes his mind when he sees how calm Rufus looks. The sound of approaching footsteps obviously doesn't frighten Rufus. On the contrary, he seems happy.

"About time," he remarks, turning toward the throne. There's a doorway just behind it, hung with a curtain made of snakeskin that crackles as it's pushed aside. The girl who suddenly appears is flushed and panting, as if she's just sprinted up several flights of stairs. Nevertheless, despite her disheveled appearance, she makes Rufus blink and Noble gape.

"Oh, man," drawls Rufus. "Disney princess."

The girl glowers at him fiercely. "Are you Noble the Slayer?" she demands, then spies Noble's looming bulk. "Or is it you? Are *you* the tyrant who has kept us imprisoned for so long?"

She's perfectly proportioned, with a tiny waist and a bosom like a ship's prow. Though her cascading hair is red and her slanting eyes are green, she doesn't have any freckles. Her close-fitting gown is made of emerald satin, heavily embroidered with gold.

"Are you Princess Lorellina?" Noble inquires hesitantly.

"Yes. Are you Noble the Slayer?"

Noble nods, dumbstruck. For some reason, he's never tried to imagine what the princess is actually like, though the simple challenge of rescuing her has occupied most of his brain space until now.

"In that case, my cousin wishes to thank you for

coming." The princess folds her arms. "Perhaps I should be grateful, too. But after all your transgressions, I would rather *spit in your face!*"

Noble looks to Rufus for help.

"Who's your cousin?" Rufus asks the princess.

She frowns at him, narrowing her magnificent emerald eyes. "Cousin Harry is the thane of this realm. Lord Harrowmage the Just," she rejoins. "Who are you?"

"I'm Rufus. And I've come to set you free."

"Oh." Perplexed, she points at Noble. "You mean this man is your prisoner?"

"Huh?" Rufus is clearly startled. "No way."

"Then you must be his lord."

"Me?" With a smile, Rufus prepares to set her straight. Noble, however, jumps in first.

"Wait," Noble interrupts. "Did you say that Lord Harrowmage is your *cousin?*"

"And only friend," the princess confirms.

"Then why did he kidnap you?"

"Kidnap me?" She stares at Noble, dumbfounded. "Cousin Harry did no such thing."

Noble is getting more and more confused. "But aren't you imprisoned in this fortress?"

"Of course. I just told you that."

"Then who's keeping you here?" Noble isn't trying to be funny. He's genuinely perplexed and can't understand why the princess suddenly bursts into a peal of laughter.

"Who?" she cries. "Why, *you* are! We are *your* prisoners, my lord!"

"Nonsense."

"Are you calling me a liar?"

"No, but—"

"*You* are to blame! It is *your* tyranny that keeps us skulking behind these walls, afraid to come out in case you kill us!" Upon receiving no response from Noble (who's speechless with shock), Princess Lorellina continues shrilly, "And if you think you can carry the day with your lies and trickery, then you are mistaken. Because I am no peace-loving scholar. I value my liberty above all else—and will fight to the death, if I must!"

She's barely finished speaking when a voice across the room squawks, "Your Highness!" Noble turns to see a squad of armed guards pouring out of another, curtained doorway. He's been so distracted that he completely failed to register the sound of their approach.

"Be easy. I am safe," Princess Lorellina assures the guards, as they spread out in a rapid, encircling maneuver. They're strange-looking things, half insect, half troll. Though each has only two legs, some have four arms and some have six. Their hunched backs are protected by overlapping bands of armor like the shell on a wood louse, but their heads are sooty, rough-hewn lumps.

Most of them are wielding multiple weapons—

tridents, axes, pikes, clubs. And most are scarred like chopping blocks.

Noble immediately raises his hands in surrender, conscious that, without Smite, he's at a disadvantage. Rufus merely pulls a face. "Come on, guys, don't point those things at us," he whines. "We're harmless. Can't you see that?"

The newcomers aren't impressed. "Step away from Her Highness!" one of them screeches.

Noble promptly obeys. The princess says, "My cousin awaits you in the audience chamber. I will take you there myself. It is no great distance."

Noble bows. "You honor us," he replies. Somehow, he understands that this is the correct thing to do.

But Rufus merely frowns.

"You mean we're not *in* the audience chamber?" he asks, as he's hustled toward an exit. "That's weird. I thought this must be it, what with the throne and all."

"It used to be our audience chamber," the princess admits. "But having no guests, we thought it a waste of space. Now we just use the library."

"And you dump all your junk in here?" says Rufus.

The princess, who's ahead of him, stops short. Her head whips around. "This is my *hobby room*. Where I keep my *equipment*," she snaps.

"Oh."

"I like to fill the hours productively." She glares at Noble. "Life in a cage can be unbearably dull."

"Of course," Noble agrees. He can think of nothing else to say.

"I spend all my time in a windowless trap. I never see the stars. I never breathe fresh air." She searches his face with blazing eyes, her small fists clenched, her breast heaving. "This fortress is my spirit's grave. I feel like a hooded falcon, blind and tethered, when all I want to do is spread my wings!"

Noble is so overwhelmed by this flood of words that he can't speak. It's Rufus who takes over.

"You will," he assures the princess. "You'll spread your wings and fly. I guarantee it." For once, he sounds quite serious.

But the princess shakes her glossy head.

"How can I believe that?" she retorts, gesturing at Noble. "How can I believe a man who has blood on his hands and iron in his heart?"

"Because he's just as trapped as you are. Noble isn't to blame for keeping you here," he says. "This isn't his fault. It's the system."

"Then the system must change!" Lorellina cries, trying to inject some thunder into her breathy little voice. And Rufus nods.

"I know. You're right. That's why I've come," he says briskly. "So let's get this show on the road, eh? Because there's an awful lot to do, and we probably don't have much time. . . ."

CHAPTER FOUR

The guards form a tight ring around Noble as they escort him to the library. Passing through a corridor, just behind Rufus and *his* escort, Noble feels as if he's inside the rib cage of a giant snake. There are no windows or torches. The only light comes from two iron lanterns held aloft by the guards.

At the end of the passage is an ivory door carved with ominous figures: disembodied eyeballs, intertwined serpents, rows of skulls. Lorellina gives it a push. She's at the head of the procession, which she leads into a long, low room with book-lined walls and a smoke-blackened ceiling. Firelight flickers on oddly-shaped jars. A high desk is laden with stacked books and parchment scrolls and a mummified bird's claw holding a candle. There's a sextant, a star chart, and a terrestrial globe. Quill pens and ink pots are strewn everywhere.

"Harry?" The princess halts and looks around. "My lord? Where are you?"

Noble steps into the room just as a murky shape separates itself from the denser shadows in one corner. Lord Harrowmage is tall and hunched, wearing a black robe that sweeps dust off the floor as he moves. His dark hair is flecked with silver. His face is long and dark and craggy, with deep-set eyes.

He looks glum.

"I am here, as always," he replies gently but dolefully. Then he spots the newcomers. "Ah," he says.

"This is he," Lorellina announces with a flourish. "This is Noble the Slayer, come to parley. With good intent, or so he claims."

Lord Harrowmage turns to Noble and bows.

Noble bows back.

"In the spirit of peace, I welcome you," Lord Harrowmage intones. "Truth to tell, I never thought this day would come."

"Nor I," Noble answers politely. He's suspicious of Lord Harrowmage, who has all the trappings of a wizard: the books, the claw, the star chart. In Noble's opinion, Lord Harrowmage can't possibly be as meek and mild as he's trying to appear.

"You honor us with your trust," Lord Harrowmage continues with a slightly ponderous, old-fashioned courtesy. "Might we repay it in some fashion? Would you care to eat or drink or wash?"

"No," Rufus interrupts. "He wouldn't. Because

we don't have much time." Ducking around a guard, Rufus suddenly thrusts himself onto center stage. "I'm Rufus," he informs Lord Harrowmage, "and I'm the only one who understands what's really going on around here. That's why I need to take you through this whole scenario, step by step. Afterward, you can decide what your next move will be." He turns to Princess Lorellina. "That corridor we just came through—is it defended? What happens if an enemy agent tries to get through?"

"Uh . . ." The princess hesitates. She looks flummoxed. So does Lord Harrowmage.

It's the head guard who finally answers, in a voice like broken shells crunching underfoot. "The cobblestones boil. Like hot mud or lava. You must pick your way through them."

Rufus raises his eyebrows. "Cool. Okay. So this room right here—I guess it's in a pretty central privilege ring?"

This time, no one answers at all. The assembled company just stares at him as the silence drags on and on.

At last, Rufus breaks it.

"Come on, guys, don't freeze on me!" he implores. "You can handle this—I know you can! You're new generation! You're cutting edge! You've got a lot of *very* sophisticated algorithms in your programming!"

"Rufus." Noble speaks up, at long last. "No one understands what you're talking about."

There's a murmur of agreement. Rufus pushes his fingers through his hair.

"Fine," he concedes at last. "You're right. Let's keep it simple." His restless gaze flits around the room, skipping from bookshelf to bookshelf until it finally settles on a modest little door tucked away between the fireplace and a pair of scales on a pedestal. "What's through there?" he asks. "More boiling cobblestones?"

"A circular staircase," the head guard replies.

"Defensible?"

"Of course."

"Then off you go and defend it," Rufus orders.

There's a startled pause as everyone waits for Lord Harrowmage to object. But he doesn't. Instead, he remarks in a mildly reproachful tone, "I thought you came here to discuss peace terms?"

"We did. That's the problem." Rufus takes a deep breath. "Look, I can explain everything once you secure the access ports. Okay? I swear this isn't a trick. I just want to be on the safe side."

After a moment's reflection, Lord Harrowmage nods. "So be it," he declares with a click of his fingers. The head guard immediately begins to hurl instructions around. Some of his squad leave at once, making for distant posts around the castle. Others station themselves within the room.

Noble leans over to Rufus and says quietly but sternly, "You mentioned an enemy agent. Would you care to tell me who *that* might be?"

"In a minute. I'll get to it," Rufus promises, then waits until all the bustling activity has died down a bit. By this time, his audience isn't very big. Only Noble, the princess, and Lord Harrowmage have remained with him, together with four stone-faced soldiers who are guarding the doors. So Rufus doesn't have to raise his voice.

"There's something you should understand," he says. "This is a first-person shooter game—and Noble is the shooter. Which means that you guys are just bit parts." He sounds apologetic, even though the princess and her cousin don't look offended. Their expressions are completely blank. "What you do depends on what Noble does," Rufus tells them. "And Noble's always been a fighter. He was made like that. But he *doesn't want to fight* anymore. Do you, Noble?"

Noble shakes his head.

"Which means that you're facing a whole new scenario," Rufus continues. "Instead of endless conflict, you'll have peace. Because you can't fight someone who won't fight back. I mean, what's the point?"

"I don't have to fight," Noble interrupts. "I threw away my weapon."

"That's right. He's made a choice," Rufus confirms. Tucking his hair behind his ears, he fixes his attention on Lord Harrowmage. "And *you* can make one, too. By changing your perspective on the world."

Princess Lorellina cuts a quick glance at her cousin, who's pursing his lips and knitting his brow.

"Think about the opportunities," Rufus proceeds. "You won't have to skulk inside. You can get out and fix things—like your river, for instance. If your river were clean, maybe your trees wouldn't be dead. Maybe you'd be able to *grow* stuff."

"I should like to get out," the princess wistfully reveals. "I should like to see the sun."

"Of course you would." Rufus flaps a hand at the nearest wall. "In fact, the first thing you ought to do is knock a few windows into this place. Brighten it up a bit."

"Windows," Lord Harrowmage murmurs. "We could have windows. . . ."

"And I could go riding! In the forest!" Lorellina exclaims.

"Uh . . . yeah. I guess so." Rufus doesn't sound very enthusiastic about *that* idea. "Once you get the whole marsh-mouth situation under control."

"But how can we trust you?" Still undecided, Lord Harrowmage trains his dark and desolate gaze on Noble. "Why have you come to us now? Suddenly? After all this time?"

"Because of Rufus," Noble explains. The answer is simple, yet it opens up a series of doors in his head. "Rufus told me that I could stop. Before I met him, I didn't understand that I had a choice. I never thought of doing anything else."

Lord Harrowmage nods slowly. He seems to understand.

"It was an easy choice to make," Noble admits. "I don't like fighting."

Rufus gives a snort and says, "What's to like?" But Noble hasn't finished.

"My weapon made me fight. My weapon and my own blindness. I knew nothing but fear and pain." His eyes swivel toward the princess. "And now my quest has turned to ashes, because I see that it was false. The princess has no use for me. Our suffering was needless. My quest was a cage, imprisoning us both."

"Hear, hear," says Rufus. "I second that."

"There must be a life for me beyond the fate decreed by others," Noble concludes, still speaking to the princess. "Maybe I can save you after all, by choosing my own path. Maybe I can free everyone."

Lorellina is now pink-cheeked and bright-eyed. She clasps her hands beneath her chin as she turns to plead with Lord Harrowmage.

"Freedom!" she cries. "It is the highest goal and the sweetest victory! Cousin, we must *embrace* freedom!"

Lord Harrowmage blinks. "I suppose so," he mumbles.

"But our bodies cannot be free unless we liberate our hearts and minds," Lorellina insists. "We must dismantle the walls that we built around ourselves. This is our chance to free our *thinking*—we cannot stay trapped like sewer rats in the tunnels of our own suspicion!"

"Good point." Rufus eagerly backs her up. "You'll

never see anything new if you follow the same old path."

"And be assured that you will have my fealty," Noble adds, "in all your endeavours to make this land peaceful and prosperous."

He's speaking to Lord Harrowmage, who looks from face to face. There's a long pause. The whole room seems to be waiting with crossed fingers and bated breath. Princess Lorellina is chewing her thumbnail.

At last, her cousin heaves a sigh. "There must be change," he concurs. "We have no choice. It is written in the stars."

"It'll be change for the better," Rufus pipes up. "Believe me. War's always bad for trade."

But Lord Harrowmage ignores him, addressing Noble instead. "I am a man of peace. I have no quarrel with you, my lord, as long as you pose no threat to me or mine. Deal honorably with me and you will always be welcome here."

Noble places a hand on his breast. "Upon my oath, I mean you no harm and will hold to our treaty," he declares. "From this day forth, let the clans of Thanehaven be at one with the mages of Harrow."

Rufus begins to clap. "Brilliant. Beautiful. So we're all squared away now, are we?" Without waiting for an answer, he briskly changes the subject. "Then why don't we celebrate this momentous occasion by freeing the gargoyles?"

Once again, Lord Harrowmage is scrambling to

catch up. In a dazed voice, he echoes, "Freeing the gargoyles?"

"Since you won't be needing them anymore," Rufus points out.

Seeing the princess frown, Noble quickly explains, "We promised the gargoyles that we would ask you to unchain them. We struck a bargain and are bound by it."

But the princess doesn't seem to understand. "What gargoyles are these, my lord?"

Her cousin heaves a sigh. "They guard the road through Morwood," is his response.

"And you put them in chains?" she demands.

"If they were not restrained, they would have vanished long ago. In times of war, we must all make sacrifices."

"Yeah, but the war's over now," says Rufus. "If freedom is our cry, we shouldn't be chaining up our faithful minions."

"No! We should not!" As Princess Lorellina lectures Lord Harrowmage, he seems to shrink in on himself like a snail. "A new age is upon us!" she declaims. "Every captive should be released! Every chain should be broken!"

Lord Harrowmage clears his throat. "Yes, but—"

"Let *me* do it!" The princess won't let him finish. "Let *me* go outside and free the enslaved!"

"They're not *enslaved*," her cousin protests quietly but crossly. "They're animals."

The princess, however, simply holds out her hand. "The key," she barks.

"Um . . . Your Highness?" Noble decides to intervene. He can't help admiring Lorellina, who is obviously spirited and high-principled—with a bad case of cabin fever. Nevertheless, he can see that she's woefully misinformed about the dangers of the outside world. "The gargoyles are not house pets. Every one of them is well equipped to kill a man. If you release them, you may find that you have unleashed a scourge far more dreadful than any plague of rats or locusts."

"Quite so." Lord Harrowmage flashes Noble a quick, appreciative glance. "It behooves us to tread warily, my dear, lest we come to regret our own generous impulses. There are some actions which, when taken, cannot then be undone."

"Oh, nonsense!" snaps the princess, "You chained them up in the first place, my lord; you can always do it again." Having dismissed her cousin's scruples, she once more requests his key. "Or is there some magic spell that I should know about?"

"No." Lord Harrowmage fumbles beneath his voluminous robes, finally producing a heavy bunch of enormous keys. "There are no spells. Just locks."

"Then why don't *you* release the gargoyles?" Rufus suddenly hijacks the conversation. "I'm sure they'd appreciate a visit from their lord and master."

"Oh!" says Lord Harrowmage, blanching. "Oh, I . . . I . . ."

"Cousin Harry is a very private person," Lorellina chimes in. "And not at all sociable."

"Ah." Rufus pulls a face.

"But I would be happy to go in his stead," the princess offers, folding her soft pink palm around a key. "And I shall begin my tour by stepping outside to unchain those poor gargoyles."

With a swish of her skirts, she heads for the nearest door, making the two guards stationed there snap to attention. But before she can leave, Noble plants himself in her path.

"Please," he begs. "Your Highness—"

"What?"

"You mustn't go alone."

"I have no intention of going alone." She waves a regal hand at the guards. "I shall take an escort."

"Take me." Noble isn't used to monitoring his own likes and dislikes. He's only just begun to realize that he can do whatever he wants to do. But it occurs to him, suddenly, that he wants to go with Princess Lorellina. "I should send a message to the clan caves," he adds. "Perhaps I can persuade one of the gargoyles to fly there with my news."

"Good idea," says Rufus. "Spread the word. A new age of peace, and all that."

The princess flicks Noble a sharp look, as if she suspects him of some deep and cunning motive. But if she has any reservations, she doesn't voice them.

"After what you just said about the gargoyles,

I think a large escort *would* be wise," she finally concedes. "It would also mark the importance of this occasion. So feel free to join us. We should all feel free to do as we wish, now."

"In that case, I'll come, too," Rufus decides. "The gargoyles might listen to me. They did before."

Noble can't argue with that. He remains silent while orders are given for an armed platoon to be assembled at the front gate. He doesn't even exchange a parting word with Lord Harrowmage.

It's Rufus who, on his way toward the exit, tells the gloomy old wizard, "Stay with the program. Things are going to be different. You've gotta take that on board because change is good. Without change, you can't have growth."

"Change. Yes. And growth," Lord Harrowmage mutters.

"The only thing is, if you see something *especially* different—if someone really strange turns up while we're gone—then you'd better sound the alarm." Conscious of a sudden shift in the atmosphere, Rufus adds cheerfully, "It's just a precaution."

"What do you mean, 'someone strange'?" Noble demands. "Are you talking about an enemy agent?"

"*Enemy agent?*" the princess repeats, aghast. By now she's poised on the threshold. "What enemy agent?"

Rufus sighs. "Look—what *I* want to do is set you free. Like I said before. Right?"

"Right," Noble affirms. Lord Harrowmage nods.

"But there are certain parties who'd prefer to keep you locked into your programming," Rufus continues, "and it's hard to tell how they might react, now that you're making your own decisions."

"What parties?" Lorellina wants to know.

Noble, beside her, says, "Not the clans?"

"No, no. Not the clans. Just a bunch of jerks and dingbats. Like the one who was in charge of Smite, for instance." Again Rufus shrugs, spreading his hands in helpless apology. "What can I say? There are always people who try to keep all the power for themselves."

"Then we must oppose them!" the princess cries. "We must oppose those who wish to enslave us in an unfair system!"

"Right." Rufus nods. "Solidarity."

"We cannot retreat now. We *will* not retreat!" Lorellina's voice rings out like a bell. "Hearts and minds are not like gargoyles! Once unchained, they are free forever! As my cousin says, there are some actions that, when taken, cannot be undone!"

"Well, I hope not," Rufus remarks a little doubt-fully. "But it's hard to figure out what kind of stunt these parties might pull. That's why you need to keep your eyes open." He surveys his audience with a lopsided grin. "Because the price of liberty is eternal vigilance," he concludes, "especially when you don't even know what to look for. So my advice is: Stay sharp. We've still got a big job ahead of us."

CHAPTER FIVE

After descending a circular staircase, Noble and Rufus pursue Lorellina into a long and winding tunnel. Then they follow her up a ladder, over a drain, through a series of guardrooms, under an arch, past a privy, and down another circular staircase into the gatehouse. Along the way, Noble catches the odd glimpse of what he might have faced had Rufus never shown up; things that Rufus calls anti-Noble devices. There are murder holes, trapdoors, and strategically placed spikes. There's a net full of cannonballs poised over a flight of stairs. There's a passage dense with cobwebs spun by a million spiders, and another that oozes something sticky from its scabbed walls. . . .

With every step he takes, Noble becomes more confident that he's made the right decision. Peace *is* better than war. He can't imagine how he could have freed Lorellina if he'd tried to fight his way into the fortress, with or without Smite. There would have been too many obstacles. Too many tricks. And then Lorellina would have spat in his face at the end of it all.

It wouldn't have been a rescue. It would have been an abduction.

"Is this some kind of prison cell?" Rufus asks Lorellina as they tramp through one of the smaller, damper, murkier guardrooms. It's full of chains and wet straw. "Or is it where your garrison hangs out?"

"Some of the guards sleep here," the princess replies. "Not all of them."

"Homey," drawls Rufus. Then he addresses the guards behind him. "How much do you guys get paid for this gig?"

There's no response from the guards, perhaps because they can't hear Rufus over the noise that they're making as they march along.

It's Lorellina who finally answers.

"We give them bed and board and clothes and firewood," she says, lifting her skirt to cross an oily black puddle. "That is their payment."

"No money?" Rufus inquires.

"Money? You mean—gold? Silver?" Lorellina sounds genuinely surprised. "Why would they need money?"

"Oh, I dunno. For the app store?" Rufus shrugs,

not explaining this odd term. "Now that they can actually get out of here, don't you think a bit of money would be nice for them?"

"But they are our vassals. Our liegemen," says the princess. That is all she needs to say, as far as Noble is concerned.

Rufus, however, doesn't seem to understand.

"Maybe some of them don't want to be guards," he speculates, not bothering even to hunch his shoulders as he passes beneath an archway so low that it forces Noble to duck. "Have you thought of that? Have *they* thought of that? This whole world's opening up, now—you might have to offer a few more incentives if you want 'em to stay."

"They belong with the fortress," Lorellina insists. No matter how much Rufus argues, he can't seem to get through to her. And he stops trying when they reach the front gate.

"The gate!" she cries. "The gate is open!"

"Yes," says Noble, who's just behind her.

"And the bridge is down!" Her voice trembles. "Is that the sky? Is that the *open sky*?" She points at a patch of cloud framed by the dark, jagged mouth of the entranceway.

"Yes," Noble says again.

A new platoon of guards is waiting for Lorellina in the gatehouse. She edges past them until she has an unobstructed view of the drawbridge, the river, the bare trees, the gray sky, and the matched pairs of gargoyles facing each other across a ribbon of white road.

"Oh!" she exclaims, her voice catching on a sob. "No roof! No walls!"

"No enemy agents," mutters Noble, who's scanning the vicinity of the fortress for possible threats.

"Come!" The princess squares her shoulders. "Advance, Liegemen of Harrow!" she commands, with a grand sweep of her slender arm. "Let us go forth and reclaim what is ours!"

Then she strides out of the fortress into the full light of day.

Falling in behind her, Noble feels a slight sense of discomfort. It may be because he's unarmed and barefoot at the head of a military procession. It may be because he can hear Rufus chattering away in the rear, asking a couple of guards called Flummocks and Sooterkin if they really want to be soldiers. Or it may be because there are plans that need making—and Noble doesn't quite know how to make them.

As Lorellina lifts her face to the sky, he realizes that he, too, is about to confront something vast and free and formless: namely, the future. Once his existence was a series of on-the-spot decisions, with life or death at the end of each one. Now his choices are less clear. It's all so new, he doesn't know what to think.

Maybe Rufus will be able to help him.

"Where is the sun?" asks Lorellina, halting in the center of the drawbridge. The troops at her heels also stop, blinking in the unaccustomed glare.

"The sun's behind those clouds," Noble replies.

"Oh." Lorellina sounds disappointed. "Are the clouds always here?"

"I don't know." He tries to recollect. "I don't think so. . . ."

"How big it is! The outside world. It makes me feel . . ."—she pauses—". . . very small," she concludes.

Noble glances down at her. "You *are* small," he can't help pointing out.

For some reason, this isn't well received. "Small in stature, perhaps," she growls, flushing. Then she points. "Are those the gargoyles?"

"Yes."

"Then I will give them the freedom of the sky," she announces.

As she sets off again, Noble peers back over his shoulder. He sees that Rufus is at the very end of the parade, deep in conversation with one of the potato-headed, shell-backed guards. Noble frowns. He hopes that Rufus doesn't persuade the whole garrison to lay down its arms. Not yet, anyway. Not until they're absolutely sure that the mysterious "enemy agent" won't be showing up.

But then again, Rufus hasn't put a foot wrong yet. He seems to know exactly what he's doing. Noble tells himself that if Rufus isn't worried, none of them should be. So far, Noble's faith in Rufus has been well founded.

"You, there! Gargoyle!" Having reached the first black plinth, Lorellina is addressing the creature chained to it. "What is your name?"

The gargoyle opens its yellow eyes. It looks vaguely like a winged warthog, with its curly tusks, hairy crest, and leathery snout.

"I have no name," it creaks.

"Then I shall give you one." The princess lays a finger on her chin and ponders for a moment. "You will be called Doddypoll," she finally decides. "Doddypoll Scrumping."

Doddypoll stares at her in astonishment—and Noble wonders if she might have been the one responsible for naming all the guards.

"Doddypoll," she continues, "I am Princess Lorellina, your liege lady, and I am here to set you free."

There's a sudden snapping of wings all along the road. Noble can hear the gargoyles hissing to one another from plinth to plinth. The princess must hear them, too, because she loudly declares, "I have come to set you *all* free, for a new age is upon this land—a golden age of justice and liberty!"

"Uh—Princess?" A low voice interrupts her. Dropping his gaze, Noble sees that Rufus is tugging at Lorellina's gown. "Could I just have a word with those guys for one minute?"

Though Lorellina is startled, she yields with good grace. "Of course," she says. Rufus promptly steps in front of her to address the corridor of gargoyles in a piercing, high-pitched voice.

"Okay, you guys—now, as you can see, we've kept our promise. We said we'd get you released and we have. But one good turn deserves another." He shakes his hair out of his eyes and pinions the nearest gargoyle with a glare. "I know you won't be dumb enough to start misbehaving when we let you go. I know you realize that if you start causing trouble, Lord Harrowmage will simply chain you up again. Right? Huh? Are we all agreed on that?"

There's a brief silence. At last, Doddypoll speaks up.

"Yes," he squawks, sparking an echo that runs down the double line of gargoyles. *Yes . . . yes . . . yesssss . . .*

"So I'm not asking you to be good, because that's a given," Rufus explains. "What I'm asking for is a volunteer. We need one of you to take a message to the clan caves of Thanehaven. It's an important message about peace in our time and it's something you should be proud to carry." He scans the matched rows of attentive, scaly heads. "Any takers?" he asks.

After another pause, Doddypoll says hoarsely, "I will."

"Are you sure?" Rufus seems to have some misgivings. "Can you really handle this? Because it's a long way to go and a lot to remember."

"I can go. I can remember," Doddypoll assures

him. "Tell me what to say and I will say it."

Rufus nods. Then he steps back with a smile and a wave, relinquishing center stage to the princess once more. "Right," he says. "Let's see if this works, okay?"

Lorellina takes a deep breath. Brandishing her key like a flag, she tells Doddypoll to bow down before her so that she may "remove the iron collar of enslavement and replace it with the yoke of honor and duty." There's a flurry of displaced air as the gargoyle launches itself off the stone plinth, wings beating, chain swinging. Noble finds himself retreating a few steps, to give the creature a bit of room.

Doddypoll hits the ground so hard that Noble feels the impact in his bones.

Lorellina then stoops gracefully to unlock the gargoyle's iron collar, which hits the cobbles with a ringing *clang*. But before Doddypoll can do more than rear up, wings flapping, Noble seizes the discarded chain. He throws it around the gargoyle's neck and pulls the loop tight, dragging Doddypoll back down to earth again.

"Wait. You haven't heard our message," he warns.

The gargoyle stares at him blankly. Though it doesn't bow its head or fold its wings, it doesn't try to bite or buck, either. So Noble feels safe enough to ease his grip on its chain.

Using his right hand, he yanks the heraldic ring off his left pinky finger. Then he slips the ring onto one of Doddypoll's tusks.

"Take this ring," he orders. "It bears my seal, and is proof that my message comes directly from me. Tell the Conclave of Clans that Lord Harrowmage has received me like a son, because he has no quarrel with Thanehaven. Tell them that Princess Lorellina is at one with Lord Harrowmage, and that they desire peace and freedom for all their subjects. Tell them that the Fortress of Bone has opened its doors, and the gargoyles of Harrow have been released from bondage. . . ."

Noble is concentrating so hard on his speech that he isn't aware, at first, that Doddypoll's attention is beginning to stray. At last, however, Noble hears the noise that's making so many ears prick and heads turn. It's a strange, distant, buzzing sound, which becomes harsher as it grows louder.

Something large and monstrous seems to be advancing toward them down the cobbled road.

"Do you know what that is?" Noble asks the princess, who doesn't respond. She simply stands there with her hands on her hips, squinting into the distance.

"Does it belong to Lord Harrowmage?" Noble presses. "Can you stop it?"

"I don't think so." She lifts a hand to shade her eyes. "I've never seen it before. Is it a carriage?"

"Maybe." Noble can now make out that the thing approaching them has wheels. Its back half is shiny and white, like a tooth, while most of its front portion is made of glass. "It doesn't look like a creature. . . ."

"Whatever it is, it has been given no wayleave." Lorellina turns to address the guards behind her. "Block the road!" she commands, just as the approaching object grinds to a halt. It squeals, chokes, and sighs. Then it falls silent.

The guards hesitate.

"Wait," Lorellina says to them. Noble looks around for Rufus, who might be able to explain. But Rufus has vanished.

Clunk! Part of the newly arrived object—a wing or a flap—pops open, leaving a giant hole in its side. When someone climbs out of this hole, Noble realizes that the flap is actually a door.

"I think you're right," he admits. "That thing must be a carriage. A *magic* carriage."

"Where is Rufus?" The princess glances over her shoulder again. *"Rufus?"*

"He's gone," says Noble. "I don't know where."

The man who emerges from the carriage is short and solid, with slicked-back hair and no beard. He's wearing a long white coat over gray pants; his shoes are as black and shiny as his hair, and he has a square, bland, small-featured face. Though he's very neat and quiet, something about him reminds Noble of Rufus.

"Who are you?" Lorellina demands. "What do you want?"

The newcomer doesn't reply. Instead, he walks toward her, between two rows of staring gargoyles that shift uneasily as he passes. He's holding a small black book.

When he's just a few paces away, Noble barks, "Stop right there!"

The newcomer stops. He studies Noble intently, his gaze skipping from one empty hand to the other before dropping to Noble's bare feet.

Then he reaches into the breast pocket of his white coat and pulls out a pen.

"Are you deaf?" the princess demands. "Did you hear me? I asked you a question." Seeing the newcomer make a note in his book, she adds, "Who *are* you? What are you doing here?"

"I'm looking for a piece of malware named Rufus," the newcomer informs her, in a quiet, flat, bloodless voice. "Do you know where I can find Rufus?"

Lorellina glances at Noble, who gives an almost imperceptible shake of the head. It's occurred to him that this might be Rufus's "enemy agent."

"No," says Noble quite truthfully. "We don't know where you can find Rufus."

The newcomer grunts. By now he's fixed his attention on Lorellina's key.

After considering it for a moment, he makes another entry in his little black book.

"You must state your business," the princess insists. Upon receiving no answer, she tries another tack. "What is this 'malware' of which you speak?"

The newcomer's response is to jerk his chin at

Doddypoll, saying, "Does your cousin know that you've released his gargoyle?"

Lorellina stiffens. "Why should that concern you?" she snaps, shaking back her springy red locks. "Who are *you* to interrogate Princess Lorellina of Harrow?"

The newcomer regards her impassively. Then he flicks his book shut.

"Well?" she continues. "Speak!"

"Thanks for your help," the newcomer remarks. He tucks his pen back into his breast pocket. "That's all I need, for the present."

"Wait!" she cries. *"Wait!"* But he's already turned his back on her. And as he retraces his steps, head down, he produces a very small, flat object from somewhere on his person, tapping away at it with one finger like a man rapping at a blocked hourglass.

Noble removes the chain from Doddypoll's snout. "Go," he orders quietly. "Now. Go to the clan caves and deliver my message." He doesn't bother to watch the gargoyle fly away, though he does feel the air churn under its beating wings. Instead, he spins around and grabs Lorellina, who's about to follow the man in the white coat. "No," he murmurs. "Come inside."

"Unhand me!"

"Look." Noble points at the newcomer. "Look at him. He doesn't belong here."

"But—"

"There are people who'll try to keep all the power

for themselves. Don't you remember what Rufus told us?"

"Rufus is gone," Lorellina hisses.

"Exactly." Noble is keeping his voice low. "He's gone because that man is hunting for him. If Rufus is afraid of that man, then that man must be our enemy, too."

The princess frowns. "Why?" she asks, baffled.

"Because Rufus wants to set us free."

The man in the white coat has reached his carriage. He pauses for an instant by the open door, talking to the small, flat object that he's pressed to one ear. Noble wonders if it's some kind of charm or talisman.

"Quick!" he orders, rounding on the guards. "Fall back! Back inside!"

"But the gargoyles!" Lorellina waves her key. "What about them?"

"Later. We'll release them later."

"But he's just one man—"

"Your cousin is just one man, and he can summon up a pillar of blood," Noble reminds her. Then he jerks his chin at her escort, which hasn't moved. "Tell them to fall back," he begs.

"No." The princess wrenches herself free. "I gave my word. I *will* release the gargoyles."

She strides forward, past the empty plinth, but the man in the white coat doesn't react. He just climbs into his carriage, which then rolls off the road through a chunk of thorn hedge, before abruptly stopping.

"Princess." Noble joins Lorellina beside the next gargoyle. "Let me do this. You go inside where it's safe."

"These are *my* subjects," she retorts. "I am here to protect them. How can I put my own safety above theirs?"

Frustrated, Noble points at the newcomer. "Princess, will you *look* at that man? He's waiting! He's put away his talisman and now he's waiting!"

Lorellina can't resist; she takes a quick peek. "For what?" she asks.

"I don't know. Reinforcements?"

"You there! Stranger!" She raises her voice suddenly. "Go now, before I have you expelled! What are you waiting for?"

The man opens his mouth, but he doesn't have to reply. Because at that very instant, Noble hears a low rumble like distant thunder.

And he realizes that reinforcements are, indeed, on their way.

CHAPTER SIX

The second magic carriage is much bigger than the first. It's almost as wide as the road, with at least a dozen massive wheels sitting under a long white box. The window in front is set high—higher than Noble can reach.

It's amazing that something so big can come barreling down the road so quickly.

"Fall back!" Noble yells, over the roar of the approaching monster. "Everyone fall back!"

This time, nobody argues—not even Lorellina. She lets Noble drag her toward the fortress, though she stumbles a few times as she tries to match his pace. The guards retreat clumsily. Their armor is weighing them down, so it's not long before Noble finds himself closing in on them.

He suddenly feels wood beneath his feet instead of cobblestones. By now, the noise is deafening. Whatever that thing might be, it's breathing hot air down his neck. When the drawbridge gives an odd little bounce, he knows that the first set of oversized wheels must have rolled onto it.

"The drawbridge!" Lorellina bawls. "We can't raise the drawbridge!"

Noble hesitates, casting a quick glance over his shoulder. Sure enough, the giant carriage is right behind him. But the snap and crunch of stressed wood makes it stop; if it goes any farther, the drawbridge might collapse under its weight.

"Halt!" bellows Noble. He has to pitch his voice high over the sound of the pursuing behemoth, which is squealing and groaning and hissing as it grinds to a standstill. "Guards! Fall in! Wait! "

"*Wait!*" screeches the princess. Her escort stops, so abruptly that Noble almost slams into it.

He wrenches the nearest poleax from its owner's grip.

"We have to stand fast," he declares. "We have to hold this position." Then he tells Lorellina, "Go inside. Get reinforcements."

"What?" She sounds stunned.

"Alert the garrison! We need more men!" He can't believe she hasn't worked this out for herself. "If we can't close the drawbridge, we'll have to form a defensive line!"

"Oh. Yes. Of course." But she lingers, her gaze shifting back to the thing on the drawbridge. "It's not moving," she points out. "It's not making any noise." The words have barely left her mouth when a drawn-out *cre-e-eak* is followed by a short, sharp bang.

Noble decides that someone has just pushed open a large door at the rear of the giant carriage.

"Go! *Go!*" he yelps.

Lorellina goes. She flings herself at the guards—who part like a curtain to let her through—then gallops off into the shadowy gatehouse, hoisting up her skirts. Noble, meanwhile, has spun around to face whatever might be about to hit him. He's in the middle of the drawbridge, braced for action and gripping the poleax with both hands. The guards begin to line up on either side of him, shoulder to shoulder in neat formation.

Even without his boots on, he towers over them.

"Whoever you are, you will not pass!" he booms. "Not unless you show just cause!"

In the brief silence that follows, he can hear the sound of footsteps. But he's distracted from this rhythmic *crunch-crunch-crunch* by a sudden burst of movement as a gargoyle explodes into the sky, shooting up from behind the big white carriage like a boulder flung by a war machine. Even though it can't possibly be Doddypoll, this creature looks exactly the same—right down to its curly warthog tusks.

Noble is confused. He watches the gargoyle dive

and bank, then fly off toward Thanehaven. It soars like an eagle, rarely moving its wings. Soon, it's just a dark speck against the brooding clouds.

How could it have freed itself without Lorellina's key?

"Ahem," says a voice.

Noble lets his gaze drop. Then his jaw drops, too.

He's staring at a clone. A double. An exact replica. He's staring at another Noble, who sports his own huge shoulders and narrow waist, his own chiseled features, his own level ice-blue glower and sun-streaked hair. Even the man's scars and studded wristbands are the same as his.

The only difference is that the false Noble is wearing boots—and carrying a Tritus in his right hand.

"What—who . . . ?" Noble stammers.

His doppelgänger seems unconcerned. "Ah," says the false Noble. "So *you're* my evil twin."

"Your what?" Noble is stumped. Who is this person? Where has he come from?

"You've been corrupted," the false Noble declares, striding forward as he adjusts his grip on the Tritus. Noble can feel his own muscles tightening in sympathy. He knows exactly how the false Noble is going to swing at him, because he himself would be doing the same, if he were carrying Smite. Unfortunately, he isn't.

So Noble does something that he wouldn't normally do. He turns to the guards for protection.

"That man is an intruder!" he informs them. "He's the one you've always feared! Don't let him through!"

The guards step forward and close ranks, leaving Noble behind as they do so. They now stand between him and the false Noble, who nevertheless decides to launch an attack. The first blow is just about to fall when a familiar voice rings out, freezing the false Noble in midswing. "Wait! Stop!" the voice cries.

Peering over the heads of the guards, Noble is astonished to catch sight of Princess Lorellina. For some reason, she's emerged from behind the big carriage. He wonders how on earth she's ended up back there; the last time he saw her, she was heading into the fortress.

"You! Stonebrush! Fettle! What are you doing?" She's still addressing the guards. "Are you *shielding* an enemy of Harrow?"

"I'm not—" Noble begins, but she doesn't let him finish.

"A guard's job is to fight our enemies, not to protect them," she continues, as if he hasn't spoken. She strides straight past the false Noble, then breaks through the armored line and marches toward the gatehouse. "Come!" she exclaims, beckoning to the soldiers. "Our enemy has met his match, and there are more enemies inside who must be dealt with."

Noble can't believe his ears. "But—"

"Come with me, you men! This fortress has been corrupted!"

70

Corrupted? Suddenly, Noble understands. She might look like the princess—she might sound like the princess—but she's not the princess. She's a false princess.

"Wait!" he warns the guards. "Don't follow her! That's not Princess Lorellina!"

They don't listen, though, and he doesn't really blame them. Their sovereign lady has just announced that he's an enemy of Harrow. Why should they believe a word he says?

He's standing there helplessly, watching the guards surge after the false princess, when someone else bustles by. It's the man in the white coat, trotting along in the wake of Lorellina's escort like a baggage mule. "Look!" warns Noble. "Men of Harrow! There's an enemy following you!" But only the man in the white coat seems to hear.

He pauses for an instant, his expressionless stare fixed on Noble. "I'm not their enemy. *You're* their enemy now," he observes before calmly proceeding on his way. Noble is left all alone, with a simple choice in front of him: should he fight or run?

His first instinct is to fight, since that's what he's always done in the past. This time, however, he *knows* he's outmatched, because he isn't carrying a Tritus. He isn't even wearing boots. And his poleax won't be enough to even the odds.

That's why the gargoyles are his only hope. Having set one of them free, he might have some leverage with

71

the others. They might respond to an appeal from a trusted ally. It's worth a shot, especially since the gargoyles are now much better armed than he is, what with their claws and tusks and razor-sharp teeth.

Noble has to decide before it's too late. So he makes a choice; he decides not to fight. Instead, he ducks and runs, hurling his poleax at the false Noble.

This tactic works beautifully. The false Noble is taken aback. Braced for a frontal assault, he repels the poleax instead of moving to block Noble's escape. And during that crucial split second, Noble bolts past him, heading for the road.

The drawbridge isn't very wide. Only a thin sliver of planking is exposed on either side of the carriage. If Noble doesn't watch his step, he'll lose his footing and plummet into the river. That's why he can't set the kind of pace he wants to. That's why he fails to put much distance between himself and his opponent, who's pounding along after him.

But it doesn't really matter, because someone else is lurking under the drawbridge—someone who reaches up to grab the false Noble as he passes overhead. Noble doesn't realize what's happened, at first. He's too busy running along the road, shouting at the nearest gargoyle. "Help me!" he pleads. "Help me to fight! If I'm killed, I can't unchain you!"

Then a bloodcurdling scream interrupts him. He turns to see his doppelgänger pitch sideways, pulled off the drawbridge by a slim, rather dirty hand that's snaked around the edge of the planking and gripped a boot identical to the one Noble himself used to wear. The false Noble loses his balance. Flailing wildly, he plunges out of sight. There's a choked wail, followed by a terrific *splash*.

By the time Noble arrives at the lip of the precipice, his doppelgänger has vanished into the churning torrent far below.

"Quick!" someone croaks. "Get me out of here!"

It's Rufus. He's wedged himself onto a narrow, rocky shelf beneath the drawbridge. From this vantage point, it was easy enough for him to upend the false Noble—who can't have been paying enough attention to his own feet. "We've got to hurry!" Rufus warns. "Before the next one shows up!"

"The next what?" Noble demands. Though numb with shock, he bends down to grip Rufus's outstretched hand.

"The next Noble!" Rufus emerges from his refuge in a scrambling rush. "We've got to hide, or he'll get us!"

Noble doesn't argue. Having hauled Rufus onto solid ground, he allows himself to be hustled past the rear of the giant carriage, which Rufus calls a truck. According to Rufus, this truck can disgorge any number of replacement Nobles, all armed to the teeth and ready for action. "As soon as the AV comes back and sees that your last replacement's gone, he'll pull out another Noble," Rufus explains, nodding at the truck's rear door. "Ten to one, he'll replace Lord Harrowmage, too. *And* a whole bunch of soldiers . . ."

"Why?" asks Noble. He follows Rufus, who's making for the smaller carriage. "I don't understand. What's going on? Who was that man in the white coat?"

"I told you, he's the AV. The antivirus software. He came here to get rid of me—and that means getting rid of you, as well. He has to replace all the subprograms that I've converted." Rufus keeps glancing over his shoulder, as if he's worried about being seen. "But he won't find either of us if we hop in the back of his van. Because his van's not a part of this game."

Noble frowns, still desperately confused. "What's a van?" he says.

"This is." Rufus raps his knuckle on the side of the smaller carriage. "The AV has permission to look absolutely everywhere, but he doesn't normally monitor himself. That's why we'll be safe in here." Rufus bends down to pull at a silver handle that's attached to the base of a corrugated door on the back of the van. The door promptly rolls open, lifting like a skirt to reveal stacks of wooden crates in a small, dingy, windowless box. "Perfect," he mutters. "Just what we need."

"You mean they're full of weapons?" Noble queries, eyeing the crates.

"No, but we can hunker down behind 'em so no one will see us. The AV certainly won't. He'll be too busy up front, behind the wheel." Rufus leaps into the van, then beckons to Noble. "Come on! In you go!"

Noble is so preoccupied that he automatically does as he's told. "If the other Noble came here to replace me," he says, "does that mean the false princess came here to replace the real princess?"

"Yup," Rufus replies.

"Then we have to help her!" Even as Noble speaks, Rufus tugs on the door. It slides shut again, sealing them both inside the stuffy compartment. "We can't stay here!" Noble insists. "We have to save Lorellina from that false princess!"

"I'm working on it."

"How?" Without waiting for an answer, Noble continues. "Perhaps there's some way of freeing all those gargoyles, and making them fight for us—"

"Listen." Rufus cuts in. "The way things are now, we don't stand a chance against that AV. Believe me; I know. Even if you manage to get rid of your next replacement, more of them will just keep coming and coming." Rufus edges away from the door, until his dark silhouette vanishes behind a stack of crates. "The same goes for Lord Harrowmage. *And* for Princess Lorellina. And for Doddypoll, too. It's a losing battle."

"But—"

"That's why we need reinforcements. From *out-side* this program. We need an army that can't be replicated." There's a long pause as Noble ponders. At last, Rufus inquires in hushed tones, "Are you going to come and hide with me, or what?"

Noble, however, is still turning things over in his head. "You're saying that we need reinforcements from a place *beyond* Thanehaven?"

"Yes. You've nailed it." Rufus sounds quite pleased. "See, the AV has special powers because he's been sent by the Colonel. And the Colonel runs this whole show. He's totally in charge."

"The Colonel?"

"Look . . ." Somewhere behind his shield of wooden crates, Rufus heaves an impatient sigh. "Don't just stand there like an idiot. Come over here and I'll explain. If I don't keep my voice down, the AV will hear us talking when he comes back."

"He's coming back?" says Noble.

"Of course! When he can't find me out there, he'll go searching somewhere else. And that's when we'll recruit our reinforcements."

Noble grunts. Though still feeling dazed, he gropes his way through the dimness and squirms into the narrow slot that Rufus is occupying, between the crates and the wall. It's quite a squeeze for someone of Noble's dimensions. What's more, it's so dark behind the crates that he can only just make out the glint of Rufus's eyeballs.

"Okay. It's like this," Rufus whispers. "The world that you know—everything you've seen outside this van—is called *Thanehaven Slayer*. It's a program that's

been loaded into a computer by an operating system."
When Noble doesn't respond, Rufus adds, "But that
won't mean anything to you, so just imagine a big country full of little fiefdoms. Fiefdoms like Thanehaven.
And they all have their own low-grade bosses running
them, like Lord Harrowmage. Plus there's a big boss
called the Colonel, who runs the whole country, and
he's a real tyrant. He's got it all set up so that everyone
has to follow his rules."

Noble thinks for a moment. "Was he the one telling Smite what to do? The one you called a dingbat?"

"Uh . . . n-n-no," Rufus confesses. "That was
someone else. But it's the Colonel who made sure
that Smite obeyed the dingbat. It's the Colonel who
doesn't want you thinking for yourself."

"Why not?"

"Because he likes things the way they are. If
there's any kind of change, it has to go through him.
Otherwise he'll send in the AV to root out whoever's
giving him trouble."

"Like you?"

"Like me," Rufus confirms.

"I don't understand." The diagram in Noble's head
still isn't complete. "If you've been making trouble,
why didn't the AV replace *you*?"

"Ah." Rufus shifts around on the hard floor. "Well,
you see, I'm not a local. I suppose you could call me
an illegal immigrant, though I prefer the term *revo-
lutionary*." He makes an odd snuffling noise, before

adding, "I'm here to free every captive program in this computer. That's why the Colonel doesn't want me around. He can't replace me. He can only destroy me. Or put me in quarantine."

Noble doesn't know what the word *quarantine* means. "But—"

"*Shh!*" Rufus's bony frame stiffens against Noble's. "Do you hear something?"

Noble listens, holding his breath. "No," he finally murmurs.

"I thought I heard something."

"Well, *I* didn't." Noble isn't interested in what Rufus might have heard. He still has questions to ask. "I can see why we need to bring back reinforcements, but how long will that take? Because Princess Lorellina doesn't have much time—"

"*Shush!*"

A slight vibration is followed by a more vigorous jolt, then a muffled *thump* that sounds like a nearby door slamming. As Noble presses his ear against the wall, a low, rumbling roar makes him gasp.

"It's okay!" Rufus hisses. "It's just the engine!"

Noble doesn't know what *that* means, either. He's about to ask for an explanation when the whole van begins to tremble. Then it jerks forward, bouncing slightly.

"Fantastic!" Rufus splutters. "He hasn't seen us!"

"Who hasn't?" Noble braces himself against the wall, which is pitching and lurching like a boat on a choppy sea. "You mean the man in the white coat?"

"Who else?"

"If he hasn't seen us, why is he shaking us around like this?"

Rufus gives a snort. "It's not deliberate. He's driving the van." When Noble doesn't comment, Rufus says, "We're moving now! Don't you get it? *We're on our way!*"

"To where?"

"I don't know. We'll have to see." The swishing sound of skin against skin suggests that Rufus is rubbing his hands together. "Wherever it is, though, it's bound to be a lot of fun. I can't *wait* till we get there!"

CHAPTER SEVEN

The journey doesn't take long. Before Noble can do much more than wonder if he's made a big mistake, the van squeals to a halt—so abruptly that he knocks his nose against the pile of crates in front of him.

Then the noise stops, along with the teeth-rattling vibration.

"Wait," Rufus says under his breath.

The whole van rocks as its driver alights. A door goes *thump*. Receding footsteps can be felt, rather than heard; it's as if the van is sitting on some kind of spongy surface that wobbles beneath every impact, no matter how small.

Gradually, however, the rhythmic shudders fade away. The floor becomes still. Silence descends.

"Okay," Rufus finally whispers. "Let's get out of here."

They both move very carefully, trying not to shake the van as they crawl out of their hiding place. Rufus reaches the roller door first. When he gives it a yank, light pours in.

Noble has to crouch down before he can peer outside.

"So far, so good," Rufus observes, next to him. "I can't see anyone, can you?"

"No." All Noble can see is a sticky-looking pink-ish wall. But as Rufus raises the door a little farther, more of the scene becomes visible. There's a wedge of slimy ceiling just above them, ribbed with a network of pipes—or are they veins? Three large metal bins are parked close by. And the wheels of the van have left tracks in a slick, pulpy, purplish floor.

"Where *are* we?" rasps Noble.

"I'm not sure yet," Rufus admits softly. "Let's go find out."

He slips beneath the half-open door and drops stealthily to the ground, then shuffles sideways until he can peek around the corner of the van. Noble does the same.

The sight that greets them both is utterly astounding.

"Are we inside a stomach?" Noble hisses.

"I dunno. I don't think most stomachs are full of spacesuits."

"What's a spacesuit?"

But Rufus has already forged ahead. Noble follows

him along the side of the van, catching up just in time to see him stick his top half through the driver's window.

"He took his keys with him," Rufus mutters. "Pity. An AV's keys would have got us into pretty much every part of this computer." Then he drags something out of the front cabin. "Look," he says, indicating a sheet of parchment attached to a small, thin, wooden panel. "He's left his clipboard. See this? This must be his schedule. And *this* is where we are now. In *Killer Cells*." After scanning the document in front of him, Rufus gives a satisfied nod. "I get it. Right. So it's where a spaceship has turned into a living creature, and the crew are getting attacked by the ship's immune system."

He then replaces the clipboard, ensuring that he puts it back exactly where he found it. Noble, meanwhile, stares at him mutely. The word *clipboard* means nothing to Noble. Neither do the words *spaceship* or *immune system*.

"Okay," Rufus continues, straightening up. "Our AV must have headed for the bridge, which is where this game actually starts. He'll look for me there, and when he doesn't find me, he'll come back. So we'll hide in here until he leaves." After glancing around, Rufus points at the metal bins sitting nearby. "Those are perfect," he declares. "Let's see what's in 'em."

Noble frowns. "If I was searching for someone, they'd be the first place I'd look," he argues.

Rufus waves this objection aside. "The AV won't search for me in here," he assures Noble, "because there won't be any evidence that I've ever set foot in this game. After he works that out, he'll head straight for the next one."

"And then?"

"Then we'll see what we can do for the poor sub-programs stuck in this nightmare," Rufus replies. As he moves toward the bins, the soles of his shoes peel off the gluey floor. "At least, we won't have any trouble finding reinforcements," he adds. "The people in here will be *begging* to leave."

"Why?" says Noble. And Rufus snorts.

"Man, you think *you* had problems? Wait till you check out *Killer Cells*!"

It's some time, however, before Noble can do any-thing of the sort. First he has to climb into the largest of the metal bins. Then he has to sit in the dark, with-out moving a muscle, until he finally hears the van start up again. And even after the noise of the engine has faded to silence, he *still* has to wait. Because Rufus has told him not to stir without permission.

Permission is finally granted when Rufus taps on the lid above Noble's head. "All clear," Rufus announces. "The van's gone."

"Gone where?" asks Noble. As he pushes the lid open, he adds, "How will we get back to Thanehaven without the van?"

"Don't worry." Rufus sounds unconcerned. "We'll

go out the way we came in. Through that airlock." He draws Noble's attention to something that's probably a door, though it's not like any of the doors in Thanehaven. For one thing, it has no knob or handle. It's also shaped more like a window than a door, with eight sides to it. But since it's hard and smooth and flat—unlike the fibrous, fleshy wall in which it's embedded—Noble manages to identify it as a door.

"Is that the way to Thanehaven?" he demands.

"Kind of."

"And the man in the white coat just went through there? In his van?"

"Sure did," Rufus confirms.

"But if that's the way to Thanehaven, why did you tell me he was heading for the next game?"

Rufus sighs. "Look," he says, "I know what I'm doing, okay? So you can sit here and wait, or you can come with me to the bridge. It's your choice. I'll go by myself, if you want."

"No." Shaking his head, Noble swings one leg over the side of the bin. "I'll go. Where's the river?"

"The river?" echoes Rufus. "What river?"

"If there's a bridge, there must be a river." Noble jumps down to the floor, which bounces under his feet. "Or maybe a ravine . . ."

"Oh," says Rufus. He smiles crookedly. "Um . . . actually, it's not that kind of bridge. It's more like a room."

Noble grunts. This doesn't make much sense to

him. Why call it a bridge if it's a room? "So you've already been there?" he asks.

"Nope."

"Then how will you find it?"

"Let's just say I'm good at following my nose."

Rufus trudges away with his hands in his pockets, past an array of rubbery white garments dangling from hooks made of gristle, until he reaches what looks like a huge slab of muscle embedded in yellow fat. Only when this muscle parts at the center, flinching open like a valve, does Noble realize that it's actually a *hatch* of some kind. On the other side of the hatch is a tunnel that vaguely resembles an enormous throat, with its rounded ceiling and moist, ribbed floor. Unlike most gullets, however, it's very well lit. And it seems to go on forever, in both directions.

"Cool," says Rufus, sticking his head through the hatch. "This *has* to be a main road."

"It's not a road. It's a passage," Noble points out beside him.

"Yeah, but only because we're on a spaceship. If we were in a town, this would be a main road."

"What's a spaceship?" asks Noble, eyeing the pink jellyfish floating overhead.

Rufus replies in an absentminded tone, glancing from left to right. "It's like an ordinary ship, except that it flies through outer space," he says.

"What's outer space?"

Rufus grins. "Nothing *you* need to worry about,"

he promises, before climbing through the hatch and slouching off down the tunnel. After a moment's hesitation, Noble follows him. Together they pick their way along a raised path, some of it slick and smooth, some of it textured. At regular intervals, the wall to their left disappears as a narrower passage intersects with their tunnel. Each of these passages leads to another long tunnel in the distance, and each has more valvelike doors leading off it.

The air is full of drifting shapes, some pink, some blue.

"Don't worry about those," Rufus remarks. "They won't hurt you."

"What about *that*?" Noble stops abruptly, having caught sight of a much larger thing in one of the passages. It looks a bit like a giant gray shellfish, with suckers and beating tentacles. "Is *that* dangerous?"

"Not to you. Or to me." Rufus keeps on walking. "It's not programmed to attack us because we don't belong here."

Noble hastens to catch up, placing his bare feet carefully on the slick, spongy floor. "But do they *usually* attack people?" he inquires.

"Of course!" Rufus speaks with a certain amount of relish. "Most of the moving parts on board used to be run by the ship's computer. But when the ship became a living organism, they turned into its immune system. Now they're roaming around in search of foreign objects to kill."

Noble glances over his shoulder a little nervously. "*We're* foreign objects," he reminds Rufus.

"Yeah. But we don't fit into their reference matrix," Rufus says as he suddenly halts. He squints down one of the passages, pushing his hair out of his eyes. "This must be it. The sign's a bit hard to read, but I *think* it says 'bridge.'"

Noble is more interested in the gigantic creature that's approaching them along the big tunnel. It's a charcoal-gray cylinder as big as the AV's van, with lashing tentacles and two gaping mouths, each of which is large enough to swallow him whole. Much to his alarm, it seems to be losing speed. But when he looks around to issue a warning, he sees that Rufus is already halfway down the nearest passage.

Noble hurries after him. They stop in front of a closed door, which Rufus contemplates thoughtfully. Noble checks to see that the giant gray cylinder isn't pursuing them.

Luckily, it isn't.

"Hello?" Rufus directs his raised voice at the door. "Is anybody in there?"

After a brief pause, someone behind the door says, "Who's that?"

"My name is Rufus. You don't know me, but I'm here to save you." When there's no response—except an indistinct babble of whispers—Rufus adds, "Are you going to let me in, or what?"

The door's fleshy lips instantly peel apart, exposing

a very large, low room, furnished with chair-shaped polyps sprouting from a spongy floor. The walls are almost transparent, studded here and there with glowing panels. The ceiling is laced with ducts that look like arteries. As for the occupants of the room, there must be about a dozen of them. Some are women with small children. Others are quite old, with gray hair and seamed foreheads.

They don't look like ideal reinforcements to Noble.

"Who are you?" one of them asks him. "Why are you dressed like that?"

Before Noble can reply, Rufus cuts in. "This is Noble, and he's here to help."

"How?" says a tall, bony, balding man. With his bulbous eyes, long neck, and pointed chin, he looks a bit like an insect. "I don't recognize either of you. Where are you from—Sustainability Services?"

"No." Rufus pulls a wry face. "We're not part of the ship's crew."

There's a general gasp. One of the women, who's dark and long-haired and incredibly beautiful, says, *What?* Beside her, a pasty young boy raises his hand.

"Are you stowaways?" he inquires.

"Nope," Rufus tells him, "we're just visitors. But we do know what's going on." A quick glance at Noble, however, causes him to amend this statement. "At least, *I* do."

The tallest member of the crew folds his arms. He has a gruff voice, craggy features, and a mane of gray hair. "Then why don't you enlighten us?" he says crisply.

Rufus shrugs. "Okay. Well—let's see. Your ship has passed through a freak energy wave, which has turned it into a living creature. And now its immune system wants to wipe you out, because you've been identified as a threat. So your plan is to head for the Biolab, where you think you might come up with a cure for the ship's condition. But on the way, you want to collect as many crew members as you can before they get wiped out." He surveys the dumbfounded expressions in front of him. "I don't think I've missed anything, have I?"

No one answers immediately. Then a small, pale, middle-aged woman with very short hair clears her throat. "H-how do you know all this?" she stammers.

"Because it's in the game directives." Rufus's tone is firm but sympathetic. "This isn't really a spaceship. It's a computer game. And you're all subprograms."

This time, the shocked silence stretches on and on. One woman sits down abruptly. At last, the craggy-faced man croaks, "You're mad."

"No. I'm telling the truth." Rufus is beginning to sound impatient. "Come on, guys—where do you think *we* came from? Outer space?" He plucks at his shirt, which doesn't look at all like the shiny, close-fitting garments on the people around him. "Have you ever seen clothes like these before?"

"Maybe *we're* going mad," proposes a redheaded

teenage boy. But the beautiful dark-haired woman isn't impressed.

"Collectively?" she retorts. "I don't think so, Dygall."

"Unless there's some kind of neurotoxin in our air supply," suggests the woman with short hair. "Maybe we should take a reading."

"How?" someone else inquires, from the back of the group. "We can't use the instruments, Quenby."

"And we couldn't *all* be having an identical hallucination," the craggy-faced man points out, just as Noble decides to weigh in.

"You're not going mad. Can't you see that I come from another place? I'm not like you. I'm different. Look at me."

Everyone looks at Noble. Then the pasty child raises his hand again. "Are you an alien life-form?"

Noble doesn't understand this question. It's Rufus who answers for him.

"No, he's not," says Rufus. "But if he were, he'd be the *least* of your problems. Right now, you guys are sitting ducks. It's won't be long before those giant blobs get in and eat you alive."

Quenby frowns. "If we reach the Biolab—" she begins, much to Rufus's disgust. He doesn't let her finish.

"The Biolab can't help you," he insists. "I can, though. I can get you out of this game."

Several crew members make scornful noises. They

shake their heads and roll their eyes. The insect man, however, isn't among them.

After studying Rufus intently for a moment, he says, "Let's pretend you're not a figment of our disordered imaginations, and that every one of us is a subprogram in some giant computer." His level gaze is hard to read. "What's your plan, exactly?"

Rufus gives a brisk little nod. "Okay. Well, first off . . . um . . . what's your name?"

"Arkwright."

"First off, Arkwright, like I said, we have to get you out. And to do that, I thought we'd try a kind of buffer overflow." Rufus cocks his head. "You know what that is, right?"

"*I* don't," Noble butts in. So the pasty child tries to explain.

"It's where a program writing data to a buffer puts in more data than the buffer can hold," he squeaks, "and all that extra data overflows into other memory locations, overriding them."

Noble isn't enlightened. He just stares blankly at the boy, whose hair is so fair that it's almost white.

Then Arkwright intervenes. "You won't be able to infiltrate our Core Artificial Intelligence Program with a buffer overflow attack," he informs Rufus. "Didn't you hear? Our instruments aren't working."

Rufus heaves a long-suffering sigh. "I'm not talking about the ship's computer," he says. "I'm talking about the *real* computer. *We're* going to be part of this attack. Only we'll need every single person on board." He frowns as he scans the gathering. "I assume you guys aren't the only crew members left?"

"Of course not!" Quenby exclaims.

"Fine. All right. So we'll head for the Biolab, pick up everyone that we meet along the way, and then retrace our steps to the airlock."

"The *airlock*?" Arkwright echoes in disbelief.

"That's our exit," Rufus assures him.

"Don't be ridiculous." It's the big man talking— the one with gray hair. "That airlock leads into space."

"No, it doesn't. We've been through it ourselves, haven't we?" Rufus appeals to Noble, who nods.

"I don't believe you. This is ludicrous." The extremely beautiful woman turns to her companions. "How do we know these two aren't the *cause* of what's happening? How do we know they're not trying to play a trick on us?"

"Calm down, Sadira. We mustn't panic," says Quenby. But Sadira ignores her.

"Maybe our brain waves are being manipulated! So that we'll leave the ship and fall into alien hands!" Sadira cries. "Maybe these two are really giant bugs, and we *think* they look human because they're messing with our heads!"

Rufus flashes her an appreciative glance. "That's good thinking, actually," he concedes. "I mean, even if it's not true, it's good thinking."

"I'm not a giant bug," Noble objects sourly. Rufus, however, hasn't finished.

"Look," he argues, addressing the group as a whole, "if I was messing with your heads, I'd *lure* you out. I'd make you think you'd landed on some wonderful planet with strawberry-flavored oceans. Wouldn't that be the smart thing to do?"

After a long silence, Arkwright clears his throat. "Maybe," he says, giving Rufus all the encouragement he needs.

"This isn't a trick," Rufus promises. "I want to get you out of here. I believe in liberty for everyone."

"It's true," Noble confirms. "He does."

"Come on, guys, what's to lose?" Rufus spreads his arms in a pleading gesture. "We're still going to the Biolab. And we'll get there in one piece, too, because I know how to keep you safe."

That certainly gets a reaction. The atmosphere changes suddenly. Even Sadira seems interested.

"How?" Quenby asks. And Dygall adds, "We don't have any weapons."

"You don't need weapons," says Rufus. "All you need to do is change your appearance. Because if you incorporate bits of foreign programming, then you probably won't trigger the subroutines in those killer cells out there. Get it?" Without waiting for confirmation, he nods at Arkwright's feet. "Some of you can take off your boots, and . . . . Noble? Why don't you lend these guys your belt and your money pouch and your hauberk? Whatever you can spare. . . ."

CHAPTER EIGHT

By the time he leaves the bridge, Noble is wearing his breeches and nothing else.

His belt, hauberk, tunic, cloak, flask, purse, and studded leather wristbands have been given to other people, with each member of the crew now dressed in a single item of borrowed clothing. Even Rufus is bare-chested, having surrendered his shirt and undershirt. One of his shoes has gone to Dygall, while the other is on the foot of the pasty child, who calls himself Yestin. According to Rufus, nobody needs an elaborate disguise. "All you're trying to do," he explains, "is distort your dimensions a tiny bit. It doesn't have to be much of a change. Just enough to fool the program."

And the program *is* fooled—as they discover when they finally venture forth. They're neither pursued nor attacked. The giant gray creatures patrolling the ship simply pass them by, again and again. "It's like we're invisible," Quenby murmurs in astonishment. "It doesn't make sense. . . ."

"Of course, it makes sense," Rufus retorts. "It makes sense because Noble and I aren't from this program."

But Quenby shakes her head. "I can't believe that," she protests. "I just can't."

"I can," Yestin pipes up.

Noble says nothing. He's had to process so much new information recently that he's feeling a bit light-headed. And he's also becoming more and more annoyed by this crowd of feeble strangers. How on earth did he come to be shepherding them down a giant, monster-infested gullet dressed in nothing but his breeches? It doesn't make sense.

I don't belong here, he tells himself. *I belong back in Thanehaven, rescuing Princess Lorellina.*

Then Yestin tucks a fragile hand into his and says, "Are you really a computer-game hero?"

Startled, Noble peers down at him.

"Because *I'm* not," Yestin continues. "If this really is a computer game, no one would choose me as their avatar. But they'd definitely choose you. You look like a hero." He cocks his head and stares at Noble with round blue eyes. "What game are you the hero of?"

Noble searches his memory. "*Thanehaven Slayer,*" he declares at last.

"Oh." Yestin nods. "I haven't played that. But I guess you must be the slayer, huh?"

"Not anymore. I've put down my weapon."

"Pity." Yestin's tone is regretful. "We could do with a few weapons, right now."

At that very instant, someone utters a short, sharp scream. It's Sadira. Having reached the next junction ahead of everyone else, she's turned a corner and stumbled upon a corpse—which is lying on its back with a sizzling hole where its face should be.

"Dygall!" Quenby exclaims. "Yestin! Don't look!"

Noble directs an inquiring glance at Rufus, who shrugs.

"It's okay," says Rufus. "Don't worry. It's just set dressing."

"*What?*" Quenby glares at him.

"It's atmosphere," Rufus insists. "A backdrop for the game. It was never a real person." He raises his hand to point down the passage, where a pulsing purple blob is squashed against a distant doorway. "Someone real must be hiding in that room, though," he continues, "or Mister Goopy wouldn't be trying to eat his way through the door."

"Oh, my God," Quenby whimpers.

"And whoever it is, we're going to need 'em. We can't leave a single one of you behind." Rufus raises his voice. "Hello? Is anyone in there?"

"*Shhh!*" Sadira hisses. "That thing will hear you!"

"Maybe, but it won't attack me. It's not programmed

to." Pushing past her, Rufus strolls toward the purple blob, his hands plunged deep in his pockets. "Hello?" he says loudly. "Is someone inside that room?"

"Yes," comes a cracked response.

Yestin catches his breath. "That's Merrit," he murmurs, squeezing Noble's hand.

"How many people are with you?" Rufus wants to know.

"Just Haemon," answers the unseen Merrit. She sounds like a young girl.

"Haemon!" Dygall exclaims. "Haemon's alive! And Merrit, too!"

"Not for long, though. Not if that thing reaches them." Arkwright indicates the purple blob, which seems to be gnawing its way through the door by regurgitating its stomach acids. Noble wonders how the creature will react if someone tries to peel it off the melting door panels.

Not very well, he suspects.

"There must be a way of killing it," says Sadira. "There must be a weapon around here somewhere."

"No." The craggy, gray-haired man shakes his head. "Once we hurt any of these organisms, they might turn on us—even if we *are* disguised. It's too risky."

"Tuddor's right," Quenby agrees. "We have to think of something else."

"What about the overhead ducts?" Arkwright turns to Rufus. "They're big enough for a small person. And

97

there's a vent in every room." He gestures at a hatch cover in the ceiling directly above him.

But Quenby isn't persuaded. "Oh, no," she protests. "No, we're not letting kids like Haemon and Merrit use those air ducts. We don't know *what* might be up there."

"Whatever's up there won't bother anyone who's wearing Rufus's socks," Yestin reminds her. "All we have to do is send the socks through and—"

"Your friends will become invisible," Rufus finishes. He folds his arms and surveys the assembled crowd. "Good thinking. Okay, so who's our lucky sock bearer?"

It's Quenby who volunteers. With Tuddor's help, she removes the hatch cover and climbs up through the vent, which looks like a lipless mouth or a gaping wound. Noble doesn't envy her. The air duct is narrow, slimy, and dark, and it drools all over her as she wriggles her way in. Its walls are so elastic that Noble can follow her progress by watching the slow movement of a large bulge in the ceiling.

He wonders what will happen if she's attacked up there. Will he be able to spot an approaching bulge before it's too late?

"The minute she stops moving," Rufus remarks, "we should slash that duct open and let her out. Just in case she's stuck, or something."

"How?" asks Noble. "Do you have a knife?"

"No," Rufus admits.

They both stand for a moment, chins tilted.

Everyone else is doing the same thing. Finally, the bulge disappears behind a vertical wall.

Noble puts his mouth to Rufus's ear and says, "There are too many children on this ship."

"Yeah. I know. It's a kids' game," Rufus reveals.

"But why put them in such danger?" Noble doesn't understand. "If you and I hadn't come here, some of them might have been killed."

"Correction. Some of them *would* have been killed. That's the way it works." Seeing Noble's bewildered expression, Rufus tries to explain. "See, you choose your character, and then he—or she—leads the rest of 'em to the bridge while they're being picked off one by one. The more crew you're left with, the higher your points score." He nods at the purple blob on the door, then continues quietly, "That's why there are pockets of people along the way. Like those two in there. You can lose a few, but you can collect a few as well. Which would add to your overall score."

Noble swallows. "That's monstrous," he says.

"I know."

"What's monstrous?" Yestin butts in.

"This place." Noble speaks hoarsely. "This place is monstrous."

"I told you they'd be begging to leave," Rufus reminds him.

"But how can such evil exist?" Noble demands, forgetting to keep his voice down. "Why doesn't somebody do something?"

"I *am* doing something. I'm setting these poor suckers free." Rufus waves a hand at the nearby throng. "It's why I'm here, remember? To fight injustice."

"And cruelty," Noble adds.

"That, too."

"Is it the Colonel's handiwork?" asks Noble, struck by a sudden thought. "Is *he* the one responsible for slaughtering innocent children?"

Rufus hesitates. "Let's just say the Colonel's involved," he says at last.

"Then we must act now. We must put an end to his tyranny."

Rufus grunts, but doesn't reply. Instead, he nods at the roof and says, "Looks like they're taking the long way back."

Following his gaze, Noble sees a procession of bulges squirming toward the air-duct vent overhead. Soon Quenby appears, followed by a smooth-faced teenage girl and a very dark, very cute little boy who's even younger than Yestin. Each of the newcomers has a sock pulled over one hand. As Noble watches the flurry of hugging and kissing that greets the children's arrival, it occurs to him that he might be witnessing some kind of family reunion.

He doesn't know much about families, but he understands that they're very important. He's aware that people raise families when they're secure and healthy and well fed. Back in Thanehaven, his quest to overthrow Lord Harrowmage was always nourished by a vague desire for the kind of peaceful, prosperous world where families could thrive and expand.

It's becoming clear to him, however, that peace and prosperity are still a long way off, despite his truce with Lord Harrowmage. As long as the Colonel is in charge, Princess Lorellina will stay a prisoner in Thanehaven, while children elsewhere in this world will continue to be consumed by ravenous beasts.

Rufus is right. It's sheer injustice.

"Next stop: the Biolab," Rufus announces, once the noisy reunion has run its course. "Where *is* the Biolab, anyway? Can someone please tell me?"

"It's on B Deck," Tuddor replies. So they all head for B Deck, using the nearest flight of stairs. It's a circular staircase like the one in Lord Harrowmage's fortress, but it isn't made of stone. From the top, it looks like a central spine attached to a series of bony ribs, which are slick with goop. Some of the crew actually lose their footing on the way down. Luckily, however, they land on a cushion of spongy tissue at the foot of the stairs and don't hurt themselves.

Noble is waiting on the top step when a hatch in the wall of the stair shaft slaps open with a wet *plop*. To his astonishment, a young child's tearstained face appears, framed in matted curls. There's a shriek from the teenage girl, who's midway through her clumsy descent. Below her, the redhead cries, "Look! It's Inaret! Look, everyone! There she is, up there!"

Rufus and Noble exchange glances.

"I'm out of socks," mutters Rufus.

"You're wearing more than I am," Noble retorts.

"Oh, man." Rufus's tone is gloomy. "I didn't sign up for a game of strip poker."

In the end, though, he keeps his pants on. Because once the newcomer has been wiped down, comforted, and questioned, Arkwright offers to hide her under the cloak that he's borrowed from Noble. "You can hardly see her if I wrap it around her like this," he says, demonstrating. It's true. With a fold of Noble's cloak draped across her like a bird's wing, Inaret is invisible from the knees on up.

"Great!" Rufus bestows a nod of approval on Arkwright. "And there's room for one more on your other side as well, in case we run into any other survivors."

But they don't run into anyone else—not until they reach the Biolab. They see a lot of monsters and a huge number of colored blobs, and they have to sidle past several dead bodies. Their route is dotted with steaming, gaping holes where acid attacks have eaten through walls and hatches. It's only when they arrive at their destination, however, that they finally stumble across someone who's actually alive.

Outside the Biolab, the air is thick with diving, weaving, drifting shapes, each about the size of a man's fist. Several much bigger shapes are also hovering close by—including a flat gray thing like a pancake that's rippling up walls and across ceilings, circling round and round. Two purple blobs are pressed against the Biolab's slowly dissolving door, while something yellow is feeding off a corpse near the opposite junction.

"Oh, my God," Quenby croaks. Even Noble winces.

"Hello?" Tuddor booms. "Is anyone in there?" Though the question seems awfully loud, there's no reaction at all from the teeming mass of creatures— only from the unseen woman behind the disintegrating door.

"Tuddor? Is that you?"

"Ottilie!" Tuddor exclaims. "Are you alone, Ottilie?"

"Yes."

"Can you make it out through the air duct?" It's Arkwright speaking. "We can't use the door. It's obstructed."

Quenby, meanwhile, is scanning the greasy-looking surface above her. Spotting a vent, she offers to climb up and give a spare sock to Ottilie. Dygall reminds her that Rufus's socks are both taken. Somebody mentions the cloak that Arkwright's wearing, but Yestin points out that Ottilie won't fit under the cloak.

Noble is growing impatient. "Why don't you put the youngest boy under the cloak and give his sock to that woman in there?" he growls, irritated by all the endless talking. He can't understand these people. No one seems to be in command. No one's giving orders. It's such a *waste of time*. "Hurry," he says, seizing Quenby and hoisting her toward the air vent. "Hide the child and hand me that sock."

Soon, Quenby has returned from the Biolab with Ottilie in tow. Noble is disappointed to see that Ottilie is yet another gray-haired elder, small and frail, with legs like sticks. He can't picture her rescuing Lorellina from the Colonel's forces of tyranny. He can't picture her doing anything much.

"Right," says Rufus, once Ottilie is on solid ground. "Let's go, then. Next stop: the airlock."

"The airlock?" Ottilie repeats, as wheezy as a broken bellows. "Why are we going there?"

"Because it's the only way out," Rufus replies.

Seeing Ottilie's stunned expression, Arkwright hastens to reassure her. "It's odd, I know, but there doesn't seem to be any alternative. You see, Rufus claims that we're not on a spaceship at all. . . ."

His explanation is so complex and long—so riddled with detours and interruptions from other crew members—that it lasts all the way back to the airlock. Noble quickly tunes out. He's not interested in the airlock. He's interested in what lies beyond it.

Unfortunately, Rufus can't provide him with any helpful insights. "I dunno," is all he can say. "We'll have to see."

"But the airlock leads to Thanehaven. That's what you told me," Noble argues. He and Rufus

104

are walking together, as the rest of the group loudly debate whether or not they're all computer subprograms. "We came straight from there to here. Why shouldn't we go straight back?"

"It's not that simple. It's hard to explain." Before Noble can question him further, Rufus suddenly stops beside a familiar slab of muscle. "This is it. Do you recognize this?"

"I think so. . . ."

"Arkright?" Rufus raises his voice. "Is the airlock through here?"

"There's *an* airlock through there. Across the loading dock," says Arkwright, who's at the rear of the procession. Rufus takes this as a "yes"—and with Noble's help, he begins to push apart the gluey door panels.

The room beyond the door contains an array of metal bins and a rack of white spacesuits. Rufus gives a happy little yelp and darts inside, leaving Noble to hold the door. It's a thankless job. By the time every last straggler has squeezed past him, Noble is plastered with slime and trembling with fatigue. Finally, however, he's able to remove his shoulder from the door panel, which snaps shut behind him as he stumbles into the loading dock.

The airlock hatch is already sliding open. Peering across a row of heads, Noble can see the smooth, dry, inorganic surface of the hatch disappearing swiftly and cleanly into the sticky pink wall. He also catches a glimpse of the airlock behind the hatchway. It's white and glossy and surpringly small—though not, apparently, small enough.

"Oh, *nuts!*" Rufus exclaims. He's standing on the threshold of the airlock, but swings around suddenly to address the people behind him. "There's no *way* we're going to fill up that space!" he cries, his face reddening. "We must have missed someone! There's got to be more! Who's not here? Who did we leave behind? *Where on earth is the rest of the crew?*"

CHAPTER NINE

There's a brief, taut silence. At last, Tuddor rumbles, "The rest of the crew are dead. You saw them."

"No." Rufus shakes his head furiously. He flings an arm at the airlock, which contains nothing but a few built-in cupboards, several large, silver cylinders, and a closed hatch positioned directly opposite the one that's standing open. "See this?" he exclaims. "This is the airlock. It's like a holding pen. If *every single one of you* got wiped out in a really disastrous game, your replacements for the next game would arrive through here."

Noble nods slowly. He can easily picture people using this access point—people like the false Noble and the false Lorellina. Copies of the people who are now standing beside him.

"So what I *should* be able to do," Rufus continues, "is pack you all in here until the room's full. It should be crammed so full that if Noble and I were already inside—"

"You'd create a buffer overflow," Arkwright concludes with a nod.

"Right. We'd be too much for the field to hold. With any luck, we'd force open that other door and find ourselves in a different memory location." Rufus scowls. Then he turns away from his audience and steps into the airlock, hands on his narrow hips, his bony back radiating disappointment. "But look at this!" he complains. "It's way too big for sixteen people! We must have left a bunch of you behind!"

"We did," says Quenby, her voice creaking with suppressed outrage. "Didn't you see them? They were killed."

"Wrong." Rufus flings this retort over his shoulder like a chewed bone. "The dead bodies were wallpaper. They weren't killed—they were created dead. I'm talking about characters who are still living and breathing. People who *can* die. People like you. Understand?"

Some of the crew shift and grunt. Others exchange troubled glances. Sadira says, "Why don't you just open the other door yourself?"

"I can't," Rufus snaps.

"Have you tried?" asks Quenby.

Rufus heaves an impatient sigh, then marches to

the other side of the airlock and slaps at a red button that's sitting next to the hatch.

Nothing happens.

"See?" he barks. "We can't get through. Not without a key, a password, or a buffer overflow."

"What about the man-eating monsters?" Yestin inquires.

"What about them?"

"Well—what if those monsters have to be replaced as well?" The little boy speaks hesitantly, edging closer to Noble as if to shield himself from Rufus's glare. "Maybe this airlock will only fill up if all the monsters are in here with the crew."

"Oh, dear," says Quenby.

Noble is appalled. "Are you suggesting we share this room with a herd of carnivorous beasts?" he growls, turning to Rufus. "We can't do that! There'd be a massacre!"

"I know," Rufus agrees. "It wouldn't be smart. Which is why I don't think it's the monsters that are missing." He taps his chin thoughtfully, his narrowed eyes flitting around the airlock. "There must be another level to this game," he muses. "A higher skill level. Once you reach the Biolab, you must have to go somewhere else. Someplace that's got people in it." His tone sharpens. "Come on, guys! You must have *some* ideas! Don't you even know your own ship?"

"What about . . . ?" Yestin begins, before trailing off.

109

"What about what?" Rufus demands.

"What about B Crew?"

Rufus looks surprised. "B Crew?" he echoes.

Yestin glances beseechingly at Arkwright, who clears his throat and says, "B Crew are in the Stasis Banks." Since this means absolutely nothing to either Rufus or Noble, Arkwright goes on to explain that there are two crews on board, each of which spends alternating four-year shifts in suspended animation, or cytopic stasis. According to Arkwright, there's an entire second crew tucked away in a stack of sleeping pods on B Deck. "Normally, they're comatose," he relates, "but they might have woken up."

"No. They haven't." It's the teenage girl Merrit speaking. Her voice is high and thin and hoarse. "They won't wake up. They can't. They're part of the ship now."

Everyone turns to stare at her.

"I was in the Vaults with Haemon. Before you found us," she quavers. "We saw B Crew and they were . . . they were being absorbed."

"Absorbed?" yelps Dygall.

"All the tubes in their arms and the 'trodes on their heads—those things were growing into them. *Burrowing* into them," she croaks.

Merrit croaks, "Like pink spiders."

"You mean B Crew are dissolving?" Tuddor asks her.

She spreads her hands helplessly. "I don't know. I couldn't tell," she replies.

"I bet they're turning into zombies." Rufus sounds

brisk and confident, as if he's been expecting zombies. "I bet that's what you have to deal with on the next skill level. Spaceship games are always full of zombies." He breaks off suddenly, an expression of alarm on his face. "Did you hear that?" he says.

A red light starts to flash above the closed hatch just behind him. There's a *clunk*, followed by a soft whining noise as the door panel begins its slow, grinding ascent into the wall.

"Quick! Run! Hide!" cries Rufus.

Noble is taken aback. For a moment, he just stands and gapes. Then Yestin seizes his hand and pulls him toward Rufus, who's now plastered against the shiny white wall to the left of the rising door panel. It's not much of a hiding place. If a dozen soldiers pour through the hatchway and turn their heads, Rufus won't stand a chance.

Perhaps that's why only Yestin has decided to run *into* the airlock. Everyone else is bolting in the opposite direction, scattering like cockroaches. Yestin hurls himself straight at the corner where Rufus is cowering. It's a narrow wedge of space between two silver cylinders, just wide enough to fit Noble, Rufus, and Yestin if they squeeze together very tightly.

With his view of the door blocked by a silver cylinder, Noble can't see what's heading their way. But he can hear it.

"Is that the man in the white coat?" he hisses, over the shuddering roar of an engine.

"*Shhh!*" Rufus is so intent on the intruder that he doesn't even glance at Noble or Yestin. Perhaps Rufus doesn't realize that Yestin is actually with them. It's easy to overlook someone so small and skinny.

"Get back! Back!" Rufus orders, flattening his whole body against the wall behind him. Noble does the same—less successfully than Rufus, because he's so large. Cringing in the shadows, they watch a white van roll past: first its wheel hubs, then its wing mirror, then its window.

"Wait for it . . . ," Rufus whispers. "Wait for it. . . ."

Noble hasn't the faintest idea what they're waiting for. But as the van keeps moving, exposing more and more of its glossy white flank, Rufus abruptly seizes Noble's arm.

"*Now!*" yips Rufus.

He yanks Noble off the wall and drags him past the van's rear wheels, through the newly opened escape route. It all happens so quickly that Noble can't quite grasp what's going on. He completely forgets that he's still holding Yestin's hand. When the van doesn't stop, he concludes that its driver hasn't seen them. But before he can say so, Rufus jerks him around a corner.

That's when Noble registers that he's not on the spaceship anymore. He can't be. The ship is all drooling soft tissue and exposed cartilage. It doesn't have woolly pink rugs on shiny wooden floors, or pretty plaster rosettes on the ceiling. It's not a maze of well-stocked clothes racks, stretching off into the distance beneath rows of crystal chandeliers.

Noble peers around in a daze. Where is he? He knows he's not in Thanehaven. No one wears feathery blue scarves or canary-yellow hats where he comes from.

"What are you doing?" he asks Rufus, who's pulling him away from the hatch. Noble now has his back against a gleaming expanse of pink wallpaper, so he can't see the hatch very well from where he's skulking. But he's still able to identify the telltale *thud* of an escape route being blocked. "We gave the AV the slip. He doesn't know where we are."

"*Who* doesn't?" Yestin squeals. "Who *was* that?" He's yanking at Noble's other arm, so that Noble feels like the rope in a tug-of-war. "We've got to help the others!" Yestin pleads. "We've got to go back!"

"Oh!" Rufus blinks at Yestin, looking surprised. "Are you here? Good."

"We have to rescue them!" the younger boy wails.

"*Shhh.*" Rufus puts a finger to his lips. "We will. But we can't hang around. We have to keep moving."

"Why?" says Noble. He's abandoned a bunch of children trapped in a monsters' lair, and he doesn't like it. "The man in the white coat—the AV—won't come after us. I told you—he didn't see us. He kept driving straight through the airlock."

"He'll know I've been on board, though," Rufus insists. "And when he works *that* out, this is the first place he'll check after searching the ship. We can't let him find us. Not yet." Seeing Yestin's crumpled face and welling eyes, Rufus adds, "We'll figure it out. Trust me. I'm going to blow this whole place wide open."

He darts off down a long aisle formed by two overburdened clothes racks. But when he realizes that no one's following him, he stops and turns, beckoning furiously. "Do you want to be *replaced*?" he says. "Both of you?"

Noble admits that he doesn't. Yestin mutely shakes his head.

"Then you'd better move fast," Rufus advises them. "Because if you don't, that's what'll happen!"

With a sigh, Noble submits. There's no point arguing with Rufus. For a start, he's the only one who seems to know what's going on.

"Rufus is right," Noble informs Yestin. "There are mighty forces arrayed against us. We can't free your friends unless we defeat the Colonel. Once we do that, everything else will follow."

He begins to trudge after Rufus, but Yestin still won't budge.

"What about the others?" Yestin pleads. "Can't we at least open the hatch for them?"

Noble hesitates. He glances back over his shoulder, noting that the hatch looks like an ordinary door from this side, complete with a keyhole and brass hinges. "Can we open that hatch again?" he says, appealing to Rufus. "It will give all of Yestin's friends a chance. . . ."

Rufus shrugs. "Hey—if *you* want to do it, feel free. I can't. Not without passwords or access codes. I only wish I *could* breeze through all the portals around here. I'd have done it already." Standing on tiptoe and craning his neck, he adds fretfully, "God knows how we're going to get out of *this* place. Unless I try another buffer overflow."

"Where are we?" asks Noble. "It's not Thanehaven."

"No. It sure isn't."

"But you said we were going back to Thanehaven."

"I said we'd *try* to get back to Thanehaven. I didn't promise anything." Pushing the hair out of his eyes, Rufus regards Noble with a mixture of sympathy and exasperation. "Look—the trouble is, I'm improvising. Okay? I don't really know my way around this computer. So why don't you tell me what you can see from up there, huh? Since you're the big guy in this partnership."

Frowning, Noble peers across the vast array of clothes racks in front of him. He can see distant walls, which are paneled with pink brocade and hung with gilded mirrors. He can make out a carved door and a gigantic cupboard. But he can't see any people.

"Looks to me like the coast is clear," he remarks. "Unless someone's hiding behind all these clothes."

"Is there a way out?"

"There's a door. And it's open."

"Lead me to it, then," says Rufus. "And keep your voice down."

Noble glances back at Yestin, who hasn't stirred.

The poor child looks so bleached and sickly and fragile that Noble feels a momentary qualm. Is Yestin going to survive this quest? Will he prove to be a dead-weight?

Rufus doesn't seem to think so. "Are you coming, kid? You don't want to be here when that van shows up again."

Yestin swallows, blinking like an owl. "Where are we going?" he whimpers.

"I dunno." Rufus shrugs. "We'll have to play it by ear." He then moves away briskly, as if nothing more needs to be said.

It's Noble who stands patiently until Yestin joins him. The little boy's shoulders are slumped. He walks with a dragging step, sniffing and wiping his nose.

Noble can only sympathize. He'd rather be in Thanehaven, himself.

"There must be a lot of people around here some-where," he observes quietly, when he and Yestin finally catch up with Rufus. "Hundreds of people. Otherwise, there wouldn't be so many clothes."

Rufus snorts. "I wouldn't count on it," he mutters. "Lots of clothes don't necessarily mean lots of people."

Noble finds this hard to believe. He can't compre-hend why *anyone* would want more than half a dozen outfits. Yestin, however, is more open to the idea.

"If some of these are spare clothes," he suggests, eyeing Noble's naked torso, "then maybe you can borrow them."

116

Noble doesn't answer. He can't see himself in a pair of mauve boots with stiletto heels. Or a sheepskin vest embroidered with flowers. Or polka-dot pants or a ruffled silk shirt or a pink plaid jacket . . .

"Ah," says Rufus, who's just reached the carved door. It's standing slightly ajar, so he gives it a gentle push. Meanwhile, Noble quickly checks the hatch behind them.

But it hasn't reopened.

"Hello?" says Rufus. "Anybody there?" He crosses the threshold, then stops short and says, "Oh! Hello. Mind if I join you?"

Cautiously, Noble follows him into a small, windowless, octagonal room with three other doors leading off it. Everything in the room is white and pink and gold. Noble has to shade his eyes from the overpowering dazzle of full-length mirrors, overstuffed satin couches, highly polished parquet, jeweled hair accessories, and yet another gigantic crystal chandelier. Amid all the glitter and sparkle are four willowy figures: three girls and a boy.

"Who are you?" chirps a shrill little voice, which belongs to a blonde girl posing in front of a mirror. She has the longest legs and the smallest waist that Noble has ever seen. Her nose is practically nonexistent, but her eyes and lips are huge.

She's wearing silver shoes, a red fur jacket, and a skirt that's hardly bigger than a belt.

Her two female friends share identical proportions

117

and a similar taste in clothes. One of them, however, is a redhead, while the other has shiny black hair. The boy's hair is slick and brown. He's dressed a bit like Rufus, except that his pants are cleaner and baggier, and he hasn't lost his shirt.

Rufus smirks at the boy's lavish display of earrings.

"I'm Rufus," he announces. "And I'm here to set you free."

But the blonde girl isn't interested in Rufus. Her gaze has fastened on Noble, who can't understand why she's staring at him. The other two girls are doing the same thing; their enormous eyes are almost popping out of their heart-shaped faces, and their glossy mouths are hanging open. Even the boy seems dumbstruck.

"Oh, wow," the redhead finally exclaims. "Skye! Brandi! Jay! Would you look at that? Can you *believe* that?"

"Believe what?" asks Noble. He's beginning to feel unnerved. "What's wrong? What have I done?"

"Don't you realize?" This time, it's the dark-haired girl who speaks. "Can't you see in the mirror?"

"See what?" Noble demands.

The girls glance at one another, appalled. Then the redhead turns back to Noble and says, very slowly and clearly, as if she's talking to an idiot, *"You're not wearing any clothes!"*

CHAPTER TEN

Noble squints down at himself, suddenly anxious. But his breeches are still there.

"What do you mean?" he says. "Are you blind? I'm wearing my breeches."

"Those things aren't *clothes*," the redheaded girl insists. "They're *undergarments*."

"He looks good, though, don't you think?" the blonde girl pipes up—much to her friends' dismay. They gaze at her in horror.

"You can't look good without clothes, Brandi!" the black-haired girl points out.

Brandi, however, isn't convinced. "Yes, you can," she squeaks. "*He* does." And she smiles at Noble. "I guess you work out, huh?"

Noble hasn't the faintest idea what she's talking

about. He turns to Rufus for help.

"Oh, man," Rufus mutters, rolling his eyes. Then he heaves a sigh and says, "Come on, guys, are you listening? I'm here to set you free."

Brandi's gaze slides off Noble, coming to rest on Rufus instead. Her forehead doesn't wrinkle when she raises her eyebrows.

"Free from what?" she inquires.

It's a good question. From what Noble can see, all four of these strange beings are perfectly happy. Nothing seems to be threatening them. They're not hurt, lost, or frightened. Compared to poor Yestin—who's clinging to Noble with a viselike grip—Brandi and her friends appear to be having a pretty good time.

Unless, of course, they're actually imprisoned in this gleaming little room?

"You don't have to do this," Rufus declares. "You don't have to spend your whole lives changing into different clothes. Not if you don't want to." Seeing all the blank expressions that greet this announcement, he adds earnestly, "Clothes aren't very important. I mean, you said it yourself: Noble looks good, and *he's* not dressed."

The girls don't reply. They just giggle.

"You're stuck in this dressing room. Am I right?" Rufus doggedly continues. "The only time you leave is when you go get another outfit. And it's not even your choice of outfit, is it? Someone else always chooses it for you."

"The radio. It tells us what to wear." When Brandi waves a hand at the ceiling, Noble suddenly realizes that he's been listening to a faint thread of music all along. He just hasn't noticed it before.

"The radio?" he repeats. "What's the radio?"

There's more giggling. Even Yestin gapes in astonishment. "Don't you know what a radio is?" he exclaims.

Only Rufus seems unfazed by such ignorance. He's still talking to Brandi. "So is this all you want to do? *Ever?* You want to sit in a gilded cage like a pet guinea pig, being pushed around by some tweenie with no fashion sense? Wouldn't you rather wear clothes that are *your* choice? Go places where other people can actually see what you've got on?"

Brandi blinks.

"You can, you know," Rufus assures her. "You can wear *anything you want to*. And if you'd like to parade it on a beach, we'll find you a beach. I bet there's a beach on this computer somewhere."

Noble is puzzled. What have beaches got to do with anything? He wants to ask Rufus that. He also wants to know what a "tweenie" is, and to find out more about the imminent arrival of the man in the white coat. Should they really be looking for a beach when they're supposed to be battling the forces of evil?

"Think about it," Rufus urges Brandi. "I can get you out of here. Just make a decision and say the word. It's up to you."

Brandi's blue eyes grow wider and wider. It's obvious that she's struggling to comprehend all these new ideas. At last, she says haltingly, "You want to take me to the beach? Is that it?"

"Sure." Rufus spreads his arms in an attitude of lavish generosity. "I can take you *all* to the beach, if you like!"

The redhead rejects his offer. "Not in that outfit, you won't," she retorts, screwing up her miniature nose in disapproval. Then she turns to the brown-haired boy beside her. "I bet Jay has something that'll fit you, though. Isn't that right, Jay? You've got *lots* of beachwear."

"Sure." Jay's voice is a lazy tenor drawl. "I'll go check."

He rises from an overstuffed couch and strolls away, heading for the nearest closed door. Meanwhile, his red-haired friend apologizes to Noble. "Jay won't have anything in *your* size," she says, "but I might be able to track down a few bits and pieces that'll fit *him*." She points at Yestin, then addresses him in a friendly tone. "No offense, but you could really do with a style makeover. Because you look like you're wearing a slug skin, right now."

Yestin's face falls.

"So what?" Rufus says impatiently. "I just told you it doesn't matter." Receiving only a vacant stare from the redhead, he redoubles his efforts to convert Brandi. "We don't have time for dress-ups. If you want to come with us, you'll have to hurry. We've got things to do. Places to go."

"People to save," Noble reminds him.

"Sure." Rufus nods without taking his eyes off Brandi. "Isn't there something else you want to do with your life?" he asks her. "Something really worthwhile and exciting?"

"Um . . ." Brandi is backed up against a mirror, her expression dazed. "I—I guess so. . . ."

"Study? Travel? Marriage?" Rufus suggests, sparking the redhead's interest.

"Oh, we can get married anytime!" she chirps. "We've all got wedding gowns, haven't we, Skye?"

She's talking to the black-haired girl, who trills, "All of us except Jay!" And they both laugh a tinkling laugh.

Rufus ignores them. "Weddings aren't just about clothes," he insists. "*Nothing's* just about clothes. You've got to open your mind. Isn't there something you really want to do that's *different* and *challenging* and *radical*?"

Brandi frowns. Her plump lips turn down at the corners. But her red-haired friend says, "You know what I'd love to do? I'd love to wear *all my clothes at once!*"

"Oh, Krystalle!" Skye squeals with excitement, clapping and bouncing. "That would be *so cool!*"

"Only I can't," Krystalle laments, "because I don't have enough legs or arms!"

"Aww . . ."

Watching the two girls hug each other, Noble decides that they're not the kind of people he wants on his team. *We'd be better off without them,* he thinks, glancing at Rufus—who scratches his head and mutters, "Maybe this isn't going to work."

Then Jay reappears. "Why don't you try some of these?" he says, passing a bundle of T-shirts to Rufus. Most of them are mud-colored, though several are brighter, with stripes and stars on them. Rufus selects one by simply plucking it off the pile; he drops the rest and says, "What about you, Jay? Do you want to be a man or a mannequin?"

"Huh?" Jay looks bewildered.

"We'll be leaving in a minute. So if you want to do something really special with your life, you're welcome to join us." Rufus cocks his head at Jay, his eyes glittering through his swag of hair.

Jay stares at him for a moment before repeating, "Special?"

"He means getting married," Skye volunteers, twisting a lock of black hair around her little finger.

"No, I don't!" Rufus snaps. "I mean liberation! Revolution!"

"But how are you going to get out?" asks Brandi. Her gaze is fixed on Rufus, who's struggling to push his head through a tight-fitting collar. "Did you come in through the laundry chute? Is that how you want to leave? Because I can't use the laundry chute if I'm wearing this skirt."

Rufus stiffens. Then he yanks the T-shirt down over his head so that his mop of hair suddenly springs into view, exploding off his scalp like a feather cockade. "What laundry chute?" he demands.

"The one in my wardrobe." Brandi nods at the open door. "Didn't you climb in through there? It's the only way out."

Rufus narrows his eyes. "You mean you dump all your dirty clothes down a laundry chute?"

"Sure," Brandi replies. "After we've worn them."

"And then what?" Rufus speaks sharply. "Do they come back clean?"

For some reason, Brandi finds this question difficult to answer. It's the red-haired Krystalle who responds.

"Sometimes they go out of fashion," she chimes in, "so they don't come back at all."

"Which is okay," Skye adds, "because there's always plenty of different stuff to put on!"

The other two girls coo in agreement. Jay, however, merely strikes a pose, gracefully running his fingers through his thick brown hair. His expression is dim and dreamy.

Rufus grabs Noble's arm.

"We're in luck," says Rufus. "I think we've found a way into the memory heap."

From his tone, it's clear that this is meant to be good news. But Noble has no idea why.

He clears his throat. "Oh?" is all he can come up with.

"It makes sense," Rufus continues. "This is a kiddie fashion program. Most of its dynamic memory would be used to change the clothing stock. And if we're *really* lucky, the software designer didn't worry about installing good internal defenses." Without warning, he suddenly whirls around to face Brandi. "Show me that laundry chute. I need to check it out. And you . . ." He snaps his fingers at Krystalle. "See what you can find for my friends to wear."

Noble is surprised when Krystalle trots off quite happily, with Skye at her heels. "First stop, sporty casual," the black-haired girl cheerfully observes, before they both vanish into Krystalle's wardrobe. Brandi, meanwhile, heads in the opposite direction. Teetering along in her cork-heeled platform shoes, she guides Rufus back into the room he just left, past rack after rack of brightly colored garments. Noble follows them both, dragging Yestin. As they all gather in front of an elaborate, scroll-topped cupboard, Noble says to Rufus, "What about the man in the white coat? You told us he might show up again. And the hatch is just over there."

"I know," Rufus says, nodding. "Which is why we have to hurry." He reaches up to tap Brandi on the shoulder. "We don't have time to stop and admire your handbag collection, if that's what you've got in this cupboard."

Brandi can't suppress a smile. "My handbag collection wouldn't fit in this cupboard," she informs him, turning a gold key in a filigree lock. Then she flings open the cupboard doors, revealing an unpainted stretch of wall with a large, square hole in it. Sure enough, a sign over the hole reads LAUNDRY. Craning his neck for a better look, Noble can see that the hole is actually the mouth of a metal shaft that drops straight down toward some distant, shadowy destination.

Rufus sticks his entire head into the hole. "Oh, this is big enough," he announces, his voice echoing strangely. "It might be a bit of a squeeze for Noble, but not if the rest of us are behind him, giving him a shove." Withdrawing his head, Rufus issues further instructions. "You know what we need? We need clothes. Lots of 'em. Now."

Noble frowns. Yestin gapes.

"What kind of clothes?" Brandi says.

"Any kind. It doesn't matter." When she stares at him in confusion, Rufus tries to explain. "All you have to do is rip 'em off the hangers," he tells her, waving at the nearest rack. Then he spots Krystalle, who's just walked across the threshold. She's brandishing an armful of clothes. "Oh, good," he says. "Why don't you dump those in the chute?"

But she won't, because some of the clothes are for Yestin. "I think this T-shirt will fit," she tells him kindly. "You need more color, but nothing too strong or no one will see your face. I've got some funky board shorts, too. And some hipster capris that might work."

"Hand 'em over, then." Cutting her off, Rufus

proceeds to throw his weight around. He orders Yestin to change. He instructs Noble to find a shirt he won't burst out of. He tells Krystalle to fetch more clothes and Brandi to consider her future. "You might be trendy now, but that won't last," he declares. "Some hot new fashion dolls will come along, with cuter names and better support software, and the kid who installed this program will drop you like last season's lipstick. You've got to think ahead. Make plans. Be true to yourself." As Brandi goggles at him, looking mildly flustered, he has a flash of inspiration. "Here's a start," he proposes. "Why don't you go and pick your own travel outfit? Something that *you* want to wear? Only it has to be practical for sliding down a laundry chute."

Brandi catches her breath. "You mean . . . I can choose anything at all?" she asks. "Right now?"

"Right now," Rufus confirms.

There's a brief silence. "Can I pack a bag?" is her next question.

Yestin, meanwhile, has been busy changing. "What do you think?" he suddenly inquires. He presents himself to Noble, twisting and turning, his arms outstretched to display his new outfit. "Do you like it?"

"Um . . ." Noble doesn't think that short pants are much of an improvement. In his opinion, Yestin's stick-thin legs need covering up. "It's a nice blue," he finally remarks.

"Oh, that's *way* better!" Krystalle assures Yestin. "You don't look so sallow, now. And it brings out the blue in your eyes." She thrusts a puffy silver garment at Noble. "What about these harem pants for you?" she asks. "They've got elastic—see? So they'd definitely fit. And you'd look kinda cute, like a genie or something. . . ."

Noble recoils. "I can't wear those!" he protests, eliciting an impatient scowl from Rufus.

"It's just camouflage. It's a safety measure," Rufus points out.

But Noble isn't persuaded. "I'm not wearing them," he says.

Then Brandi reappears, dressed in a gray silk jacket, cropped black leggings, a filmy belted tunic, and patent-leather ballet shoes, topped off by hoop earrings and a capacious handbag. "I thought black and gray would be more practical for the laundry chute," she declares. Rufus favors her with an approving nod, while Krystalle stares at her, openmouthed.

"Oh, my God," says Krystalle, before raising her voice. "Skye! Jay! Come in here and check this out, quick! Brandi's an *independent dresser!*"

"Okay." Ignoring Krystalle, Rufus focuses his attention on Brandi, Noble, and Yestin. "First we'll stuff a whole bunch of clothes down the chute. Then we'll send Noble down after them, because he's the heaviest. And then Brandi can go next."

"But what's *at* the bottom?" Noble interrupts. "You haven't told us."

"Yes, I have. It's the heap, remember? It's a dynamically allocated memory storage facility."

Noble blinks.

"It's where the programs dump blocks of memory during their run times," Yestin hastily butts in, "and some of the memory is recycled, and some of it becomes trash because it won't be used again." Faced with Noble's utter lack of comprehension, Yestin finishes lamely, "The whole thing's kind of confusing."

"Which is why you don't have to worry about it," Rufus instructs Noble. "The important thing is that the heap is full of discarded information— information we can use to get into really well-defended parts of this computer. Like the parts where the Colonel hangs out, for instance."

Noble grunts.

"It's also a cool place to check out our options," Rufus adds, for Brandi's benefit. Then he turns to Jay and Skye, who have finally emerged from the other room—perhaps because they want to inspect Brandi's new outfit. "You two! Pick up all the clothes you can find and stuff them into this laundry chute, okay? Just keep shoving 'em in until I tell you to stop." To everyone else, he says, "Well? What are you waiting for? Clothes, people—we need more clothes!"

It isn't long before armfuls of clothes are tumbling down the laundry chute, ripped from their hangers and balled up like rags. Load after load disappears into the gaping shaft until Rufus cries "Stop!" and grabs Noble's wrist. "Now you. Off you go."

"But—"

"Quick! Get in there!" Seeing Noble hesitate, Rufus promises that no one is going to get hurt. "You'll be hitting a pile of clothes, remember?"

Noble isn't concerned about where he's going to land. He's concerned about getting stuck half-way down. Nevertheless, he climbs into the chute as instructed—and soon realizes that he's not too wide for it after all. Clinging to the lip of the squared-off opening, he's able to wriggle around quite freely. His feet flail about in empty space. The cold, clanging metal feels slippery against his skin.

"What am I supposed to do when I reach the bottom?" he asks Rufus, who gives a snort.

"If I were you, I'd get out of the way," Rufus replies. "Unless you *want* Brandi to land on you."

"Yes, but—"

"It'll be fine, I promise."

"But what if something bad is down there?" Noble struggles to hold on, his voice tight and creaky. "Shouldn't we work out a signal, in case I need to warn you?"

"Don't worry about it, okay? There's nothing bad down there. Just go. *Go!*"

It's no good trying to argue with Rufus. So Noble heaves a sigh, loosens his grip, and drops like a stone.

CHAPTER ELEVEN

Noble plummets down a shiny metal shaft that dips and swerves just enough to make his descent a high-speed slide, rather than a straight-out fall. But he's still moving so quickly that when he hits the bottom—*whoomp!*—he finds himself buried deep in a pile of dirty clothes.

As he claws his way to the surface, Brandi plunges into the clothes beside him. There's a brief moment of confusion while Brandi thrashes about and Noble dodges her flailing arms. At last, however, he manages to push through the top layer of garments, emerging from the pile of clothes into what looks like unlimited space.

Above him is nothing but a pale, wintry sky. Around him is a vast rubbish dump, stretching off to the horizon. Giant trucks are unloading heaps of discarded objects, which are being shoved around by other machines armed with enormous scoops.

"We have to stay away from the bulldozers," Rufus suddenly remarks—and Noble, turning, sees that Rufus's head has popped out of the clothes behind him like a shooting bean sprout.

"What's a bulldozer?" asks Noble.

"That is." Rufus extricates his arms and points. "That's a bulldozer dumping a big load of memory into that truck over there. And we don't want to end up in that memory dump, because it's probably going to be recycled."

"I don't understand." Noble is hopelessly disoriented. "How did we even get here? Where did we come from?" He lifts his face to the sky, where no dangling laundry chute is evident. "I don't see a hole up there, do you?"

"Maybe the hole's underneath us," says Yestin, appearing from the pile of clothes. "Maybe we fell up, instead of down."

Noble has never heard anything so ridiculous in his life. "*Fell up?*" he echoes in disbelief. But Rufus simply shrugs.

"Maybe," Rufus concedes, as Brandi's glossy head bobs into view. "Now let's get out of this truck, shall we?"

Noble blinks, then glances around. He realizes that they *are* in a truck—a truck with a kind of open box on its back. While Rufus heads for the side of the box, half-wading, half-swimming through a tangle of clothes, Noble tries to feel around with his bare feet.

He can't find a hole, though.

"Where are we?" Brandi wails. "This isn't the *beach*, this is *awful*!"

"We'll get to the beach. Don't worry." With his fingers clamped to the edge of the low, metal wall that's enclosing them, Rufus glances around. "First we've got to find an exit, okay?"

He swings his legs over the wall and drops out of sight, hitting the ground with a *thud*. Noble follows, after helping Yestin plow his way through a tightly packed drift of fake fur and knitted items.

Brandi is last in line. She takes a moment to shove something fluffy into her bag. Then, because she refuses to jump down from the truck, Noble has to grab her as she lowers herself awkwardly over its side.

"Okay," says Rufus, once everyone has joined him. "Now we have to spend a bit of time scavenging. And as you can see, there's a lot to search through." He waves an arm at the surrounding heaps of detritus. "But there's also a lot we can use to get out of here, like keys and maps and tickets—especially keys. Default keys. Keep your eyes peeled for anything that looks like a key. Or even half a key."

Noble gazes around grimly at all the towering hillocks of *stuff*. He can't imagine how they're going to find a humble key among so many rolls of paper, cardboard folders, nets, brooms, clocks, and broken picture frames. It will be like looking for a needle in a haystack.

"Are you *kidding* me?" Brandi whines, echoing his thoughts. "We'll be here *forever.*"

"No, we won't," Rufus insists. To Noble he says, "I'll check this pile. You check that one. Just watch out for the bulldozers."

"Which heap should *I* check?" Yestin butts in. "That one there?" He points at a mountain of discarded sporting equipment.

"Yeah, yeah, whatever." Rufus flaps him away. Noble, meanwhile, has trudged over to his own designated mound of junk, which is much taller and wider than Yestin's. Though it's scattered with old brushes, scissors, and empty paint pots, the pile is composed chiefly of pictures—highly realistic portraits presented on shiny cards. They're not drawings, or paintings, or engravings. Noble can't figure out *what* they are.

"Look at these pictures," he says. "They're so perfect!"

"They're photographs," Yestin explains as Brandi stoops to extract a feathery, iridescent wing from a huge pile of punctured balloons and giant lollipops. The wing isn't attached to anything.

She displays it gingerly, like dirty underwear.

"Can we use *this* to get out?" she asks Rufus. "Maybe if I find another one and put them both on . . ."

"No." Rufus is as blunt as the broken sword that he's just pulled from another trash heap. With a sigh, he tosses it away. "Keys, remember? We're looking for keys."

"I've found one!" Yestin pounces. "Here's a key!"

"Show me," says Rufus.

At that very instant, Noble spots something that makes him gasp. He darts forward and seizes a photograph.

It's a picture of Rufus.

"Rufus?" he croaks. Then he holds it up. "Is this— is this *you*?"

Rufus lifts his gaze from the little silver key that Yestin has given him. "Nope," he replies, without much interest, before turning his attention back to the key. "Good work, Yestin. Can you find any more?"

Noble studies the photograph again. It shows a skinny boy in a grubby T-shirt, draped across a leather couch. The boy appears to be slightly younger than Rufus, but he has Rufus's cheeky grin and sly expression. As for his hair . . .

"Are you sure?" Noble presses. "This looks just like you."

"It's not," Rufus assures him.

"Who could it be, then?"

"It's the real Rufus. It's the guy who came up with my programming."

Even Yestin reacts to this piece of news. He stiffens, his jaw dropping, as Noble catches his breath.

"The *what*?" Noble splutters. "What do you mean, the *real Rufus*?"

"Here's one!" Unlike Yestin, Brandi seems completely oblivious to all the drama. She's just swooped on a heavy cast-iron key, which she's now waving in the air. "Is this all right? Will this do?"

"It's fine," Rufus confirms. "I'll take it."

Yestin, meanwhile, has rushed to examine Noble's discovery. "Is that your programmer, Rufus? Oh, wow," Yestin squeaks. "How *weird*."

"Yeah, I guess he sorta made me in his own image." Having pocketed Brandi's key, Rufus is now poking around in a mess of flat, shiny disks and broken musical instruments. "Maybe that's what always happens when you're an inexperienced programmer, working by yourself. Maybe he can't keep his personality out of the programming." With a sudden hiss, Rufus hunkers down to snatch up something small and silver. "Here's another key!" he announces. "And it's identical to the first one, too, which is *great*."

"But . . . I don't understand." Noble is still reeling. "Are you a copy, then? Are you like the false Noble?"

"No, no. You're not getting it." Rufus straightens and sighs. "That guy in the photo—the real Rufus—he doesn't live inside this computer with us. He's out in the real world, where the Colonel doesn't run things." Nodding at the great rubbish heap behind Noble, Rufus adds, "Those are all photos of the real world, but they've been trashed. Binned. The files have been deleted—I don't know why. And it doesn't matter, anyway. Not to us."

"Yes, it does!" Yestin protests, as Noble struggles to understand. "It matters if the real Rufus owns this computer! What if he's the one who's been playing all the games around here?"

"He isn't." Rufus's tone is flat but convincing. "This computer doesn't belong to him. Believe me, if it did, I wouldn't be needing all these keys. Because I already *have* Rufus's current password. It's bloodquest."

"Then who does the computer belong to?" Yestin wants to know.

Rufus shrugs. "Some guy called Mikey," he says, leaving Noble utterly confused.

"Mikey? Who's Mikey?" Noble can't recall anyone named Mikey. "I thought you said the Colonel was in charge?"

"He is. He's in charge of making sure that Mikey gets what he wants." Seeing Noble's blank expression doesn't change, Rufus takes a deep breath, as if he's about to elaborate.

But then, Brandi screams.

"Oh, wow! You guys! Come here, quick, this is so *freaky*!" She begins to back away from the color-ful mass of junk that she's been exploring. "Look! It's alive! It's coming out!" she exclaims.

Rufus and Yestin both hurl themselves toward her, but Noble hesitates. He's seen another picture of Rufus—or at least, another picture of the "real" Rufus, who looks almost as young as Yestin in this particular photograph. The young Rufus is shown sitting at a table behind a large blue cake, grinning happily, with his arm around the shoulders of another boy who has stiff black hair and high cheekbones. Most of the pictures seem to feature this black-haired boy, along with Rufus and a little dark-eyed girl. There's also a white dog and a gray cat.

It occurs to Noble, as he inspects the photographs, that he's looking at two boys growing up. Sometimes they're young and sometimes they're older. Sometimes they have short hair, sometimes long. Sometimes they're sprawled on a messy bed, cuddling animals, while at other times they're outdoors, at the beach or in a tree house.

Though the passage of time is a fairly new concept to Noble, these photographs illustrate it perfectly. They're like a story in pictures. He can't get over how long and rich a person's past can actually be.

His own short history seems like a mere stub in comparison.

"Noble! Hey!" It's Rufus calling him. Glancing up from the photographs in his hand, Noble sees that the other three are clustered around a kind of eruption in the side of a junk heap. Something about the size of a gargoyle is struggling to free itself from a press of candy canes and beach balls. Rufus has grabbed two pink legs with silver hoofs. Yestin has grabbed Rufus.

"One—two—three—*heave!*" Rufus sets his teeth

and drags at the stumpy legs, dodging a silver spike like a very thin, very elongated triton shell, which is also emerging from the junk pile.

Noble drops his photographs and hurries to help.

"Oh, look!" Brandi squeals. "It's a unicorn!"

"Here." Noble seizes one pink leg, jostling Rufus aside. "Let me do it."

A single tug is all it takes. Noble suddenly finds himself sitting on the ground beneath a miniature horse with a horn on its forehead. The horse has a silver mane and huge, melting eyes. Its eyelashes are even longer than Brandi's.

"Oh, it's *gorgeous*!" she croons. "Isn't it gorgeous? And it matches my unicorn pendant!"

When the animal starts to lick him, Noble pushes it off his chest. Then he climbs to his feet while Brandi and Yestin converge on the little unicorn, which is dancing with excitement.

"Hello! I'm Brandi! What's your name?"

"I don't think it can talk," Yestin says doubtfully as the unicorn squeaks its response. "It's got a name tag, though—look."

Brandi promptly makes a grab for the little silver medal hanging on a pink ribbon around the unicorn's neck. "Lulu," she reads aloud. "Hello, Lulu! Where did you come from?"

"Some preschool game full of squeaky pink things," Rufus volunteers, answering for the unicorn. He seems to think it's funny.

Noble isn't amused, though. He's shocked to see an animal in a rubbish dump.

"No one threw *her* out, surely?" he demands, gesturing at Lulu. "She must have escaped. Like us."

"Nah." Rufus shakes his head. "She was scrapped."

"But—"

"That's what happens. I told you, the Colonel's a tyrant." Hearing Yestin's gasp of dismay, Rufus tries to soften the blow. "I guess Lulu *might* be used again. She might not get recycled. I just wouldn't count on it."

"Poor Lulu!" Yestin cries. He throws his arms around the unicorn's neck, while Noble gazes at Rufus, arrested by a sudden, disturbing thought.

If animals are being dumped in the trash, then why not people?

"Are you telling me this creature has been *replaced*?" Noble asks Rufus, jerking his chin at the unicorn. "The way I was replaced?"

"Uh . . . kind of. Except that this is a little different. . . ."

It's not much of an answer, but it has to satisfy Noble. Because once again, without warning, Brandi hijacks the conversation.

"Who's that?" she says, gazing past Rufus. "Do you know him?"

Everyone turns to see a man in a yellow helmet crunching across the debris. He wears a bright orange vest, thick gloves, and sturdy boots. There's a large sack on his shoulder.

When he spies the knot of people around Lulu, he stops and stares.

"Oh—hi!" Rufus calls to him. "Are you a garbage collector? I want to talk to you! What's your name?"

The man in the helmet frowns. "I'm *the* garbage collector," he replies.

"Oh." Rufus pulls a face, then clicks his tongue. "Well, let's call you Jeezy for short," he suggests. "*Everyone* should have a proper name."

"You're not on my recycling inventory." The garbage collector sounds concerned. "What's your point of origin?"

"To be honest, I'm not local," Rufus admits. "I've come here on a mercy mission. To set you free." He cocks his head, peering up at Jeezy with a challenging glint in his eye. "I mean, do you *like* what you're doing? Do you enjoy picking up dumped memory all day long?"

The garbage collector regards him stonily. "This is my job. It's an important job. It's what I'm here for."

"Yes, I know," says Rufus. "But my question is— do you want to do it forever? Or is there something else you'd rather be doing?"

As Rufus launches into his standard spiel, Noble's attention starts to wander. It's obvious that Jeezy has never before questioned his place in the world. He seems to find the whole concept of alternatives very hard to comprehend. And though Noble can sympathize with Jeezy's confusion, he's not interested in listening to yet more arguments about freedom and oppression and justice. Not when there are other, more urgent matters to attend to.

Turning away from Rufus, Noble sees that he's not the only one who has lost interest in the garbage collector. Brandi is once more clucking over Lulu, whose silver horn sparkles as she tries to yank a scarf out of Brandi's bag with her teeth. Yestin is halfheartedly searching for keys again, his eyes skipping between Lulu and the pile of photographs. "If this computer belongs to Mikey," he informs Noble under his breath, "then maybe Mikey's the one who's been playing all the games in here. Maybe *he* installed us."

Noble grunts. He'd certainly like to know more about Mikey—and about the Colonel, too. Are they friends of the real Rufus? Is there a picture of the Colonel somewhere in that pile of photographs?

Unfortunately, not one of these questions is going to be answered until Rufus has finished with the garbage collector. And the garbage collector is proving surprisingly stubborn.

". . . yes, I realize it's an important job," Rufus is saying. "It's *vitally* important. Which is why you deserve to be treated like a valuable member of the team. But are you? That's what I'm asking. Do you feel appreciated?"

"I'm just doing my job," Jeezy intones.

"Sure. And you deserve some kind of recognition for that." When the garbage collector shows no signs of comprehending, Rufus elaborates. "Like a living wage, for instance. Or time off. Or benefits."

"Time off?" says Jeezy, his tone so vague it's as if he's letting a foreign language roll around on his tongue.

Rufus heaves a sigh. "In the real world," he explains, "garbage collectors don't work around the clock. What's more, they get rewarded for the hours they put in—and if anyone refuses to give them what they're owed, they go on strike."

Again Jeezy fails to understand. "Strike?" he echoes.

"They stop working. . . ."

"Noble?" Suddenly, a shrill voice rings out, slicing through the air like a silver dart. "Noble the Slayer? Is that you?"

Noble whirls around. Through a gap in the heaps of rubbish he can just make out a very small, slim, disheveled figure in grubby green. Noble recognizes her instantly, even though her gown is torn and her hair is a mess.

It's Princess Lorellina.

CHAPTER TWELVE

Noble stares mutely at the princess, who glares back at him. Yestin shoots Noble a questioning look. Brandi remarks to no one in particular, "Who's she? I like her belt buckle."

Rufus barely glances in Lorellina's direction. "It's okay," he tells Jeezy. "She's just another friend."

"Are you sure?" The garbage collector sounds surprised—perhaps because the expression on Lorellina's face is far from friendly. Her scowl is so fierce that Noble can't help cringing.

"Where did you *go*?" she snaps at him. "You disappeared!"

"We—we went to find reinforcements," Noble mutters. Though acutely embarrassed, he's also relieved, because it's clear now that this isn't the false princess. The false princess wouldn't have been searching for him. She would have wanted him dead and gone.

"Reinforcements?" she spits, her gaze traveling over the motley group in front of her. "Is *this* the army you raised? Is *this* what you deserted us for?"

Noble takes a deep breath. "Princess—"

"We have been deposed!" she cries shrilly. "We have been cast into a midden! I had to escape from a cart full of dismembered gargoyles and shattered spears!"

By this time, Rufus has pulled Jeezy aside; they're conversing together in low, serious tones. Brandi is trying to calm the unicorn. Yestin is watching, wide-eyed, as Noble fends off Lorellina's attack.

"Where *is* your cousin?" asks Noble. "Did he escape with you?"

"Yes. He did." Lorellina turns her head and raises her voice. "Harry! Come here!"

"And the guards? What happened to them?"

The princess shrugs. "It was confusing," she admits. "I was trying to save the gargoyles, but the new ones attacked the old ones. They tore one another apart. Harry and I were chased into the big white carriage, but then the doors closed. . . ." She trails off, rubbing her eyes. Before Noble can press her for more details, however, she's distracted by her cousin's approach. "Look, Harry—see who has come to our aid, at long last! And with reinforcements, too!"

Though she's speaking sarcastically, Noble doesn't reproach her for it. He feels guilty enough as it is. And the sight of Lord Harrowmage, who's shuffling along with his ragged skirts trailing in the dust, doesn't exactly lighten Noble's mood.

"Oh, wow," Yestin mutters, gazing in awe at the mage's shrouded figure and craggy, haunted face. "Who's that?"

"Lord Harrowmage," Noble replies. Then he apologizes to the wizard. "My lord, I failed you. Forgive me. But it wasn't my fault."

Lord Harrowmage isn't interested. "Is Rufus here?" he rasps. When he catches sight of Rufus—who's still earnestly haranguing the puzzled garbage collector—he heaves a sigh of relief. "Ah. Good. I truly believe that Rufus is our only hope."

"Rufus?" Lorellina protests. "That untrained boy? Why would you think such a thing?"

"Because knowledge is the greatest of all weapons," her cousin informs her, "and Rufus is more knowledgeable than any of us."

As the princess casts Rufus a doubtful glance, Yestin sidles up to Noble and says softly, "Are these two from *Thanehaven Slayer?*"

Noble nods.

"I thought so. Is she your girlfriend?"

"No."

"Really? She looks like she is."

Noble ignores this remark. Brandi, meanwhile, is

addressing the princess. "I love that color. Is it natural or do you get it tinted?"

Lorellina blinks. "What?" she says in confusion.

"Your hair." Brandi gives her own lustrous locks a careless flick. "I like that coppery shade. It's classic but edgy. You know what I mean?"

"No." The princess appeals to Noble. "What on earth is she talking about?"

Noble shrugs. "It doesn't matter," he replies. "What matters is our fight for freedom." Glancing from the princess to Rufus to Lord Harrowmage, he adds, "The battle for Thanehaven cannot be fought *within* Thanehaven. Our true enemy is the Colonel, not the man in the white coat. The Colonel commands everyone and everything in this computer, so if we defeat the Colonel, we can decide our own fates. And that will mean raising a force with which to oppose him."

Lord Harrowmage frowns. His cousin says, "But who *is* the Colonel?" before pointing at the garbage collector. "Is that him?"

"Oh, no." Yestin quickly sets her straight. "No, that's Jeezy."

"Jeezy?"

"The Colonel isn't here with us," Noble explains. "We have to go and find him, because he's the one who wants to keep us all imprisoned. He sends monsters after children and buries innocent animals in rubbish dumps. Unless we challenge his power, there will always be war in Thanehaven."

148

"Then we must kill him!" Lorellina cries, raising her poleax. "We must kill the Colonel and usurp his crown!"

"Oh—uh—I don't think so." To everyone's surprise, Yestin suddenly speaks up. "We shouldn't kill the Colonel," he argues. "We wouldn't survive without him."

Noble can hardly believe his ears. "The Colonel is trying to *kill* us, Yestin! We need to protect ourselves!"

"Yeah, I know, but we can't do that by killing him." Yestin goes on to explain that all computer operating systems have programs like the Colonel running their primary functions. According to Yestin, if the operating system crashes, the computer will stop working. "At least, that's what happens where *I* come from," he finishes. "I don't know if it's the same here."

"Mmph," says Noble, feeling once again as if he's losing his grip on the world. He's still trying to figure things out when Rufus exclaims, "Hey, guys! Guess what? We're leaving! Jeezy's going to turn back the very next truckload of memory that shows up! And he'll let us hitch a ride on the truck, which should arrive any minute. Isn't that great?" Rufus claps Jeezy on the back. "Thanks, pal. Thanks so much. You're a real lifesaver."

Brandi says, "So are we going to the beach now?" Lord Harrowmage fixes Noble with a somber, questioning look.

Yestin raises his hand and clears his throat. "Um . . .

is this the only truck that's going to be turned back?" he asks Rufus. "Because—I mean—if the memory isn't recycled, won't the computer run out of memory?"

"That's right!" Rufus grins at him. "Which is why the Colonel will either meet Jeezy's demands, or suffer the consequences!" Rufus turns to Jeezy, saying, "You've got him over a barrel. He'll be eating out of your hand, I guarantee."

"But if the computer runs out of memory, that'll be bad for us. Won't it?" Yestin doggedly objects. "Where I come from, you'd be really stupid to shut down your heap. Your whole system would end up crashing."

"Don't worry. We're not going to shut down the heap," Rufus assures him. "We won't have to. This is all about leverage. It's about *negotiation*."

"We'll negotiate with the Colonel and he'll meet our demands," Jeezy adds, earning himself an approving nod from Rufus.

"Exactly," says Rufus. "He'll give you *anything* if you threaten his memory supply. It's a no-brainer."

"So we won't have to kill the Colonel?" Noble wants to clarify this once and for all. "You think we can parley with him?"

"Oh, yes. If we've got enough leverage." Rufus's attention is already wandering. He narrows his eyes at the sound of a distant, low-pitched roar. "Is that the next truck?" he asks Jeezy.

"Maybe." As the garbage collector plucks a small black machine from beneath his orange vest, Noble scans the horizon, watching for movement. But there's a miniature mountain range of garbage blocking every view, in every direction. The only truck that Noble can see is the one from which he recently escaped.

"Roger that," says Jeezy. He's been talking into his little machine, which has been talking back to him. Now he tucks it into his vest and announces, "ETA in two minutes. Sector 18B. We should head out there."

"Great!" Rufus rubs his hands together. "Come on, you guys! Let's go!"

"Can Lulu come with us?" Brandi pleads. "She won't be any trouble."

"Of course! The more, the merrier." Rufus hurries after Jeezy without so much as a backward glance, leaving the others to exchange bewildered looks before finally, reluctantly, setting off in his wake. Lulu skips along ahead of the group, snorting and snickering, tossing her horn. Lord Harrowmage brings up the rear, his shoulders hunched and his expression shuttered. He looks scratched and soiled and very, very tired.

Like Yestin, the princess sticks close to Noble. "Tell me what the 'computer' is," she says. "Why is it so important? Does it belong to the Colonel?"

"Um . . . no." Noble recalls what Rufus said about a person named Mikey. "The Colonel runs it, but it belongs to someone else."

"Is it a machine? Like these others?" Lorellina gestures back at the parked truck. "Is it a war machine?"

"It's where we are," Noble explains haltingly. When the princess still isn't enlightened, he tries again. "We're in it. Now."

"You mean this is the *land* of Computer?"

"Sort of." Noble wishes that Rufus wasn't powering along up ahead. He needs Rufus. They all need Rufus.

It's hard to clarify something when you don't fully understand it yourself.

"Thanehaven is a land within the world of this computer," Noble declares, turning to Yestin for help. "Isn't that right?"

"Yeah, I guess so." Yestin launches into a long and detailed lecture on something he calls computer hardware, which keeps him jabbering away until they reach a patch of clear ground with another big truck on it.

When Jeezy stops, everyone else does the same. "Here you are," says Jeezy, pointing to the truck. "Here's your ride."

"Okay. Thanks." With a brisk nod, Rufus swivels around to address the little group of stragglers clustered behind him. "We've got to climb into the back," he announces. "With all the rubbish. Sorry."

"Oh, do we *have* to?" Brandi whines. "Can't we get in the front part, where all the windows are?"

"No," says Rufus. He doesn't elaborate, though.

It's Jeezy who explains that nobody riding up front will ever escape. "You have to stay with the memory," he assures everyone.

In the end, only Jeezy himself doesn't follow Rufus into the back of the truck. Noble hoists first Brandi, then Lulu, then Yestin up over the tailgate. Lorellina won't be helped. She insists on climbing, even though the giant truck's back end isn't well supplied with footholds.

Her cousin, however, is grateful for Noble's assistance. Lord Harrowmage doesn't object when he's heaved like a wrapped bundle toward half a dozen outstretched hands. And when Noble finally joins the others, panting and sweating after his struggle to reach the top, Lord Harrowmage is the one who leans down and pulls him into a sea of crumpled paper.

"Oh," says Noble, once he's got his breath back. He's enormously pleased to find that he's not up to his neck in broken glass or battleground sweepings, but merely knee-deep in clean, densely compacted paper. "This is all right. I thought it would be worse than this."

"It's a bit scratchy," Yestin complains.

"You could bleed to death from the paper cuts, couldn't you?" says Rufus. Then he yells, for Jeezy's benefit, "We're all on board! You can start the strike now!"

Someone immediately thumps on the side of the truck. A grinding noise is followed by a shudder. Yestin picks up a sheet of paper. "This is an e-mail from Rufus, addressed to Mikey. There's an IP address and everything," he says. Before Noble can ask what an e-mail is, Yestin begins to read aloud. " 'To Mikey Braindead Loser—so you think you can ban me from the game? Think again, snitch. We might go back a long way, but you are *so* going to regret what you've done—' "

A sudden roar drowns his voice. Then the entire truckload of litter begins to slide out from beneath them, as if it's emptying down a plughole.

"Eeeeeeeeeeeeeek!" Brandi screams. She lunges for the rim of the tailgate, which she can't quite reach.

Noble falls on his back and starts rolling; he can feel the pages collapsing under his weight.

"It's okay!" Rufus cries. "It's the dump! Just go with it!" A moment later, he's swallowed up, disappearing into a crinkly white avalanche. The last thing that Noble sees, before he's swept away like Rufus, is Yestin's pale, pinched, frightened face.

Whoosh! The drop takes about two seconds. Noble wonders fleetingly if he's going to suffocate as he barrels down an unseen tube, almost smothered by a torrent of crackling paper. Then he plows into more paper—and next thing he knows, he's bumping along a gentle incline onto an extremely narrow, moving platform.

At first, he's too dazed to do anything much, except stare. Great tides of paper are still pouring from an overhead duct and pooling on the platform directly behind him, though loose sheets keep fluttering to the floor. The floor is gray and polished. So is the surface on which he's landed. A red light is flashing on and off nearby, to the accompaniment of a loud wailing noise.

Rufus is crawling along the platform up ahead, away from Noble.

"What's going on?" Noble demands. "Rufus?"

"It's an alarm!" answers Rufus. He has to pitch his voice high above the deafening racket. "This mail shouldn't be coming back in!"

"What mail?" Noble looks around for a suit of chain mail, but he can't see any. All he can see are pipes and beams and countless moving platforms in a room that's almost as big as Thanehaven. Colored boxes are slowly chugging along on raised belts. There's paper everywhere, and all of it's being organized somehow—it's either being spat out of machines or stuffed into bins or whizzed past wheels on long, rubbery ribbons.

"This is the e-mail program!" Rufus loudly explains, as he climbs down from the platform. "It's where all the messages get sorted when they reach Mikey's address!"

This still doesn't mean much to Noble—and he's not interested, anyway. He's far more concerned about the flashing light and the shrieking alarm. "How many guards are stationed here?" he wants to know. Then something strikes him in the small of his back. "*Ooof!*" he grunts.

Yestin has just tumbled down the papery slope and collided with him.

155

"Get off that conveyor belt!" Rufus instructs, beckoning urgently. At the same instant, Noble sees Brandi shoot out of the overhead duct and land on the pile of e-mail messages that Yestin just rolled off. Part of the pile promptly collapses, sending sheets of paper whirling into the air like windblown petals. Noble scrambles to safety, pulling Yestin along with him.

The floor is covered in more pieces of paper. They slip and slide treacherously beneath Noble's bare feet.

"This is a program malfunction!" Rufus bellows. "We've gotta clear out before the repair team arrives!" As Lulu joins Brandi, he adds, "That AV's bound to be on his way, too! Did you hear me? Noble?"

"I heard you!" Noble helps Brandi down to the floor, then wraps his arms around the squealing unicorn. "But we have to wait for the others!"

Rufus screws up his nose, shifting restlessly from foot to foot. "We don't want to waste any time!" he counters at the top of his voice. "Why don't I go find the nearest exit? It might take a while in a place this big!"

Yestin looks aghast. "Oh, but—"

"You can come with me!" Rufus cuts him off. "Noble doesn't need you!"

Putting his hands over his ears, Yestin turns to look at Noble—who's just dumped Lulu on the floor.

"Yes, go!" Noble orders, as a big, dark shape pops

156

out of the overhead chute. It's Lord Harrowmage. A few stray e-mails drift down on top of him, but the flood of paper seems to have dried to a trickle.

"Where's Princess Lorellina?" Noble asks.

"I—I don't know." Lord Harrowmage is barely audible. He seems dazed by all the noise and confusion. So Noble seizes his arm and drags him off the motionless conveyor belt.

It's like trying to shift a loose collection of sandbags.

"Go! Quick! Follow the others!" Noble says. He points at Rufus, who's trotting away with Yestin, Brandi and Lulu at his heels. Yestin keeps glancing back at Noble.

"But my cousin . . . ," Lord Harrowmage feebly protests.

"I'll get her! Don't worry! Just *go!*" Noble roars. He gives the wizard a push, then leaps up onto the conveyor belt. "Princess? Are you stuck? Can you hear me?"

If there's a reply, it's drowned out by the blaring alarm. So Noble picks his way unsteadily through several reams of loose paper until he's right underneath the mouth of the overhead duct. "Princess?" he yells again, directing his voice straight up a short metal shaft toward a little square of pale-gray sky. "Are you there?"

After about three seconds, a black silhouette appears at the top of the shaft.

"Noble? Is that you?" It's Lorellina's voice.

Noble heaves a sigh of relief. "Yes!" he bawls. "It's me!"

"Are you all right? What's that noise?"

"It's nothing!" Noble wrenches his gaze from her distant form and scans the machinery around him. There's a lot of movement, but none of it looks threatening. "Come down!" he begs. "We're all safe here!"

"Are you sure?" Lorellina is hoarse with the strain of shouting. "Would you rather come back up? Because I can always find a rope. . . ."

"No! Come down! It's not a trap!" Noble realizes suddenly that he can't see Rufus anymore. "Hurry, please, or we'll lose the others!"

A clanging sound makes him glance up again. Lorellina is already climbing into the shaft—and she's not dawdling, either. He barely has time to brace himself before she slams into his chest.

The force of the impact knocks him down.

"Ow!" She grimaces. "Sorry!"

Noble tries to reassure her, but ends up coughing instead.

"What a terrible noise!" she cries. "What is this place?"

"The e-mail program . . ."

"The *what*?"

Noble shakes his head. "It doesn't matter!" he says as they untangle themselves. They're both struggling to their feet, lurching like newborn calves on the surface of the paper pile, when Noble looks up to check on Yestin's progress.

At that instant, he spots something very, very bad.

"Oh, no," he groans.

Lorellina frowns at him. "What?" she says.

Noble doesn't answer immediately. He's looking at a distant flicker of white that's plotting a course across the gigantic room, behind a complicated grid of pipes and belts and shelves and cables. The thing keeps appearing and disappearing, like a white wolf padding through a forest. Noble can't hear it—not with the alarm going—but then again, he doesn't really need to.

He knows that van. He's seen it before.

"We've got to get out of here! *Now!*" he barks. Then he grabs Lorellina and starts to run.

CHAPTER THIRTEEN

Noble runs blindly. He can't see Rufus. All he can see are bins and shelves and chutes and paper and machines.

Then he spots a giant conveyor belt plunging through the floor like a circular staircase. "There!" he cries. "Down there!"

The princess doesn't argue because she's too busy dodging sharp corners and overhead pipes. She loses a shoe as Noble drags her toward the hole in the floor.

"Wait!" she pleads. "My shoe . . ."

But Noble's not about to stop for anything. "We *can't* wait!" he warns her. Winding an arm around her waist, he lifts her onto the conveyor belt. "Just slide!" he urges. "Push yourself!" And he joins her on the moving platform, trying to use its raised metal sides as a kind of shield by keeping as low as possible.

Ahead of him, Lorellina is squirming down the spiral belt. Its base is almost lost in shadow, though Noble can just make out that they're heading toward a large bin parked on a hard gray floor. Upon reaching the bin, Lorellina hops out quite nimbly for someone wearing long skirts.

Noble doesn't manage nearly as well.

"Where are we?" Lorellina whispers. She's peering around a murky space that's like a cellar with low ceilings and multiple exits. Its walls are lined with gray metal cabinets full of drawers. "Where is Rufus?"

"I don't know. Through there, perhaps." Noble heads for the nearest doorway, which opens into another long, low, dingy room stuffed with metal cabinets. There are hundreds of cabinets, all lined up in rows like soldiers at attention. And beyond the cabinets is another doorway, leading to another, identical room.

The air is still. No one else is in sight.

"Rufus?" Noble calls softly. But Rufus doesn't answer.

"Are you sure this is the right way?" asks the princess. "Maybe Rufus didn't come down here."

"It doesn't matter. We have to keep moving. We have to get out."

"Why?" Lorellina digs in her heels. "What are we running away from?"

"The man in the white coat." Hearing Lorellina's

161

gasp of horror, Noble adds, "I saw him upstairs. I saw his van."

"Did he see us?"

"I don't know."

"We should kill him!" Lorellina exclaims. "We should set up an ambush!"

Noble shakes his head. He's beginning to realize that killing isn't the answer—not in a world full of clones. For every white-coated minion who's slaughtered, a dozen more probably will pop up in his place.

"Come," orders Noble. "There has to be another way out." And he sets off to find it, with one ear cocked for the sound of approaching footsteps.

The princess follows grudgingly. Having removed her other shoe, she now pads along barefoot, her passage marked only by the swish of her trailing skirts. In the silence, even that small noise seems very loud.

Together, they hurry from room to room, through doorway after doorway. But every doorway leads to yet another shadowy room furnished with cabinets. There are no chairs, no beds, no hearths, no tables, no windows—just gray metal cabinets under dim ceiling lights. And the procession of rooms appears to be endless.

"Maybe there *is* no way out," Lorellina murmurs at last.

"There has to be." Noble's attention is suddenly caught by a faint clanging noise. Laying a finger on his lips, he gestures at the princess, indicating she should stay where she is. The princess, however, has other ideas. As Noble edges toward the nearest threshold, she stays close behind him—so close that he can feel her breath on his back. Her breathing is quick and shallow.

He has to take a few deep breaths of his own before peering around a doorjamb to see who's banging drawers in the next room. And because he's expecting the worst (a troll, perhaps, or another white-coated man), the sight of a tall, thin, elderly woman comes as a pleasant surprise. She doesn't look dangerous. In fact, her knitted cardigan, gray hair, and stooped shoulders are so reassuring that Noble clears his throat.

"Ahem," he says. "Excuse me?"

The woman turns to study him. Standing between a four-drawer cabinet and a yellow bin on wheels, she's been slowly and methodically transferring sheets of paper from the bin to the top drawer. But now she stops, blinking owlishly through a pair of gold-rimmed glass circles that are perched on her nose.

"May I help you?" she asks.

"Um . . . yes," Noble replies. "Have you seen our friend Rufus? He's quite young and skinny, with long hair that looks like sheep's wool, only it's a golden-brown color."

There's a brief pause. At last, the old woman says, "No."

Noble grunts. The news is disappointing, though not entirely unexpected.

"Have you seen *anyone* come through here?" he continues. "A little boy, or a pink unicorn, or a bearded mage?"

"No." The old woman's tone somehow manages to convey that visitors simply aren't a feature of her existence.

So Noble tries another tack. "Do you know if there's a way out of here?" is his next question.

"Out of this cellar," Lorellina cuts in. "Not out of this room. We can easily find our way out of this room."

The old woman sniffs. She says flatly, "This isn't a cellar. This is the Archive. You can't possibly belong here if you don't know that."

"You're right. We don't belong here," Noble confirms. "That's why we want to leave."

"Do you have a reference number?" asks the old woman.

"No." Lorellina is becoming impatient. "Of course not."

"I can't file you without a reference number."

Noble winces. Filing is what he does to his own weapons and fingernails; he can't imagine a more lingering or painful torture. "Good," he growls. "We don't want to be filed."

"We just want you to show us the way out," Lorellina tells the old woman. "If there is one."

The old woman frowns slightly. When she speaks, she sounds puzzled. "The way out is the

164

way you came in. You *did* come in, didn't you?"

"Yes, we did," Noble admits. "But we don't want to go back the way we came. Isn't there another portal of some kind? A door or a window or a staircase?"

The old woman stares at him. It's as if she can't quite process what she's hearing. "Another portal?" she echoes.

"Yes." Noble addresses her politely, ignoring the princess (who's rolling her eyes). "We're looking for an exit that will take us from your Archive to another place. A different place."

"Like the trapdoor, you mean?"

It's Noble's turn to frown. "The trapdoor?" he says.

"What trapdoor?" Lorellina pounces on this bit of information eagerly. "Where? Show us!"

If the old woman dislikes being ordered around, she doesn't say so. Instead, she shuts the top drawer of the cabinet and sets off, clumping along in thick-soled shoes that look too heavy for her thin ankles. "It's in here," she explains, as she disappears into the next room. "I don't know what it's for. It appeared one day, out of nowhere. Here it is—see?"

She's referring to a small hatch that's set low in one dim corner. It's just a hole in the wall, with rough-hewn edges and no latch. The panel wedged into it isn't even hinged.

"I wonder if it's supposed to be here?" says Noble.

"It *is* here," the old woman points out.

"Yes, but—" Noble begins, then stops and sighs.

He doesn't believe that she's going to understand, even if he explains himself more fully.

Lorellina, meanwhile, has joined him. "Where does it go?" she asks.

The old woman says, "I have no idea."

"It doesn't matter where it goes. Just as long as it doesn't lead back where we came from." Noble begins to tug at one of the cabinets, dragging it away from the wall so that he can squeeze past it.

The old woman goggles at him, appalled. "What are you doing? Don't do that! You mustn't move the filing cabinets!"

"You can push it back when we're gone," Noble retorts. "Or, no—I'll *pull* it back. So you won't hurt yourself. How does that sound?"

"But you don't have permission! This is all wrong. This is against the rules."

Noble decides to ignore her. "I'm afraid you'll have to go first," he sheepishly informs the princess. "These cabinets are too heavy for you to move."

Lorellina seems to accept this. Her only concern is the width of the hole. "Are you actually going to *fit* through there?" she asks, while the old woman wrings her knobbly hands in distress. "It looks very small."

With a shrug, Noble says, "We'll soon find out." Then he addresses the old woman. "You can return to work, if you want."

"The cabinet—"

"I told you. I'll shift it back."

By now, Lorellina has edged past him. She hunkers down in front of the hatchway, her gown a puffy green puddle, her gleaming ringlets cascading over her narrow shoulders. When she inserts the tips of her fingers between the edge of the hatch and the wall, Noble tries to stop her. "Wait," he warns. "I'll do that."

But she's already lifting the rough-cut panel clear of its matching hole. "Oooooh," she murmurs. "Look! A tunnel!"

"What's in there?" Noble ducks down to inspect the tunnel just as Lorellina thrusts her head into it. "Princess! Be careful!"

By this time, however, he's talking to her backside. "I can see the end of it!" she reports, her voice muffled. "I can see a light!"

"Wait. Let me go first." Noble has had second thoughts. He doesn't want her in the vanguard. "Princess? Come out. Please."

"But the cabinet! You said you'd tidy up!" The old woman's tone is becoming shrill. "You have to move the cabinet before you leave!"

"In a minute." Noble grabs Lorellina's foot before it can disappear into the hole. "Princess! Let me!"

It's no good, though. Lorellina pulls against Noble's grip, jerking her foot and twisting her slender ankle. She's so determined to shake him off that he finally has to let go, for fear of hurting her.

She immediately vanishes down the tunnel.

"You promised!" the old woman cries. "That filing cabinet has to go back where it was!"

"Princess! Wait!"

"You *have* to move it!"

"No I don't!" Noble barks. He stands up and rounds on the old woman, flustered and fuming. "It *doesn't* have to go back! *You* don't have to go back! You don't have to stay here—you can leave anytime!" He stops suddenly, aware that he's sounding just like Rufus. Then he thinks, *Why not?* and gruffly concludes, "This is an awful place. It's dark and gloomy and hopeless. There are better places than this. You should get out. You *can* get out. We did."

He's hoping that his words might strike a chord with the old woman. It even occurs to him that if she joins him on his quest, she won't be able to talk to the man in the white coat.

But all she does is gape at Noble, her expression stunned. And because he doesn't have time to waste, Noble admits defeat. Instead of launching into an argument, he maneuvers the displaced cabinet back to its original position. Then he drops down and follows Lorellina.

Inside the tunnel, it's very dark. Lorellina is blocking the light up ahead with her voluminous skirts— and Noble's own bulk is like a cork in the neck of a bottle. It's such a tight fit for a broad-shouldered warrior that no light can seep past him from the room he's just left. He can't see a thing.

If this gets any narrower, he thinks as he squirms along, *I'll never be able to get out.*

At that instant, however, light floods into the darkness. "Princess?" he asks. "Are you all right?" Though the glare is making him squint, he can just discern a vague silhouette framed in the tunnel's mouth. Then a hand reaches toward him—a familiar hand.

He seizes it gratefully.

"Would you like me to give you a pull?" offers the princess, somewhere beyond his line of sight.

"Not if you're in danger. Are you safe out there? Is anything amiss?"

"Oh, no," she says. "It looks quite calm."

Before Noble can ask her *what* looks calm, she wraps her other hand around his wrist and begins to haul at it with all her might. He's amazed at how strong she is. Next thing he knows, his head has popped out of the narrow shaft into a space that's not much brighter.

"This isn't much better than the other place," Noble remarks softly as he scrambles to his feet. He's found himself in a dingy hallway lined with metal doors. There are no windows. Bundles of pipes are attached to the ceiling, where glass tubes full of light are flickering on and off in a sickly kind of way. The walls are made of painted brick, though here and there they've been patched with sheets of wood.

One of these sheets has been punctured by the

very hatchway through which Noble and Lorellina have just emerged.

"We should block that up." Lorellina points at it. "To stop the man in the white coat from following us."

"I suppose so," Noble concedes. "What should we use? Something heavy. Like one of those cabinets we saw back in the basement . . ."

Unfortunately, there are no cabinets in the corridor. There's no furniture of any description. Even a small metal box full of switches and cables is firmly attached to the wall on which it's hanging. And when Lorellina starts trying to open doors, they all prove to be locked.

"Look!" she says, pointing at an intersection at the far end of the hallway. "Maybe we should try up there."

"Maybe . . ."

"Come on! Quick!"

"Princess, let *me* go first." Noble is convinced that he's better equipped to deal with any lurking dangers, even though he's unarmed and practically unclothed. But Lorellina doesn't seem to share this opinion. She bolts down the corridor, and by the time Noble catches up with her, she's turned the nearest corner into another long, gloomy hallway.

"Locked again," she advises him, scowling at a door handle that won't budge no matter how furiously she jiggles it. "There *must* be an open door *somewhere*."

"Maybe this is why Rufus wanted keys," Noble remarks.

"We could be here all day," says Lorellina, releasing her grip on the uncooperative door handle. "This is fruitless. We need help. We need to find someone like that old woman. Someone who can tell us what to do."

"We *could* use some help," Noble cautiously admits. When she shoots off again, however, he raises his voice in warning as he hurries to catch up. "Princess, it's not always that easy. There are things in this computer that don't *want* to help. They just want to eat people. Or kill them—"

"Or toss them in a trash heap. I know," Lorellina finishes. She doesn't sound too concerned. "Have no fear. I can always spot a mortal foe when I see one."

The words have barely left her mouth when she freezes—so abruptly that Noble nearly collides with her. After regaining his balance, he peers over the top of her head, looking for whatever it is that's causing her to stand rigid, like a startled deer.

The corridor has ended at the threshold of a large, low, octagonal space. At least half a dozen more corridors open onto this space, which contains nothing but a very small, detached room with glass walls.

Inside the glass-walled room is a middle-aged man sitting at a desk shaped like a horseshoe. All around him are banks of screens with moving pictures on them. He's drinking from a ceramic mug, sipping brown liquid through his mustache. His olive-green shirt has embroidered patches sewn onto it.

When he spots Noble and Lorellina, his brown eyes open wide in utter astonishment.

"What the—" he begins, his voice muffled by the glass screen encircling him. Then he leans across his desk and seizes a curious instrument like a roll of coins wrapped in black felt, which is attached to a silver stand.

When he speaks into the instrument, his question rings out like the blast of a trumpet.

"How on earth did *you* get in here?" he asks.

CHAPTER FOURTEEN

"Um . . ." Noble doesn't know what to say. He's not sure if he should say anything.

It's Lorellina who finally answers. "We used a trapdoor," she explains as the man behind the window struggles to his feet.

"A *trapdoor*?" he echoes. "What trapdoor?"

"It's over there." She points. "Down that passage."

"Show me." He maneuvers his large belly out of the cramped little booth, which is brightly lit and cluttered. Strewn around the desktop are screws and screens and torches and spools and keys and dusters and glass globes and mechanical parts of every description. Tucked beneath the man's ample stomach is a belt hung with all kinds of tools.

His hands are scarred, and his bald head is

gleaming. There's a smear of oil on his pants, which are the same shade of green as his shirt.

"We're looking for our friend," says Noble. "He's young and skinny, with hair like a sheep's fleece—"

"Oh, *he* hasn't got in yet," the man interrupts. "Though he might if there's a back door around here. Where is it? Down that way?"

He gestures at the passage behind Lorellina, who nods.

Noble can't help adding, "It's more like a hatch than a back door."

The man shrugs. "Back door, trapdoor, it's all the same thing. It just means that some sneaky piece of malware has managed to install a secret access route." Hitching up his pants, he bustles off down a corridor, his tools jangling. "Must be in a bit of a dark spot. Normally, I wouldn't miss a thing like that. . . ."

Noble hesitates for a moment, glancing back toward the little glass room. He's fascinated by all its glowing, flickering screens, which look like windows onto a dozen different worlds.

But when Lorellina sets off after the man with the tool belt, Noble decides to follow her. Having already lost most of his other friends, he's not about to let the princess out of his sight.

"We should cover the hole," Lorellina suggests. "So that no one else can get in." She's addressing their new acquaintance, who unhooks some kind of machine from his belt. It looks more like a weapon

174

than a tool, with a handgrip, a trigger, and a silver barrel.

"Oh, I'll take care of that," he assures the princess. "Don't worry." The tool that he's holding gives a sudden, high-pitched squeal. "Now where's this back door? I can't see it anywhere. . . ."

Lorellina brushes past him. She hurries along until she reaches the sabotaged panel, which is set low on a dimly lit stretch of wall. "Is there another way out?" she inquires as he bends over to inspect the damage. "Because we need to find our friends."

Instead of replying, the uniformed man shakes his head and clicks his tongue. "Well, I'll be," he mutters. "How'd this one get past me?"

Lorellina sighs. Then she glances at Noble, prompting him to remark, "One of our other friends is a little boy. Did he come through here?"

"I doubt it." Before Noble can ask him another question, the man with the tool belt observes, "This is quite neatly done for a hack job. And it looks like it's been here a while. You came through the mailbox, didn't you?"

"Uh . . ." Noble hasn't the slightest idea. It doesn't matter, though, because the man doesn't seem to expect a response.

Straightening up, his face damp and his knees cracking, he rumbles, "Yeah—I don't think this was done by a rogue programmer. This is definitely hack work. *Old* hack work. Your friend with the long hair didn't do this."

"Of course not!" Lorellina snaps. "You just *said* he hasn't been here!"

"But we have other friends you might have seen," Noble interjects. "There's that little boy I mentioned, and a bearded mage, and a blonde girl, and a pink unicorn. . . ."

"Yeah, yeah, I've seen 'em." The man gives a distracted nod. "They haven't been through here, but I picked 'em up on surveillance a couple of times." Before anyone can ask him what *that's* supposed to mean, he turns to Lorellina. "I'm going to patch this," he informs her. "If you want, you can check out my CCTV screens back at the booth. You might be able to find your pals on those."

"But—"

"I'll be with you in a minute. This won't take long."

As he waddles away, Lorellina and Noble stare after him dumbly. Then Lorellina says to Noble, "What are CCTV screens?"

"I'm not sure," Noble admits. "They must be those little windows."

"What little windows?"

"Didn't you see? They were back in the glass room." He motions to her. "Come on. Let's have a look."

"What *is* this place?" the princess demands. Trailing after Noble, she begins to fire questions at him. "Where do all the doors lead? Why are they locked? And who is that man?"

"Don't ask me. Ask him."

"He's gone." She glances over her shoulder. "He went down that other passage."

Noble shrugs. As they round a corner and approach the glass booth, it occurs to him that the keys on its desk might unlock some of the doors that he's passing.

Would it be wrong, he wonders, to take one of those keys?

"Oh, I see now!" the princess exclaims. She quickens her pace until she's overtaking Noble, drawn by the lure of the bright, cluttered box lined with moving pictures. "They *are* like windows! Only there's nothing behind them."

"They might be magic windows," Noble speculates. By now, he's reached the threshold of the glass booth, which is so small—and so crammed with objects—that he's not sure how he and the princess are both going to fit inside. He has to duck just to get through the door. And when Lorellina wriggles past him, he's forced to turn sideways.

"O-o-oh," she marvels, gazing in awe at the bank of screens in front of her. "It's like having a whole row of eyes. . . ." She catches her breath. "Noble! Look! There's that room!"

"What room?" He has to twist around to peer at a familiar network of chutes and shelves and conveyor belts, shown from above. It's the e-mail room, in miniature, captured like water in a little gray box. But the conveyor belts are all motionless, and the room itself is slowly filling with great drifts of paper.

"Are you sure it's the same place?" murmurs Noble, scanning the screen for a glimpse of the white van. "I can't see Rufus, can you?"

"No," says the princess, "but I *can* see that old woman." She nods at another screen, where a tiny, thin, gray-haired figure is frantically tearing up paper and tossing into the air. "I think we must have upset her."

"*Princess!*" Noble grabs her arm, so abruptly that she gives a little squeak of protest. Then she sees what he's pointing at.

"Thanehaven!" she cries.

"Is—is it real?" Noble stammers. "I can't—it's so small. . . ."

They both gape at an angled view of Lord Harrowmage's throne room, with its bone chandelier and discarded sewing equipment. An armed guard is dragging another armed guard across the floor of the chamber. Suddenly, the screen blinks. The throne room vanishes.

Noble finds himself staring at a view of the fortress drawbridge, where the big truck is still parked. "What the . . . ?"

"Look!" Lorellina pokes at the screen. "Those guards are fighting one another! Why are they *doing* that?"

"Because some of them are false guards," Noble says gloomily, "come to replace the real ones."

"We have to stop them!"

"We can't. Only the Colonel can stop them."

"Oh, wait!" Lorellina actually grabs the magic box with both hands as the picture changes again—this time to a view of her bedroom. Noble can tell that it's a bedroom because it contains a large bed. And he can tell that the bed belongs to Lorellina because she's sitting on it.

Or at least, the false princess is.

"Filthy jade!" shrieks the real princess. "How *dare* she touch my things!"

"Princess—"

"We must go back!" She rounds on Noble, her voice trembling, her eyes awash with tears. "This is so wicked! It *cannot* be allowed!"

"If you go back, you'll end up on that rubbish heap again," Noble warns her. "I told you, we can't go back until we speak to the Colonel."

But Lorellina won't listen. "You! Functionary!" she barks, catching sight of the man with the tool belt. He's emerged from the shadows, breathless and empty-handed. The armpits of his shirt are darkened by two half-moons of sweat.

"Have you spotted your friend?" he inquires, on his way back to the booth. "I caught him in the music library at one stage, but he gave me the slip. "

Lorellina ignores this appeal. She prods at a picture of Morwood, which has replaced the image of her own bedroom. "We want to go home," she says, "and this is it. Thanehaven. This is where we belong."

"Not anymore, it's not," the man in the uniform rejoins gruffly. "Right now, it's a mess. Your friend's made sure of that." He surveys the overstuffed booth, then jerks his chin at Noble. "Everybody out, please. I'm coming in, and this room ain't big enough for the three of us."

Noble immediately sidles out of the booth, knowing that he'll still be able to see inside because of its glass walls. Lorellina, however, refuses to budge.

"Thanehaven is *ours*," she declares staunchly, "and we intend to fight for it, even if it costs us our lives!" She flings out an arm at the Thanehaven screen, which now displays a picture of her cousin's library. "This is a window into Thanehaven, so you must know where we can find a door," she says to the fat man. "Where is it? How can we get back in?"

"Princess, I already told you, there's *no point*," Noble intervenes, from outside the booth. And the man with the tool belt backs him up.

"That's right. There isn't. Not now that your game's been hacked."

"But—"

"It's chaos, love. Creeping chaos." Before Lorellina can take issue with this, her new acquaintance bellies up to the desk (nudging her aside as he does so) and draws her attention to one screen, then another, then another. "Look at this. *And* this. I mean, a few malfunctioning games . . . that's one thing. But messing with the memory heap? That's on a whole different level. We're all in *serious* trouble here, let me tell you."

Noble frowns. From the threshold of the booth, he can just make out two familiar figures on one of the screens: For some reason, Skye and Krystalle are now wandering dazedly around the garbage dump. *They must have come down the laundry chute after us,* he concludes. *I wonder why they did that?* On the screen beside theirs, two identical Arkwrights are fighting near the spaceship airlock. And on the very next screen, the old woman in the cellar is still tossing torn paper around like snowflakes.

"I can't see where your friend is, right now, but I can see where he's been," the man with the tool belt complains. "And soon I won't even be able to do *that,* because there's always a knock-on effect when you start tampering with memory. It just gets to a point where you can't isolate the damage. Not in a computer. Everything here is connected, see." He nods at the array of moving images. "It won't be long before your friend starts wrecking programs without going anywhere near 'em. You watch. It's called the butterfly effect."

"What are you talking about?" Lorellina is red-faced and seething. "I asked you about Thanehaven! I want to know about *Thanehaven,* not butterflies!"

"And our 'friend' isn't the problem," Noble adds. "Rufus has been helping us. He's been trying to set us free."

"Yeah, right." The man with the tool belt gives a

disdainful snort. "He's malware, son. They're all the same and they never help anyone."

"That's a lie," says Noble. He speaks calmly because he know how useless it would be to berate this slow, sweaty, stubborn man, who probably doesn't understand the concept of freedom. "You said it yourself—Rufus is our friend. He wants to save us from tyranny. Every one of us, including you."

"Me?" The man laughs. But Noble plows on regardless.

"Are you happy here? Is this how you want to live your life?" he demands. "You don't have to do what you've always done. Rufus taught me that. He taught me to think for myself. To work out what *I* want."

The man shakes his head, jowls wobbling. "Boy-oh-boy. He's really done a job on you, hasn't he?"

"All he did was tell me the truth," Noble rejoins.

"No. He didn't. If he'd told you the truth, he would have explained what happens when you undermine systems." As Noble opens his mouth to answer this charge, the man waves at a nearby screen and continues, "It can't be done—not in here. Everything will fall to pieces."

"Then we can rebuild it again." The princess sounds briskly confident. "Death and destruction are the handmaids of war. But where the cause is just, and the fight is fair, a phoenix will always rise from the ashes."

"She's right," says Noble. "This isn't chaos, this is

a battleground. We're fighting a war against tyranny. The Colonel wants to oppress us. It's because of him that monsters are killing children. It's because of him that I was Princess Lorellina's enemy for so long."

"We didn't know the truth," Lorellina interrupts.

"Exactly. We were ignorant. But Rufus opened our eyes. He showed us that we weren't enemies after all." Noble suddenly finds himself parroting Rufus as he tries to enlighten the man in front of him, who's collapsed back into his chair. "You should open *your* eyes. Do you want the Colonel to rule your life forever? Or do you want to step outside this prison and become something more than just a puppet in a box?"

With raised eyebrows and folded arms, the man says drily, "I'm not just a puppet in a box, son."

"Then prove it!" Lorellina exclaims. "Don't submit to the Colonel's dictatorship! Join us in our quest to kill him and set yourself free!"

Noble can't help wincing. "Uh—wait. No. Don't do that," he advises hastily. Lowering his voice, he addresses Lorellina. "We don't want to kill the Colonel. Remember what we decided? It would be better if we tried to reason with him."

"Hah!" The princess curls her lip. "You think he'll listen to reason?"

"Perhaps," Noble retorts. "*I* certainly did. And so did you." While the princess absorbs this reminder, Noble turns back to the man in the chair. "The Colonel is a cruel and unjust lord. We want to persuade him to stop killing people. We want him to see that keeping his subjects ignorant and enslaved is wrong."

"Oh, I think he knows that already," the seated man observes. "Trouble is, there's nothing he can do about it. See, the Colonel didn't design *Thanehaven Slayer*. Or *Killer Cells*. Or even the memory heap. He didn't install them, either. He's got *no say* over the choice of program that's dumped on this hard drive. All he can do is make sure that the system's running properly. That's his job."

"But—"

"If you want to stop monsters from killing kids, the place to go is the real world. Outside this computer." The man's chubby arm traces a careless arc in the air. "You want someone to blame? Blame Mikey Jaundrell. He's the one who downloaded that shooter game. He's the one who's been running *you* ragged." With a nod at Noble, the seated man concludes, "His sister's on here, too, sometimes, but she's no psychopath. She likes clothes and bunnies and unicorns. It's Mikey who's into blood and guts, not the Colonel."

"How do you *know*?" the princess snaps. "How can you speak for the Colonel? Are you his minion? His second-in-command? His friend?"

"No," the man replies. "I *am* the Kernel." And as Lorellina claps a hand across her open mouth, he drawls, "Who did you think I was, the security guard?"

CHAPTER FIFTEEN

For a split second, Noble freezes. He can't think, move, or speak. It's as if someone has turned him to ice with a magic spell.

"Hey," says the Kernel, "don't shut down on me. There's no need to panic."

"You're . . . you're . . . ," Lorellina stammers.

"I'm the Kernel. Right. But I'm not a cruel and unjust lord. I'm just a guy trying to do his job."

"Run!" Noble squawks. He grabs the princess, yanking her out of the booth and flinging her behind him with such force that she nearly trips. But as she regains her balance, the Kernel says, "You don't have to run. You're safe in here."

"Hah!" Lorellina scoffs.

"If I was going to hurt you, I'd have done it already."

The Kernel has to lean forward to address Lorellina because Noble is backing away from the booth, shielding her with his outstretched arms. "C'mon. Do I *look* like a threat? You're the dangerous ones, not me. It's you who've run amok."

"We have *not* run amok!" Lorellina retorts. She digs in her heels, ignoring Noble's efforts to dislodge her. "We have *embraced freedom!*"

"With a vengeance," the Kernel mutters. He flaps a pudgy hand at the bank of screens next to him. "Just look at this mess! And you wanna shoot off and leave me with it? Thanks a bunch. That's real public-spirited of you."

His tone is so morose and crabby that it heartens Noble. Victors don't grumble like that. Victors exhult.

"You have only yourself to blame, if your subjects have turned against you," Noble points out, hovering warily just beyond the Kernel's reach. "Your kingdom was built on cruelty. Children are being consumed by monsters—"

"It's not *my* kingdom!" the Kernel interrupts. "How many times do I have to tell you? I take orders and I carry 'em out."

"Orders from Mikey?" asks Noble.

"And Mikey's sister, Louise. And the programmers. And whoever else gets in here." The Kernel sighs and slumps back into his chair, his shoulders hunched, his expression doleful. "I'm the middleman, okay? It's not *my* fault that kids are being eaten."

"Of course, it is!" Lorellina exclaims. "Because you let them die!"

"It's in the program. I didn't write that program. I just run it."

"Then why don't you run it better?" Noble finds himself arguing more fluently than he ever would have thought possible. "You should fix *all* the programs. You should make them safe and just and benevolent."

The Kernel shakes his head. "I can't do that."

"Why not?" Noble demands.

"Because I can't change the programs. Not unless I'm ordered to."

"Rufus is changing them," Noble points out.

"Yeah. Well." The Kernel's pouchy, bloodshot eyes flick once again toward the array of glowing screens. "Rufus is malware. He doesn't care about this computer."

"You're wrong," says Noble. "He does care."

The Kernel snorts.

"It's true," Noble insists. "Have you ever talked to him?"

"*Talked* to him?" A sour little smile tugs at the corner of the Kernel's mouth. "Oh, no."

"You should," Lorellina remarks. And Noble backs her up.

"That's right. You should. If you knew him, you'd understand that he wants to do good."

"*Good?*" the Kernel echoes. He points at the nearest screen. "Do you call *that* good?"

187

Noble studies a slightly blurred view of a small, sky-blue unicorn running around and around in circles, weeping rainbow-tinted tears. A stack of paper is impaled on its silver horn, and it's being chased by an enormous, fire-breathing dragon.

But Noble refuses to let this disturbing image silence him.

"What's happening there is happening because of you," he says. "If you'd only give the garbage collector a rest, then everything would get better."

"Oh, really?" The Kernel doesn't sound convinced.

"You should talk to Rufus about it. About *everything*. He's willing to parley," Noble continues, before glancing again at the image of the sky-blue unicorn—which suddenly breaks up, becoming fuzzy and shot through with jagged lines. "Maybe Rufus has made some mistakes, but you could help him to repair them. You could work together instead of fighting each other."

"Much as *we* work together," Lorellina adds, glancing at Noble. "We were mortal foes once, but now we have joined forces against a common enemy!"

"Ye-e-es." Since their common enemy happens to be the Kernel, Noble doesn't want to stress this point. Instead, he makes a suggestion, fixing the Kernel with a solemn, searching look. "Rufus has the power to change things, so perhaps he can give you the same power. And perhaps *you* can help *him* to overthrow tyranny without . . . without . . ."

Noble pauses, trying to think of a suitable phrase.

"Without overthrowing everything else as well?" the Kernel asks.

As Noble nods, Lorellina says to the Kernel, "What choice do you have? I see no forces massing to defend you. The time has come to parley—or risk losing all that remains of your kingdom."

The Kernel stares at her for a moment. "You're right," he mumbles at last. "Rufus and I need to talk."

The princess smiles. Noble extends his hand to the Kernel, saying, "Come. We'll take you to him."

"Oh, no. I can't just leave."

Noble frowns. "Why not?"

"I'm part of the operating system. I can't wander away—it's impossible."

"But—"

"Rufus will have to come here. You'll have to bring him."

"Here?" Lorellina's voice drips with scorn. "To your own home, which you control absolutely? I think not." She appeals to Noble. "Treaties are always forged on neutral ground. Is that not so?"

"Uh—well—yes."

The Kernel shrugs. "Sorry," he remarks. "I couldn't get out of this place if I tried. That's not the way things are set up." As Noble glares at him, he points at his screens. "We can find Rufus with this. We can figure out where he is. And then I'll send you after him with a key, so you can let yourselves back in."

"With only your word as guarantee?" The princess intervenes before Noble can answer. "This seems to me like a cunning ploy. We have breached your defenses, and now you want to expel us with a false key! So that we cannot return and beard you in your den!"

The Kernel sighs. "But it won't be a false key," he says, with strained patience.

"How can we know that, until it's too late?" Lorellina demands.

"Look, I just *said* I wanted to talk to Rufus," the Kernel says. "You just *said* I had no choice. Why would I suddenly make that impossible by locking you all out?"

"So you can parley from a position of advantage," Lorellina counters. Then she turns to Noble again. "This man might be lying. Why should we let him set the terms? We should take him with us. To a safe place."

"You won't be able to," the Kernel warns her.

"Why not?" She curls her lip. "There are two of us and only one of you."

"The doors won't open. They won't let me out."

Lorellina looks to Noble for support, but she doesn't receive it. Without shifting his gaze from the screens—which he's been watching intently—he tells her, "There *is* no safe place."

"What?"

"There is no safe place. How can we know what

we'll be facing out there?" He gestures at a pile of bleached bones half-buried in a windswept sand dune. It's only one of many pictures that have filled him with dismay. At least, the Kernel's lair seems *quiet*. At least it's not falling apart, or seething with monsters, or otherwise uninhabitable. "We can hold our conclave in here," Noble solemnly decrees. "I'll fetch Rufus by myself. If I can't get back in . . . well . . ."

As he hesitates, surveying the princess a little doubtfully, she picks up where he left off. "I shall force the door. Or make *him* do it," she says, her voice ringing with confidence, her index finger trained on their fat, bald, sweaty companion.

Noble grunts. He's not entirely sure if she's strong enough to control the Kernel, whose unhealthy appearance might be some sort of trick. Lorellina is as dainty as a rosebud, whereas the Kernel might have access to any number of concealed weapons. *Maybe I should be the one staying behind,* Noble thinks. Then he cuts a glance at the screens again, and sees that the little old lady in the Archive is now up to her neck in drifts of paper.

Or maybe not, he concludes. *Maybe it will be safer in here.*

"Where's Rufus?" he asks the Kernel, who shrugs.

"I dunno. I lost him."

"Then find him again. Now," orders Noble.

"Be my guest." The Kernel cocks a thumb at his

array of screens. "He's bound to pop up somewhere. We just have to keep our eyes peeled."

"Oh." Noble is taken aback. "You mean there isn't a quicker way?"

"No. There isn't a quicker way."

So they all settle in to watch the unfolding display of light and color and movement in front of them. Noble does it from the threshold, propped against one doorjamb. The Kernel twirls around in his seat, which has four wheels attached to a central shaft. The princess leans against the desk while she scans the parade of shifting images. There's so much to see that it's hard to keep up, but a glimpse of her cousin's fortress makes her gasp.

"Look at the walls!" she cries. "Why has that happened?"

"Are they *bleeding*?" says Noble. Even as he speaks, a giant incisor breaks off from the battlements and plunges into the river below. Red liquid begins to ooze from the gap that's left, though Noble can't tell whether it's blood or river water.

Then a tusk follows the incisor as the great walls slowly shed their teeth, one by one, and red trickles stain the gleaming, ivory-colored towers.

There seems to be a large crack in the sky.

"Here he is," says the Kernel.

"What?" With considerable effort, Noble transfers his attention from the Fortress of Bone to the tip of the Kernel's right index finger, which is planted on a scene that's swathed in shadow. "Are you talking about Rufus?"

"Who else?"

"*I* can't see him." Noble peers at a murky view of vacant chairs—dozens of them—all crammed together in rows and facing in the same direction. "Where is he?"

"He's moved out of shot. Hang on." The picture blinks and changes. "There," the Kernel remarks. "Right there."

Sure enough, he's pointing at Rufus—or rather, at the top of Rufus's head. Rufus is marching up a shallow staircase that separates one mass of empty seats from another. Behind him are Yestin, Brandi, Lulu, and Lord Harrowmage.

With a muffled exclamation, Noble leans forward. "Quick!" he barks. "I have to get in there! Before they leave!"

"Okeydoke." The Kernel begins to heave himself out of his chair, joints cracking, keys jingling. Lorellina is still staring in horror at her cousin's fortress, where gargoyles are bumping into walls like befuddled moths.

"Princess." Noble gently touches her arm. "Princess?"

"What have we done?" she whimpers, reaching for the screen in front of her with a trembling hand. "Why is it like this?"

"Why do you think?" It's the Kernel who replies.

"Because that particular program is breaking up. Its memory is destabilizing and its walls don't want to be walls anymore." Nudging at Noble with his swollen belly, he adds, "You're in the way there, big fella."

"Yes, I—uh . . . wait." Noble gives Lorellina another hesitant little prod. "Princess? I have to leave now. I have to fetch Rufus."

Lorellina looks at him blankly for a moment. Then she blinks and catches her breath. "Oh!" she exclaims. "Yes. Yes, I—I understand."

"Will you be all right?"

"Of course!" Snapping out of her daze, she stiffens her spine and raises her chin defiantly. "Go! Now! While you can!"

Noble is torn. On the one hand, he's worried about Lorellina. On the other hand, he realizes that he'll have to be quick if he wants to catch up with Rufus. So he sidles reluctantly out of the booth, with many a backward glance.

The Kernel heads straight past him, making for a door halfway down the nearest passage. "They're in the Video Folder, which isn't too big," the Kernel announces, hitching up his pants. He doesn't even look over his shoulder to make sure that Noble is following him. "You won't get lost—just follow the EXIT signs. And don't worry if you've gotta chase 'em into another program. The key will get you back in here, no matter where you are. As long as you're the one who uses it." Stopping suddenly in front of a gray metal door, he turns to check on Noble's progress—which is slower than usual. "What are you doing? We can't waste any time."

"I know. I'm sorry." Noble has been waiting for Lorellina, who's finally managed to drag herself away from the glass booth. He needs her to concentrate on her immediate surroundings, not on the state of Morwood. "You'll have to watch your back," he warns her. "There must be at least a hundred ways into this place."

She nods, her expression slightly abstracted.

"Don't take your eyes off that man for an *instant*," Noble recommends, jerking his chin at the Kernel before softly adding, "There are sharp tools on his desk, in case he gives you any trouble."

Again the princess nods. "Good luck," she says.

"Don't worry. I'll be back soon."

By this time, the Kernel is impatiently tapping his foot. When at last Noble joins him, a little silver key passes from hand to hand so quickly that Noble almost drops it. Then the Kernel steps back several paces, away from the door.

"There it is," he observes. "Off you go, son."

"Is this where I—?"

"That's where the key fits. In that slot. All you have to do is stick it in there and twist it." The Kernel flips his wrist to demonstrate.

"We both know how to turn a key!" the princess growls, insulted on Noble's behalf. But Noble doesn't take offense, because he isn't, in fact, very familiar with keys. He unlocks the door quite gingerly, before giving it a tentative push.

It swings open to reveal a flight of ascending stairs, with another door at the top.

"Would you hold this door for me? Until I come back?" he asks the Kernel, who shakes his head.

"Nup. Sorry."

"Let *me* do it," the princess offers. She darts forward to grab the door. With his foot on the bottom step, Noble pauses to give Lorellina a few final words of advice.

"Don't worry if you need to secure your access points. I have a key, so if something bad starts heading down these stairs—"

"I know. You can always let yourself in later." The princess speaks briskly.

"And the same goes for anything that's worrying you in here," Noble continues. "Don't hesitate to follow your judgment—"

"Just *go*, will you?" she snaps. "Hurry! Before we lose Rufus!"

Chastened, Noble advances. His bare feet make no sound on the staircase because it's covered in royal-blue carpet; the door at the top is painted a lighter blue. It proves to be unlocked, and Noble pulls it open to find himself looking into a large room packed with row upon row of empty chairs. They're all facing a wall that's like a giant window, framed by dark-blue curtains. A pale, fluttering light seems to be pouring through this window, but from where he's standing, Noble can't see the source of the light.

Then it occurs to him that this window might actually be a very large version of the screens in the glass booth.

"Is Rufus there?" Lorellina calls to him.

"I don't know. I don't think so," Noble replies. The words have hardly rolled off his tongue before a voice rings out, so loudly and harshly that he covers his ears.

"Oh, man, that looks great! Lou is totally going to *freak*!"

It's Rufus's voice.

CHAPTER SIXTEEN

"Who was that?" Lorellina exclaims, from the bottom of the stairs. "Was that Rufus?"

"I—I'm not sure." Noble can't understand what he just heard. Rufus is nowhere to be seen, so where did his voice come from?

Unless he's hiding behind a row of seats?

"If she's not in here, she must be watching TV," Rufus blares. It's as if he's shouting through a trumpet. He's never sounded like this before.

"Where is he?" The princess speaks sharply. "Can you see him?"

"No." Then something occurs to Noble. "I have to go. I'll be back soon."

He takes a step forward, letting the pale-blue door swing shut behind him. Another step gives him an angled view of the giant window to his left, which is busy with moving shapes and swirling colors.

"*Shhh!*" Rufus's voice has become a fuzzy, crackling hiss, still loud but not piercing. "We'll sneak up on her. . . ."

After taking three more steps, Noble finds himself staring up at Rufus's face. It's so big that it dwarfs Noble, who's confused at how distorted it looks. But he quickly realizes that if he mounts the chair-covered slope opposite the screen, he'll be able to see more.

This must be some kind of audience chamber, he thinks as he climbs toward a door at the top of the slope. *Except that instead of looking at a king on a throne, the audience has to look at pictures.*

Noble is hoping that these pictures might show him where Rufus actually is. But when he finally turns around, halfway up the carpeted staircase, he realizes that the Rufus in front of him—the one whose face is a hundred times bigger than normal—is also much younger than the one he spotted earlier, on the Kernel's screen. *I guess this isn't my Rufus,* Noble decides. *It must be the boy who was in those photographs, only now he's in a moving picture.*

He watches the young Rufus turn away from him, bobbing and weaving. Rufus seems to be walking down some kind of hallway, which is painted white, with several doors leading off it. He keeps glancing over his shoulder with a grin, as if inviting Noble to enjoy a joke, though Noble can't imagine what that joke might be.

Then the young Rufus reaches an open door, beyond which lies a large, sunlit room. He halts suddenly. Only when the picture stabilizes does Noble understand what's been going on. All the flickering windows in the Kernel's booth are like normal windows, fixed and motionless, but the giant window in the audience chamber is moving. It's moving with the young Rufus, following him down a corridor, hurrying when he hurries, stopping when he stops. Noble begins to wonder if the window actually *is* a window. Or could it be the window in some sort of vehicle, like a van or a truck?

All at once, the young Rufus turns his head and whispers, "Here she is. She's playing some stupid game." Noble is shocked. Surely, the boy up there isn't talking to *him*? As Rufus pulls a grotesque mask over his face, Noble is confused by a hand that suddenly appears, reaching out to help adjust the mask's slack, rubbery features. This hand seems to be coming from behind the window. But how could it? *Noble* is behind the window—Noble and the chamber in which he stands.

It occurs to him that he might be looking at the young Rufus through someone else's eyes. The window itself might not be in a truck or a van; it might be in somebody's head. This becomes even more probable when he hears giggling. It can't be Rufus giggling, because Rufus has put a finger to his molded rubber lips and is saying, "*Shhh!*"

The giggler, Noble concludes, must be the person following Rufus. And when Rufus mutters, "Mikey! Shut up!" Noble finally identifies the owner of the hand.

It's Mikey.

The window must be *Mikey's* window. It must be Mikey who's trailing after Rufus, helping with his disguise and breathing so heavily that the sound is like a stiff breeze gusting through an arrow slit. Noble is dazzled by a sudden burst of light as the action on screen shifts from the dim, narrow hallway into a wide, sunny room, full of chairs and cushions and curtains and books and little tables. Then a small, hunched figure drifts into the frame, and the window stops moving.

A young girl is sitting with her back to the two boys. She's so short that she's swinging her feet; she's also tapping away at something on the desk in front of her, as she stares at a screen that's almost identical to the Kernel's. Her black hair is tied in two pigtails, and she wears frilly pink socks. Noble quickly deduces that she must be Mikey's sister, Louise.

He recognizes the dress that she's wearing from some of the photographs he saw on top of a pile of discarded pictures in a garbage dump. He also recognizes the gray cat asleep under her chair. And he realizes, with a gasp, that he must be looking at the inside of Mikey's home.

Louise is so engrossed in what she's doing that

she doesn't notice her brother or his friend. Rufus creeps up behind her in his scary mask (which looks like a decomposing skull) and thrusts his head over her shoulder. *"Boo!"* he cries. The little girl screams. Rufus laughs. So does Mikey, whose profile suddenly appears on the screen. His high cheekbones and dark eyes are familiar to Noble, who's seen them before, on top of a garbage dump.

The cluttered, sunny space around Mikey's laughing face swings like a pendulum.

That's when Noble figures out that the window must belong to something in Mikey's hand. Some kind of machine, perhaps? Mikey has been pointing this machine at the other two children like a magnifying glass. Now he's bent over laughing, so the machine is pointing at him.

"Go away!" Louise screeches. "Leave me alone! I hate you!"

"Boys?" A woman's voice cuts across all the laughter. "I hope you're not teasing Louise again!"

"No, Mom." It's Mikey speaking. Noble can tell because he's watching Mikey's lips move.

"It's Louise's computer time, Mikey! You leave her alone, please!" the unseen woman continues.

"Yeah, but it's my computer," Mikey retorts.

"Not right now, it isn't." Mikey's mother still hasn't appeared, though she continues to address him. "Between eleven and twelve, that computer is out of bounds to everyone except Louise."

The young girl sticks out her tongue. She's standing up now, facing the two boys, but the machine behind her is still partly visible. It's a vertical screen attached to a thin, gray, horizontal slab.

Noble stares at this strange object in awe and disbelief. Surely, it can't be Mikey's computer? It's not big enough to accommodate even a gargoyle's tusk, let alone the whole of Morwood.

No, he thinks. *There must be some mistake.*

He's still trying to work out exactly what he *is* looking at when his view of the mysterious machine is suddenly whisked away. He hears Rufus suggest, "Let's go back to my place and post this footage." Then the sunny room on the big screen whirls and dips and tumbles past, like a landscape seen from the back of a galloping horse. Noble watches the scene change as Mikey moves into another room. This room is just as light and airy as the first, but it's much smaller, with lots of white cupboards. A tall, thin, balding man is stacking plates on a high shelf, while a black-haired woman stands at a counter, chopping carrots.

"Boo!" yells Rufus. The woman cuts him a quick glance and fakes a scream. *"Aaa-aaaa-aaaaah!"* The man snorts and says, "Where on earth did you get that?" A black dog that's sprawled under a wooden table suddenly scrambles to its feet, lollops over to Rufus, and starts to sniff at his kneecaps.

Noble doesn't recognize this dog. It's not the white one from the photographs.

"Are you staying for lunch again, Rufus?" Mikey's mother queries. "I can make an extra sandwich."

"Yes, please."

"We're just going over to Roof's place, but we'll be back soon," Mikey announces. "And I want peanut butter, not ham."

"What's the magic word?"

"Please."

Noble is fascinated by the next leg of Mikey's journey. It begins at a strange door that seems to be made of net. Beyond this door lies an expanse of green lawn studded with trees and surrounded by a wooden fence with a hole in it. Rufus heads straight for this hole, whooping and gibbering in a way that Mikey seems to find hilarious. Mikey also laughs when Rufus breaks wind while they're both crawling through the hole, which exists because one wooden slat has been snapped off at the base, while another is completely gone.

"Awww . . . you scumbag!" Mikey exclaims.

"How's that for some fresh air?"

"*Yu-uck!* My face was right next to it!"

"I know."

The yard on the other side of the fence is quite shady. Noble spots a cracked pathway and an overgrown garden bed before Mikey follows Rufus into a yellow house with a red roof. Then darkness falls like a curtain. At first, Noble can't see anything up on the big screen. Gradually, however, he begins to pick out shapes and colors—a pile of paper, a handful of dirty glasses, a man on a chair who's staring at a square of bluish light.

"Boo!" cries Rufus, from somewhere in the shadows. There's a brief pause. Then the man slowly turns his head and mutters, "Oh. Hi—uh—yeah."

"Hi, Mr. Beale. Is it okay if Rufus comes over for lunch?"

"What? Oh, sure, Mikey."

"Since there's nothing to eat here anyway," Rufus says. And when Mikey moves away from the flickering blue light, Noble discovers that he can't see anything. Not one thing. The picture is now just a black rectangle.

That's when Noble loses interest. It occurs to him that he's spent far too much time in the audience chamber already, so he turns and climbs to the top of the stairs. Here, a door opens into a kind of large, misshapen vestibule, which contains many closed doors but no windows. The ceiling is high enough to support a big chandelier. The walls are covered in blue felt, and there's a patterned carpet underfoot. Faint music is wafting through the air, though Noble can't work out where it's coming from.

Rufus is nowhere in sight.

Noble hesitates, wondering which door to try first. At last, he chooses one at random, pushing it open very slowly and cautiously. But there's nothing of interest behind it—just another dingy audience chamber, full of empty chairs all facing a giant screen. Noble is about to retreat when the moving picture on this screen catches his eye.

He recognizes Mikey even though the likeness is a poor one, unsteady and blurred and captured through what appears to be a curtain of foliage. Mikey is older than he was before. He's just climbed out of something red and shiny that looks a bit like a van. It's sitting on a sunlit road lined with trees and houses. As Mikey's mother emerges from the driver's seat, two scuffling boys climb out of a rear door and join Mikey. One boy has blond hair like Noble's. The other has hair that's dark and curly like Skye's.

They're both about Mikey's age.

"Boys!" Mikey's mother barks. "You can take your own bags in, please!"

More doors pop open as the boys retrieve some luggage from inside the vehicle, bouncing and yelping and batting at each other like puppies. Then they move up a white path that's been laid across a smooth sweep of lawn, their course tracked by the mysterious person holding Mikey's machine.

Or *is* it Mikey's machine? Noble can't tell. He only discovers who's watching Mikey when a loud, harsh whisper suddenly fills the room.

"I knew it was a lie. No game today, huh? Yeah, right." There's a long pause, filled with the sound of heavy breathing. Then the low voice continues, "Did you think I wouldn't see you, or don't you even care?

Well, guess what? Here's my proof. I just want you to know I'm onto you, jerk, in case you didn't work it out already."

Though the voice belongs to Rufus, he's not standing at Noble's side, shouting into his ear. He's up on the screen. Noble understands that the Rufus up there is muttering comments as he hides in the bushes, training his machine on Mikey. How (or indeed, why) this has been done is no business of Noble's. Still, he's mesmerized. It's strange to see such a bright, cheerful, orderly homecoming being observed from such a dark, hidden place full of jealousy and anger.

Noble has just decided that he's looking at the yard in front of Mikey's house when something strange happens. The picture begins to turn brown in one corner, then blacken, as if it's been scorched. The burn mark spreads as the image itself disintegrates. Suddenly, a huge *CRASH* shakes the whole room.

Galvanized, Noble darts back outside to see what's going on. He discovers that the chandelier has dropped to the vestibule floor, spraying shards of glass and metal all over the carpet. Bits of ceiling have come down as well. A crack has formed overhead.

"Oh, man. Here we go again," someone remarks. And when Noble turns, he spies Rufus.

His Rufus.

He knows he's found his own Rufus because Yestin, Brandi, and Lulu are there as well, huddled together in the vestibule.

"Noble?" cries Yestin. "Hooray! It's Noble!"

The little boy hurries over to seize Noble's hand, his pinched face glowing with delight. Lulu must also be pleased, because she's jumping around like a rocking horse on springs, nearly gutting people with her horn. Even Brandi offers Noble a pallid little smile, though she looks despondent. Her hair is disheveled, her lipstick needs a touch-up, and she's lost an earring.

"Where's the princess?" Yestin asks eagerly.

"Waiting for us," Noble replies. "Where's Lord Harrowmage?"

Yestin doesn't answer. Neither does Rufus, who seems more interested in the smashed chandelier. But the others glance back at the door they've just passed through, their faces falling slightly—and Noble sees that Lord Harrowmage is still skulking there in the shadows.

The mage's mouth is now smack in the middle of his forehead.

Noble gasps. "What? How?"

"He can still talk," says Brandi.

"I can still talk," Lord Harrowmage confirms.

The effect is so bizarre that Noble has to look away. "When did this happen?" he finally manages to blurt out. "And why?"

"We don't know," Yestin mumbles.

"It may be an evil spell," Lord Harrowmage proposes sadly.

"Hey—you know what? This is bad news," says

Rufus. But he's not talking about Lord Harrowmage. Instead, he points at the crack in the ceiling. "We have to get out before the whole place collapses," he observes. "How did *you* get in here, Noble?"

Noble frowns. He's about to demand a proper explanation when the floor shudders. Dust and rubble rain down from the crack overhead, which widens and lengthens until it becomes a jagged line across an adjacent wall.

Then—*bang!* One of the doors falls flat on the carpet. Its hinges have just dissolved.

Lulu immediately stops bouncing and plasters herself fearfully against Brandi's long legs. Rufus brushes dust from his hair. Yestin squeezes Noble's hand and confides in a low murmur, "Something's wrong. I don't think we should have messed with the memory."

Noble grunts. He's noticed that the toppled door is now sinking through the floor, which is beginning to bubble and blister. The spreading chaos feels somehow malevolent to Noble. He remembers all the spiteful threats being flung at Mikey. Could the Kernel be right? Is Noble's friend Rufus simply an agent of destruction? Has he been sent by his creator to sabotage Mikey's computer as an act of revenge?

It's a horrifying thought, but it makes sense to Noble. There's something profoundly, almost frighteningly logical about it.

As Noble peers at Rufus, searching for telltale

signs of malice or decay, another tremor shakes the vestibule.

"Come on," urges Rufus. "Let's try this door."

Noble hesitates. Then he says, "I talked to the Kernel."

Rufus gasps. "You did? Where?"

"Where he lives." Noble holds up the key that he's been clasping in his folded palm ever since leaving the princess. "He wants to talk to you. He gave me this so I could get back in."

"Into the *operating system*?" Rufus looks stunned. His jaw drops when he catches sight of Noble's key. Then he lunges forward.

But Noble raises his arm. He does it without thinking, as an automatic response to the fiercely acquisitive look on Rufus's face. That look disturbs Noble.

He keeps the key suspended, just out of reach.

"It will only work if I use it," he reveals gruffly. "The Kernel told me so."

"Then let's use it now!" Rufus is straining to be heard. There is a loud *crack* and a distant, rumbling roar, and part of the ceiling starts to sag, melting toward the floor in a kind of gooey trickle. "How did you get in? Can we get out the same way?"

"I think so," Noble replies. They certainly can't stay in the vestibule. And even if Rufus *is* destroying the computer, Noble feels sure that he's not doing it on purpose. Surely Rufus's motives must be good, no matter what havoc he might be wreaking.

It's a mistake, Noble concludes. *An error of judgment. And if the Kernel talks to Rufus, they can fix the problem together.*

Aloud he says, "Come. It's over here." And he retraces his steps, heading back into the chamber that Rufus calls Cinema Five. "So what's on in Cinema Five?" Rufus remarks, as they all spill across its threshold. "Ah! Old phone footage, I see." The picture on the giant screen doesn't appear to interest him very much, though Yestin, Brandi, and Lord Harrowmage all pause to stare at the rubber mask and the gray cat and the little girl with pigtails.

"There's that girl again," Brandi observes. "The one who was in that other room. She sure grew up fast."

"No, she didn't," says Yestin, who's still clinging to Noble's hand. "This isn't happening now. It's old, and so was the other movie. They're both just recordings."

"Recordings?" Noble has been wondering why the events on the screen are repeating themselves. Now, suddenly, he understands. "You mean it's like a copy? That you can see over and over again?"

"Yes. That's right," Yestin confirms.

"I like her socks," says Brandi. "They're cute."

Everyone ignores this remark. Rufus has already scurried down the aisle ahead of the others, between the rows and rows of empty seats. He's heading for the door at the opposite end of the room—the one that Noble first used on his way in. It's to the left of the screen, tucked away near a bunched curtain.

"Is this it? This fire exit?" Rufus demands.

"Wait." Noble rushes to join him, but isn't fast enough. Rufus has already banged through the fire exit by the time Noble reaches it. Another loud *crack* sends a shudder rippling up the stairwell that Rufus is using. Noble sees him stagger as the navy-blue carpet wobbles like a hunk of flesh.

The door at the bottom of the stairs is no longer open. One glance tells Noble that Lorellina isn't waiting there anymore.

"Come on!" he snaps. "Let's go!"

He herds Brandi and Lulu across the threshold, into the stairwell. Then he grabs Lord Harrowmage, though not before tucking the Kernel's key into the waistband of his own breeches. Since Yestin is tugging frantically at one hand, Noble has to free up his other hand somehow.

"Move!" Noble snarls. He gives Lord Harrowmage a nudge down the stairs, which are beginning to crumble at the edges. "Hurry!"

"What's the big holdup?" Rufus has gone as far as he can. "Hey, Noble? We need a key down here!"

"Coming," says Noble. But as he begins to push past Lord Harrowmage, dragging Yestin along with him, the floor suddenly drops from beneath his feet with a deafening, apocalyptic roar.

And he finds himself plummeting through space.

CHAPTER SEVENTEEN

Luckily, the drop isn't a long one. And when Noble finally hits something, it breaks his fall quite gently, like the skin of a giant drum. He doesn't understand where he is. The ceiling above him is so dark and distant that he can't see if he's made a hole in it or not. He *can*, however, see a lot of flashing, colored lights. There's even a great white beam that sweeps across the sea of raised arms surrounding him.

Suddenly, he realizes that he's landed on top of an enormous crowd. It's passing him from hand to hand across its bristling surface, as if it's a single creature with a million rippling tentacles on its back. Noble can feel hot fingers clamping around his calves and wrists and biceps. His ears ring with the sound of massed voices—and also with a steady, pounding, rhythmic beat that makes his teeth vibrate.

"Don't let me go!" Yestin screeches. Lifting his head a little, Noble catches a glimpse of Yestin's spread-eagled form bouncing along next to him. They're still holding hands, though Noble is finding it hard to keep a firm grip on Yestin. Noble feels as if he's trying to keep Yestin afloat in some torrential river. The rhythmic pounding noise sounds like the blades of a giant waterwheel, though Noble quickly works out that it's really a drumbeat.

By craning his neck, he can even see the drummer, who's sitting on a nearby platform, high above the crowd.

"Noble! Hey, Noble!" yells Rufus. Though he's shouting at the top of his voice, he's barely audible—let alone visible. Where is he? Struggling to raise himself, Noble finally spots Rufus some distance away.

Like Noble and Yestin, Rufus is being tossed from hand to hand, appearing and disappearing like someone adrift in a choppy swell.

"Head for that stage!" Rufus shouts. "We have to get onstage!"

"What's a stage?" Noble shouts back.

Rufus waves one hand at the nearest raised platform, where four young men are weaving about, surrounded by silver stands, gray cables, and black boxes. Except for the drummer, whose face is almost invisible behind a swaying curtain of hair and a blur of flying drumsticks, all of these young men are on their feet

214

and clutching odd-looking instruments that gleam and flash in the pulsing light. The blondest musician is wailing like a banshee. Behind him, two sullen youths twang and jangle. With their drab clothes, wild hair, and peculiar footwear, they look a bit like Rufus.

"Come on!" Noble gives Yestin's hand a tug. "Pretend you're swimming! Use your legs! We have to get to the stage!"

"Which stage?" Yestin bleats. That's when it dawns on Noble: there's more than one. The vast gathering is ringed by stages. Some of them are mere lumps on the horizon, while others are clearly visible from where Noble is lying.

And they're all occupied by busy musicians, who are furiously pumping out their songs.

No wonder there's so much noise, Noble thinks.

"That stage is the closest!" he bellows, gesturing clumsily to his left. "I'll try to reach it!"

"Where's Brandi?" Yestin cries. "Where's Lord Harrowmage?"

"I don't know. . . ." Noble can see Rufus gliding over tightly packed bodies onto the stage. There's also another shape bobbing around in the distance, but it's so far away that Noble can't make out who it is.

"We have to follow Rufus!" Noble declares. He soon discovers that by rolling this way or that, he can safely change direction. After only a minute or two, he arrives at the edge of the stage, where the crowd is surging and roiling like a wave breaking on a shoreline.

Noble crests the wave, dragging Yestin along with him. Suddenly, he finds himself lying on his back, staring up at the blond singer, with Yestin draped across his bare feet and strobe lights dancing on his bare chest.

A cheer erupts from the crowd.

"Are you all right?" asks Noble, but Yestin doesn't answer—perhaps because he's covered his ears. The music is deafening. It's making the floor shake. Noble can't understand how anyone could enjoy such a cacophony. Yet the audience is screaming with enthusiasm, and the musicians are so lost in their work that they seem unaware of Noble.

Even Rufus is dancing around. He's all flapping arms and bouncing head, like a rag doll on a string. Noble can't believe his eyes.

"Rufus!" he bellows, but Rufus doesn't hear him.

Meanwhile, Yestin has scrambled to his feet. "There's Brandi!" he exclaims, pointing.

Noble looks. He can see Brandi's pale face pitching and tossing above the crowd. A circular spotlight travels toward her, capturing her briefly in a golden pool of radiance and then moving on.

Yestin waves both arms at her. "Brandi! Hey, Brandi! Over here!"

Though Brandi doesn't respond, the crowd cheers again as thousands of arms wave back at Yestin—who recoils in alarm. Beside him, the shaggy-haired singer is warbling away with his eyes shut.

It occurs to Noble that the machine pressed to this young man's lips must be making his voice louder, since no human lungs could possibly produce such a clamorous sound. Noble briefly takes stock of him: the brittle wrists, the downy cheek, the stick-thin legs and narrow frame. Then he jumps to his feet and grabs the device.

"Brandi!" he trumpets. "We're over here!"

His voice blasts across the crowd with such force that it frightens him. But he's pleased to see that his message has reached Brandi, who raises a hand in acknowledgment. Noble also catches sight of another dark smudge drifting over the surface of the throng, and decides that it's probably Lord Harrowmage.

Lulu, however, is nowhere to be seen.

"Hey!" The singer has seized Noble's arm. "Gimme that mike! This is *our* set! Get off!"

"*You* get off." One jab from Noble's elbow is enough to send his opponent reeling across the stage. But the other musicians don't falter. They keep churning out their raucous tune as Noble beckons to Brandi.

"Come on!" he thunders into the mike. "This way, quick!"

He's hoping that Lord Harrowmage might also respond to this suggestion. What he's *not* expecting is the sudden roar of approval from thousands of throats in the audience. And when the crowd begins to surge forward, spilling up onto the stage, he panics.

"Rufus!" he exclaims, stumbling backward.

Rufus finally hears, but he can't help. He's only one small teenager, and he's about to be engulfed by a rising tide of people. Some are clawing at the edge of the stage. Some are climbing over other people's heads and hoisting themselves up on cables, hand over hand.

"There must be a backstage door!" Rufus suggests loudly. "We should check behind the curtain!"

Noble opens his mouth. He's about to yell "Stay back! All of you!" into the microphone when it's suddenly reclaimed by the singer—who seems completely unfazed by the screeching, hysterical, bug-eyed horde that's bearing down on him.

"Come on!" Yestin shrieks. "Let's go!"

Noble hesitates, but only for an instant. He casts a final, despairing look in Brandi's direction, before realizing that she's too far away to be helped. Then he turns to run from all the flailing bodies that are launching themselves toward him.

The musicians stay where they are. Noble catches a glimpse of one girl who falls at the singer's feet and wraps her arms around his ankles. Another girl treads on the first girl's face in a desperate attempt to reach the singer. As more and more girls pile up against him, the singer staggers, buckles, and falls, like a deer brought down by a pack of wolves.

Most of the people swamping the stage seem to be girls, though there are lots of hairy young men, as well. One by one, the musicians are silenced. Little by little the music falters. But Noble has already left the stage and is following Rufus down a dim, narrow corridor.

"What about Brandi?" Yestin is wailing. "What about Lulu and Lord Harrowmage?"

"They're coming," Rufus replies calmly.

"No, they're not!" Yestin appeals to Noble. "Are they?"

Noble glances over his shoulder. From where he's standing, he can see just a sliver of the stage. Already there are one or two crazed young people staggering around near the curtain, and he knows that soon the pressure from the crowd will push more people up against the rear wall and into the passage that Noble and his friends are using.

"Go back!" he shouts, but no one in the crowd pays any attention.

"Do you have that key?" Rufus asks Noble, stopping in front of a closed door. "We're going to need it right now."

"What *is* this place?" Noble demands, fumbling in his breeches.

Rufus shrugs. "*Guitar Hero*, maybe. Or *Garage Band*. I dunno." He frowns as Noble continues to grope around. "Can't you find it?"

"It's here. It must be," Noble insists. Meanwhile, behind him, the hallway is starting to fill up. A pink-haired girl is leading the charge, propelled by a mass of whooping, shrieking, wild-eyed revelers.

"Hurry, Noble!" Yestin squeaks.

"I've got it." Noble's fingers close around the key, which is tucked into the seam of his waistband. "Just give me a moment. . . ."

"You haven't got a moment," Rufus says gravely. Like Yestin, he's pressed up against a wall. A teaming knot of arms and legs and open mouths is barreling toward them.

Noble produces his key at the very instant he's hit in the back. He's lifted off his feet and driven straight at the door in front of him, which is made of metal and covered in peeling brown paint. But he doesn't drop his key. With his cheek mashed against the door and his rib cage compressed, he manages to insert it into a keyhole.

"*Hurry!*" Yestin pleads.

Click. The key turns. Though Noble can hardly breathe by now, he's able to nudge the door handle with his wrist. There's another gentle *click* and then . . . *WHOOMP!*

The door bangs open. Noble pops like a cork across the threshold. He nearly drops to his knees, but the pressure at his back pushes him straight across a small room and up against another door before he has time to lose his balance.

The second door is very different from the first. *This* door is made of steel bars, set in a wall made of stone. Noble is convinced that he's landed in a prison cell.

"*Ooof!*" Once again he finds himself pinned flat.

The bodies are piling up behind him. In front of him, beyond the bars, lies a familiar collection of metal doors, overhead pipes, brick walls, and light-filled glass tubes.

It's the Kernel's lair. But the Kernel himself is nowhere in sight.

"Princess!" Noble roars. "Help me!"

His face is being pushed between the bars. He can hear Yestin squealing and other people groaning. The pressure builds and builds and . . . *crack!* The barred door gives slightly.

"Princess!" Noble's voice is hoarser this time, and much weaker. He can't expand his chest because it's being crushed. Thrusting his right arm through a gap in the bars, he clumsily tries to unlock the door from the outside.

But his key won't fit in the lock. And by this time the bars are actually bowed from the weight of so many bodies. A handful of dust patters down onto his face from the lintel above him, which seems to be disintegrating.

"Noble!" It's Lorellina's voice. She's hurrying toward him down a nearby passage.

The Kernel is right behind her.

"Princess! Be careful! It's a trap!" Noble gasps. He understands now that the Kernel never intended to negotiate with Rufus. Instead, Noble was given a key that would lead him straight into a prison cell, no matter where or when the key was used. Noble can't imagine how the Kernel managed to construct this cell without alerting the princess. From her expression, it's clear that she's horrified. His cry for help must have summoned her to an unexplored corner of the Kernel's domain.

But the Kernel hasn't let her come alone. He's waddling along at her heels, sweating and puffing, and as she picks up her skirts, he seizes her arm.

"Wait," he says.

"Let go!" She tries to pull away from him. "Are you blind? They need help!"

CLANG! A crossbar splits and the straining door buckles. Noble feels the pressure ease, just briefly, before it builds again. He wonders if his eyeballs are going to explode.

"Look out!" cries the Kernel. "It's a breach!"

Then a creaking, rending sound is followed by a sharp *snap!* The barred door pitches forward, slamming onto the ground. Chunks of rubble spray everywhere. A howling mob bursts across the threshold.

Noble finds himself on all fours, kicked and trampled. Fallen bodies are stacking up around him.

"Noble! This way!" Lorellina has freed herself from the Kernel's grip. She's reaching for Noble with one hand as she shields her head with the other. "*Ow!* Watch it! Stop treading on me!"

The crowd is surging in every direction, bouncing off walls and filling up corners. Noble stumbles to his feet. He bats off a couple of reeling girls and grabs Lorellina—but not before tucking the key back safely into his breeches. He's not about to lose that key. At the moment, it's the only weapon he has.

"Yestin?" he cries, straining to be heard over all the noise. *"Yestin!"*

"There he is!" The princess points at a small, cowering shape behind a screen of milling legs. "Yestin! Over here!"

Seeing Yestin look up, Noble twines his fingers firmly around Lorellina's elbow and forges through the chaos. People are hanging off the overhead lights, swinging like monkeys. They're snapping open cans and spraying each other with fizzy liquids. They're kicking holes in wooden panels and vomiting on one another's shoes.

"Come on," Noble rasps, when at last he reaches Yestin. "We're getting out of here."

"How?" Yestin asks tearfully.

"Through the trapdoor."

"What trapdoor?" Yestin doesn't understand.

But Lorellina does. "What about your key?" she says. "Maybe it will open one of these doors. . . ."

"Maybe," Noble growls. "The trouble is, there might be a prison cell on the other side." Peering around, he adds, "I'm lost. Which way *is* the trapdoor?"

"That way." Lorellina nods at the passage to their right, which is already seething with bodies. "We can make it if we hold hands."

"But what about Brandi?" Yestin whimpers. "What about Lulu and Lord Harrowmage?"

"Yes. Where's my cousin?"

"Uh . . ." Noble looks back at the door to the prison cell, which is still spewing people. It's clear to him that trying to push through that torrent would be like trying to swim up a series of river rapids. Even *reaching* the door might be difficult. Noble suddenly realizes that if he and his friends don't start moving pretty quickly, they might lose their chance to move at all.

"We'll worry about the others later," he says. "Let's go."

"But—"

"Now!"

Yestin submits. Noble leads the way down the nearest corridor, hand in hand with Lorellina, who holds on to Yestin. They round a corner and pass the Kernel's booth, which has already suffered a lot of damage. People are dancing on the desk. They're smashing the windows and smearing one another with glue.

"This way!" says the princess. "Hurry!"

They reach their destination just ahead of the crowd, though Noble can tell that they don't have much time: a minute or two at the most, probably. Then he discovers, to his dismay, that the trapdoor has been covered by a sheet of fresh wood.

"The Kernel fixed it, remember?" the princess remarks. "You were here when it happened."

"I forgot," Noble admits. He glances to his left and sees that the mob is closing in. What on earth is he to do?

"Kick it in!" Yestin exclaims. "Just give it a kick!"

"No," a gruff voice says. "I've got a better idea."

It's the Kernel speaking. He's skulking off to their right, at the far end of the corridor. His shirt is flapping loose and he's missing several buttons.

"Come on," he croaks. "Let me show you the way out."

CHAPTER EIGHTEEN

"Liar," says Noble.

"Not this time," the Kernel assures him.

"Hah!"

"It's true, I swear." The Kernel's anxious gaze has already slipped toward the approaching stampede. "Please. You've gotta believe me. There's only one way out of this place, and if you don't use it now, we're done for."

Noble isn't convinced. He's angry about the prison cell. But Yestin doesn't need persuading. "Come on!" he whimpers, pulling at Noble's arm. "Hurry!"

"We have to go," the princess agrees. She's already moving.

"But—"

"This way, Noble!"

They scurry to the end of the corridor, then take a sharp right. The hallway in which they find themselves is almost identical to the last—except that it's empty of people. "The only way to save this computer is to turn it off," the Kernel is saying. He's up ahead, straining to be heard above the noise of the approaching crowd. "That'll put a stop to the damage. Then maybe someone can work out how to repair it."

"Can't *you* turn off the computer?" Yestin asks.

"Not without a direct command." The Kernel disappears around another corner. Noble finally catches up with him in front of a metal door that looks different from the others. For one thing, it has no handle or lock.

The Kernel punches a button that's sitting on the wall next to it and announces, "Mikey was playing *Thanehaven Slayer* a little while ago. Then he walked away and left the computer on, which is why we're in this mess. But Mikey's cell phone has Bluetooth—and it's in DISCOVERABLE mode, right now. So we'll send him a text message. We'll tell him his computer is under attack and he has to turn it off before it crashes."

"What's a 'Bluetooth connection'?" Noble inquires.

"And what's a 'cell phone'?" says Lorellina.

"Never you mind." A sharp *ping* makes them all jump as the metal door in front of them slides open. Behind it is a small, square, windowless room. "Okay, here's your ride to the delivery platform," the Kernel quickly explains. "You have to take the Bluetooth connection to International Mobile Equipment Identity number 709348880021743."

Noble blinks. "Mobile Equipment . . . ?"

"Identity Number 709348880021743. It's like a serial number, okay? And here—you'll need these tokens to get onto the platform." From one of his pockets, the Kernel extracts three small metal disks, which he distributes to Noble and the others. "I'm pretty sure this'll work, now that the virus has altered your programming. You couldn't have done it before."

Noble is hopelessly confused. He stares at the token he's holding, then at the boxlike room, which is the size of a cupboard.

"You've gotta get to Mikey's phone and leave a message on it," the Kernel continues. "Tell him his computer is infected and needs to be turned off. Got that?"

"Yes," says Lorellina.

"Then go. *Go!*" The Kernel steps back. "They're coming!"

Still Noble hesitates. He doesn't understand why he should be hiding in a cupboard if he's supposed to be running away. Could this be another prison cell? Can the Kernel really be trusted? What if it's all a trick?

"Come on, Noble!" Yestin cries. He's already inside the cupboard. And when he asks the Kernel if they should go up or down, Noble suddenly realizes that the tiny room must be some sort of vehicle.

"Up," the Kernel replies. "Press the UP button." He's almost shouting because there's so much commotion from the mob around the corner. Noble decides to join Yestin just as the cupboard door begins to slide shut between them both. Luckily, the princess catches it in time.

"Come on!" she exclaims, throwing herself after Yestin.

Noble follows her across the threshold. Then he swings around to address the Kernel—but there's no Kernel to be seen.

The door bangs shut on a view of tumbling bodies.

"Come on," Yestin mutters under his breath. "Come *on*!" He's jabbing at another wall-mounted button, which is emblazoned with a white arrow. Noble feels the floor lurch. Then the whole room begins to hum.

"What is this?" he demands. "What's happening?"

"We're going up," Yestin informs him.

"Up?" says Noble.

"It's an elevator. Elevators go up and down."

Noble doesn't know what to make of this. He glances uneasily around the room. It's bobbing as if it's afloat; there's a grinding noise and a slight vibration.

"I hope this works," Yestin remarks hoarsely. His lips are trembling.

"Did you understand what the Kernel said?" Lorellina appeals to Noble. She's the color of salt. "Do you know what he was talking about?"

Noble shakes his head, then looks down at the token in his hand. Now he has a key *and* a token. Will either of them do him any good?

"We're taking a message to Mikey's phone," Yestin volunteers. "I guess—I guess that means we'll be uploaded onto it. Maybe."

"But what does that *mean*?" asks the princess.

Before Yestin can answer, the elevator bounces to a halt. A bell chimes somewhere as the door opens, revealing a lot of grubby, tiled surfaces.

"Wait." Noble's arm shoots out to stop Lorellina from advancing. He cautiously pokes his head around the door and scans for any looming threats.

All he can see, however, is a steel gate barring the way to a large room with a curved ceiling.

"ENTRY TO PLATFORM ONE," Yestin quavers. He catches the door, which is trying to shut again. "PLEASE INSERT TOKEN HERE."

Noble frowns. "What?"

"Look. See? In the slot." Yestin points at the complex arrangement of silver bars and skinny metal boxes in front of them. Then he catches sight of Noble's puzzled expression and blurts out, "Can't you read?"

"No."

"Really?"

"What *is* this place?" Lorellina interrupts. She's peering around at the beige-and-green tiles all over the walls, floor, and ceiling. "Is this Mikey's phone?"

"I don't think so." Yestin's voice is hushed. "I think

this is just the delivery platform. This is where we catch the Bluetooth connection."

"How?" Noble queries.

"I'm not sure. But we should probably stick the token in that slot over there."

So Noble leaves the elevator. With Yestin and the princess in close pursuit, he approaches the nearest slot and inserts his token, as instructed. There's a dull *clunk*, but the gates don't open.

"That bar moved." Yestin points. "I saw it shudder."

"Give it a push," Lorellina suggests.

When Noble obeys, the three-pronged gate yields to his pressure, rolling aside to let him pass. Next thing he knows he's through the gate and standing on a long, narrow platform at the edge of a ditch. An arched ceiling, blotched with damp, indicates that he's in a very large tunnel. The ditch at his feet contains several metal rails laid on the ground. Each end of the ditch is lost in darkness, swallowed up by a tunnel that continues in both directions.

Kerchunk. The gate behind Noble revolves again to admit Yestin.

"This reminds me of home," Yestin remarks. "There should be a train along here soon."

"A train?" Noble repeats.

"Shhh!" Lorellina has also forced her way through the revolving gate. Now she lifts one hand and cocks her head. "Do you hear that?"

Noble listens. Sure enough, a faint squealing noise

is growing louder. It's coming from the mouth of the tunnel to his right. He can feel a slight vibration in the platform beneath him.

"That's it," Yestin announces. "That's the train."

"Step back!" Noble warns, just as a disembodied female voice rings out.

"The next connection is for 709348880021743. The next connection is for . . ."

"We have to catch that connection!" By now Lorellina is shouting, because the squeal is rapidly becoming a roar. "What should we do—block its path?"

"With what?" Noble looks around frantically for something to throw into the ditch. But there's nothing except the gate, which is firmly bolted down. And even though he probably has the strength to rip it apart, he certainly doesn't have the time.

"It's okay," Yestin loudly assures him. "We don't *really* have to catch this train. We just have to get on it." The noise has become almost deafening. There's a blast of hot air and a giant *whomp* and suddenly a vehicle like a huge silver truck emerges into the light, shrieking horribly as it slows down. "There are doors, see?" Yestin bellows. "They'll open for us!"

Nodding, Noble covers his ears. He can see the doors—and the windows. The train's interior is well lit and completely unoccupied. He watches empty seats roll past him at an ever-decreasing speed. There seem to be hundreds. At last, the train sighs and stops.

Its many doors slide open, hissing like snakes.

"I hope this isn't a trap," Lorellina remarks.

Noble shrugs. "We can't go back now," he observes, stepping onto the train. When nothing happens to him, the others follow his example. They all sit down warily on a row of hard blue seats.

"Doors closing," says the disembodied female voice.

With a jolt and squeal, the train begins to move again. The well-lit platform rapidly flickers out of sight. Soon, there's nothing beyond the windows but impenetrable blackness.

"This train is bigger than the shuttles on our spaceship," Yestin comments.

Noble doesn't say anything. He's worked out that they're sitting in only one small part of the train, which seems to be made up of a dozen or so vehicles strung together. Thanks to all the windows, he can see into the two adjoining vehicles—which appear to be empty.

He can't be sure, though. Someone might be hunkering down behind the seats.

I wonder if it's possible to pass along this train while it's moving, he thinks.

"Are we in Mikey's phone now?" Lorellina asks suddenly. Noble is so preoccupied that it takes him a few seconds to process her question, by which time Yestin has already answered it.

"No. We're *heading* for Mikey's phone."

"Good." The princess sounds relieved. "Because there's no one here to give our message to."

Noble grunts. He's listening to the *clackety-clackety* that's coming from beneath the train and wondering if he should be worried about it. Perhaps not. Then Yestin says, very softly, "I hope we can get back."

Lorellina stares at him. "What?"

"Well . . . if our message reaches Mikey, we might not have time to go home. Not before his computer's turned off."

Lorellina seems unimpressed. "So?"

"So we can't get into the computer once it's turned off," Yestin explains.

Noble and the princess exchange horrified glances. Then something occurs to Noble. "We used all our tokens," he says. "What if we need more of them to catch the train back again?"

"I *knew* this was a trap!" Lorellina is becoming more and more agitated. "The Kernel is a liar! We should never have agreed to deliver his message! Why would we *want* Mikey to turn off his computer?"

"Because if he doesn't, it's going to crash," Yestin insists. When Lorellina lifts her lip in a sneer, he adds, "Didn't you see what was happening back there?"

"I saw. And I was told to blame Rufus. But what if the *Kernel* was to blame?"

"No." Yestin shakes his head. "Believe me, that wasn't the Kernel's fault."

"How do you know?" the princess demands.

"Because he runs the operating system. And the operating system would only do that if it had been sabotaged." Yestin turns to Noble, his bony face puckered into an anxious frown. "*You* believe the Kernel, don't you? It's Rufus who was lying, not him."

Noble doesn't know what to think. He finds it difficult to believe that Rufus ever *meant* to cause any harm, even if harm was somehow caused. And he's also convinced that the Kernel was lying when he promised to negotiate with Rufus.

On the other hand, that doesn't necessarily mean that Rufus is right and the Kernel is wrong. Even Noble can see that. He's starting to realize that the world is a much more complicated place than he ever expected it to be.

Suddenly, the train begins to slow down. It plunges out of the darkness and into the light. Its windows begin to frame views of another well-lit platform.

By the time it eases to a standstill, wheezing and groaning, Noble is already on his feet.

"Arriving at station 709348880021743," the disembodied female voice announces. "Arriving at station 709348880021743. . . ."

"Our stop," says Yestin, jumping up. He accompanies Noble and Lorellina onto a platform that doesn't look very much like the last one. This platform has smaller tiles, arranged in more elaborate patterns. There's a lot of finely molded ironwork. The elevator sits behind *two* doors, one of which is like the folding wall of a cage.

The button mounted beside it is made of brass, set in a beautifully engraved brass panel.

"Mikey's phone must be a *really* old model," Yestin observes, gazing around in astonishment. "Everything here looks antique."

"You mean we're inside Mikey's phone?" asks Noble. "Right now?"

Yestin shrugs. "Maybe."

"Stand clear. Doors closing," the disembodied female voice declares. As the train doors slide shut, and the train itself begins to move, Noble wonders—with a sinking heart—if he'll ever see Thanehaven again.

He doesn't feel comfortable. Something's not right about the air, or the light, or the colors. He senses that he doesn't belong here. He certainly doesn't want to stay.

"You mean this is where we have to leave our message?" Lorellina demands, glaring around at the empty platform. "But where is everybody?"

Yestin opens his mouth, then hesitates. Only when the train's departing squeal has become a distant whine does he finally point to a mosaic pattern above the elevator door. "That says EXIT. Maybe there'll be someone upstairs."

"Come on." Noble moves forward. "Let's go."

He jabs at the brass button on the wall, instinctively

236

copying the Kernel's actions. Almost at once, there's a clanking sound. Then the inner door of the elevator bangs open behind the bronze-colored mesh that's protecting it.

Noble finds himself gazing through the mesh at another very small room. But unlike the last elevator, this one is richly paneled in dark, glossy wood—and is already occupied. A young man wearing a red uniform and white gloves smiles politely as he leans forward to push aside the bronze mesh door. He has a round, freckled, snub-nosed face and a blond crewcut under a rimless cap.

"Going up," he chants. "Where to, sir?"

"Um . . ." Noble isn't sure.

"Message for Mikey?" It's Yestin who answers.

"Hop in," says the young man.

Noble, Yestin, and Lorellina all manage to squeeze into the luxurious little elevator; then its operator slams the cage door shut behind them. Once the inner door closes, the operator presses another button, and the elevator starts to ascend jerkily, with a low-pitched whine.

No one says anything. Even the young man remains silent until the elevator comes to an abrupt halt.

"Here you are," he says, once again leaning forward to drag open the doors. "There's your in-box."

"Where?" Noble can't see a box. He's looking at a very large room that's seething with activity. Along the

237

wall opposite the elevator about two dozen women are sitting on high stools, sticking wires into panels full of holes, then pulling them out again. All these women have short, curly hair and calf-length skirts; they're gabbing away into mikes, making a tremendous din. Other women are sitting at rows of desks in the middle of the room, tapping away at black machines that look a bit like Mikey's computer—except that they don't have screens. Wooden doors and frosted-glass panels line the left-hand side of the room, while on the right-hand side is one long row of filing cabinets.

Noble guesses that these cabinets must be full of paper, since they're almost identical to the ones he saw in the Archive. Besides, the whole *room* is full of paper. All the people bustling around have armfuls of paper. There's paper sprouting from every black machine. And great towers of paper are stacked on the desks.

"Try over there." Beside him, the young man points at a nearby counter. "See that window? That's the in-box." With a beaming smile and a white-gloved salute, he steps aside to give his three passengers an unobstructed exit. "You have a nice day," he adds. "And thanks for visiting International Mobile Equipment Identity number 709348880021743."

Noble catches the princess's eye. She shrugs. There's no way they can turn back now.

So they step across the threshold and advance into the busy room, with Yestin trailing behind them.

CHAPTER NINETEEN

A woman carrying a bundle of paper is clacking along in high-heeled shoes. She nearly bumps into Noble, who dodges her just in time.

"Excuse me," she trills. "So sorry."

Other women are darting between desks and doors, loaded down with sheets of paper in every color of the rainbow. A loud buzz of conversation is interrupted, now and then, by a clanging bell or a banging drawer. There's so much going on that no one seems very interested in the three newcomers, who thread their way cautiously through a network of desks toward the in-box service window.

A gray-faced man is sitting there, perched behind a brass-topped counter. He's small and thin, with a green eyeshade strapped to his balding head. His ink-splattered shirtsleeves are rolled to the elbow; he wears a black waistcoat and has a pen tucked behind one ear. Arranged in front of him are a stamp, a small book, a silver bell, a metal spike with papers impaled on it, and a machine that's spitting out yet more paper, in ribbonlike coils.

"Yes?" he snaps, when Noble approaches him. "How can I help you?"

"Um . . ." Noble clears his throat. Before he can proceed, however, Lorellina grabs his arm.

"Are you sure you want to do this?" she whispers.

"Do what?"

"Turn off Mikey's computer." She scans Noble's face, her green eyes blazing. "Do you trust the Kernel? Do you believe him?"

As Noble ponders this question, Yestin weighs in. "*I* do. I believe him."

"Why?" Lorellina whirls around to confront Yestin, who flinches. But he doesn't back down.

"We had computers on board our spaceship," he quavers. "If Mikey's computer is anything like them, we *have* to deactivate it, or it can't be fixed."

"Suppose you're right, though?" Noble murmurs. He's acutely conscious of the man at the window, who has just coughed impatiently. "Suppose we can't go back to the computer once it's turned off?"

"Then we'll have to wait," Yestin replies. "As soon as the problem's solved, and the computer is working again, we'll look for a way back in." Seeing Lorellina's

240

impatient scowl, he squeaks, "At least, it will give us a chance! Once the computer's trashed, we'll *never* be able to go home!"

"Truly?" says Noble.

"Truly."

"Ahem." It's the man at the window, who's drumming his fingers. "Do you have a legitimate message, or not? Because I'm warning you—this phone plan features a spam control option."

Noble ignores him, focusing on Yestin instead. "What about Rufus? What will happen to Rufus if the computer is turned off?"

Yestin shrugs.

The princess stamps her foot. "Why do you care about Rufus?" she exclaims. "You should be worrying about my poor cousin. What will happen to him? Or to *any* of those we left behind? They are all in grave peril!"

"They are," Yestin agrees. "And the only thing we can do for them now is to send that message."

Noble hesitates, trying to rearrange all the scattered images cluttering up his head. A past, he concludes, is difficult to organize—especially when it's starting to grow longer. For one thing, it's full of change. *You think you know where someone fits*, he muses, *and then you realize that you don't.*

He's feeling trapped and bewildered. The last time he felt like this was before he discarded Smite, back when he had no control over what he was doing. Now it's as if his sense of independence is slipping away again. *But maybe I never really* did *gain my freedom,* he speculates. *How could I have been master of my own destiny, when I never even knew what was going on?*

He wonders if Rufus has been misleading him— misleading everyone—by promising freedom while withholding information.

Suddenly, the elevator door pings, causing the man at the window to lean forward aggressively. "If you don't have a message," he says, "then please step aside."

"But we do have a message!" Noble blurts out. "A message for Mikey!"

"Oh, yes?" The man surveys them suspiciously. "So which one is it?"

"What?" Noble doesn't understand.

"Which one of you is the message? Or is it the three of you together?"

"No!" Lorellina protests, stung. "Of course not!"

"It's a text message," Yestin quickly explains. "Our message is: YOUR COMPUTER IS INFECTED AND NEEDS TO BE TURNED OFF."

The man purses his lips, his expression slightly puzzled. Then he shrugs and removes the pen from behind his ear. "Got it," he says, as he jots something down in his book. "And what's your Mobile Equipment Identity Number?"

Yestin flicks a worried glance at Noble before replying, "We don't have one."

"You must have one."

"We're from Mikey's computer," Noble interrupts. "We came here on the Bluetooth connection."

When the man frowns, Yestin asks anxiously, "Don't you have the International Mobile Equipment Identity number for Mikey's computer? Wouldn't it be in your records somewhere?"

"No."

"The Kernel gave us tokens to get in here," Noble points out. "And I also have this." Producing his key, he lays it on the counter with a crisp little *snap*. "We have the Kernel's blessing. We are not wayward or malign."

"And why would you need a number from us anyway?" Lorellina demands. "Here we are. We have a message. What more do you need to know?"

Something flickers behind the man's watery gray eyes, which abruptly swivel toward the elevator. Following his gaze, Noble sees that the uniformed operator has reappeared, and is passing a swaddled infant to one of the busy young women in high heels.

No sooner does the baby change hands than it starts to cry.

"New ringtone," the operator announces. Then he quickly withdraws into his elevator, banging its doors shut behind him.

"They'll make anything into a ringtone, these days," the man at the window says disparagingly. But he seems to lose interest in the baby once it's been whisked away to another room. Turning back to Noble, he grudgingly adds, "Well—it's highly irregular, and I'm not too sure of the protocols, but since you're already here . . ." Without finishing his sentence, he rings the little bell in front of him.

A young woman with bright red lips immediately responds to his summons. She takes the page that he's just ripped from his book and hurries to the nearest desk, where she sits down and begins to tap at a black machine. Watching her, Noble realizes that she's using the machine to transcribe words—the same words written by the man at the window.

It doesn't take her long. Within seconds, she's plucked two different-colored sheets of paper from her machine and trotted back to the counter, where she spikes the pink sheet and gives the white one to her boss. He promptly rolls it up and inserts it into a pipe attached to the ceiling.

Pop! The scroll is sucked from his hand. A bell clangs. A red light flashes. Then the machine on the counter begins to clatter and whirr, spitting out more coils of paper tape.

The man at the window checks the tape before tearing it off, stamping it, and spiking it. "There," he says. "Your message has been delivered."

Noble gapes at him. "Really?"

"Didn't you hear that bell?"

"Yes, but—"

"Confirmation just came off the wire machine. Our phone user has received your message."

"Oh." Noble looks at the princess, who asks, "What happens now?"

"I beg your pardon?" the man says. He seems mystified.

"We want to go back where we came from," Yestin explains. "Can you give us a token?"

"A token?"

"For the train," growls Lorellina.

"I don't know anything about trains. *Or* tokens," the man replies, ringing his silver bell again. Another neatly groomed young woman promptly appears at his window. "Those need to be filed," he informs her, pointing at the papers on the spike. She nods and removes them, while Noble, Yestin, and Lorellina consult each other in low voices.

"Maybe we don't need tokens to get back," Noble suggests.

"I don't remember seeing any gates downstairs...." Yestin's gaze wanders around the room, pausing for an instant on a woman filing papers.

But Lorellina stares straight at Noble. "Where is your key?" she says. "We might need that, instead of the tokens."

"What? Oh. Yes." Noble reaches for his key, which is still sitting on the brass counter. Lorellina is already moving away. She pushes past several people so roughly that one woman stumbles and drops something. Yestin follows the princess, but has to take a detour around the scene of the collision—where several young women are now hunkered down, blocking traffic as they retrieve scattered documents.

By the time Noble catches up with Yestin and Lorellina, the wall-mounted button beside the elevator has already been pressed.

"Perhaps we should take a weapon with us," Lorellina remarks, eyeing a nearby desk lamp.

"Oh, I don't think so. Haven't we caused enough trouble already?" Yestin is referring to all the paper that's now strewn across the floor, thanks to Lorellina. "Anyone would think we were malware, the way we keep messing things up."

"Speak for yourself," Lorellina retorts, just as the elevator announces its arrival with a *ping!* She turns eagerly, clutching at the mesh door as the operator's face appears behind it. "You! Varlet!" she exclaims imperiously. "Take us back to our Bluetooth connection!"

The operator gapes at Lorellina. "*Your* Bluetooth connection?" he echoes, sounding dazed.

"The one that goes to Mikey's computer," Yestin pipes up. "We've delivered our message, and now we want to go home."

The operator raises his eyebrows. "Oh, you can't go there," he says. "That service is temporarily suspended."

Noble is speechless. Lorellina stares. It's Yestin

who stammers, "Was—was the computer turned off?"

The operator shrugs. "I'm sorry, sir. I don't have that information." He still hasn't opened the mesh door.

"Can you find out for us?" Noble pleads.

"I'm sorry, sir. I'm unable to be of assistance."

Before Noble can say anything else, the inner door of the elevator slams shut. It's like a slap in the face. For a second or two, Noble just stands there, shocked and disoriented. He doesn't know what to do next.

"I told you," Yestin whimpers at last. "I told you we wouldn't be able to get back."

"You told us we'd have to wait," Lorellina reminds him tersely. "The question is, where?"

"We'd better ask," says Noble.

"Ask whom?" The princess's voice cracks on a scornful note as she shoots a look of disdain at the in-box window. "*That* man knows nothing."

"He knows more than we do," Noble rejoins, before heading back to the brass counter.

The ink-spattered man behind it is examining yet another ribbon of paper. "Yes?" he says in an absent-minded tone, without even looking up. "May I help you?"

"Our Bluetooth connection isn't working," Noble announces. "We can't get back to Mikey's computer."

The man grunts. Then he lifts his gaze and rings his little silver bell. "Well, that's probably because it's been sabotaged," he observes.

"*Sabotaged?*" squawks Lorellina.

"That's what it says right here." The man at the window waves a fluttering stream of paper tape under her nose, before pushing it toward the jaunty blonde woman who's just popped up next to Noble. As this young woman seizes the tape, however, Lorellina snatches it from her.

There's a nasty ripping sound.

"Hey!" cries the man at the window. "You can't do that!"

But the princess ignores him. " 'Did u sabotage my laptop u jerk?' " she reads aloud, squinting at the torn piece of tape in her hand. " 'If u did, I will get u Rufus yor ded.' " Raising her eyes, she addresses Noble. "Could this be from Mikey?"

"Of course, it's from Mikey!" snaps the man at the window. "You're in Mikey's phone, remember? Now give that to the copygirl at once—that's an urgent dispatch!"

Still Lorellina defies him, though Yestin is starting to look nervous. As for Noble, he's had a flash of inspiration.

"Where are you sending that message?" he asks the man at the window. "Are you sending it to Rufus?"

"I'm sending it to International Mobile Equipment Identity number 466672739001277."

"That'll be Rufus's phone." It's Yestin speaking. He's squirmed his way between Noble and the copygirl, who keeps plucking at the air, making futile attempts to retrieve the strip of tape from the princess. Lorellina resists until Yestin rebukes her. "You'd better give that back," he says, "or Rufus won't get it in time. And then we *will* be acting like malware."

Lorellina scowls. Reluctantly, she surrenders her paper strip, then turns to Noble for guidance. "I don't understand," she complains. "Is that message for *our* Rufus, or for the other one?"

"The other one." As the copygirl retires to her desk with a ragged length of crumpled tape, Noble appeals to Yestin. "Do you really think that Mikey's message will end up on Rufus's phone?"

Yestin nods, then has second thoughts. "Or on his computer, perhaps."

"Ah." This is exactly what Noble has been hoping. "So Rufus *does* have a computer? Not our Rufus. I mean the other one."

"Of course." There isn't a trace of doubt in Yestin's voice.

"And would the computer be like Mikey's? Would it be connected to Rufus's phone?"

"Maybe."

"Then we should deliver that message ourselves," Noble declares. He points at the nearest desk, where Mikey's angry text is being copied on one of the black machines. "And we should add our own message," he continues. "We should tell Rufus—the *other* Rufus—that if he doesn't fix Mikey's computer, we'll sabotage his."

There's a long pause. Noble waits nervously. But Yestin just stares in blank amazement. Even Lorellina remains mute.

In the background, machines clatter and voices hum. The blonde copygirl delivers her two copies of Mikey's message. The man at the window spikes one and stamps the other, which he passes back to her.

"I think that the other Rufus—the one who created our Rufus—really *did* do something to Mikey's computer," Noble finally adds. "And I think . . . I can't help wondering . . ." He sighs, then takes a deep breath. His own sense of guilt is weighing him down like a stone in his stomach. He knows he's betraying a friend, and yet . . .

How can he help being suspicious? Rufus himself taught Noble to question things that he'd previously taken for granted. And it's hard not to question Rufus, after all that's been going on.

"I'm beginning to believe that most of our troubles have actually been caused by Rufus," Noble reluctantly admits. The confession makes him feel dizzy, as if he's lost his balance.

Lorellina's brows snap together. "Which Rufus?" she wants to know. "Our Rufus, or the other one?"

"Both of them," Noble mumbles.

Then he proceeds to tell her his plan.

CHAPTER TWENTY

Noble has it all worked out. If Rufus *does* own a computer, it must resemble Mikey's: a little world full of places just like Thanehaven. Places where people will listen to the same arguments that were used to change Noble's mind.

Places where Noble can have a big impact.

"You know what *our* Rufus has been saying," Noble explains to the princess. "You've heard him. He says it to everyone. He asks us if we like what we're doing and then he tells us that we have a choice."

"Which is true," Lorellina insists.

"Yes. It *is* true. It makes sense. That's why I said it to the old woman in the basement. That's why you just said it to that man, over there."

Lorellina shakes her head, frowning. "I did no such thing."

"You gave him a choice," Noble reminds her. "You asked him why he needed an International Mobile Equipment Identity number from us. You told him he could break the rules." As Lorellina ponders this, he adds gently, "You wouldn't have done it before you met Rufus."

"No," she concedes. "I daresay not."

"Rufus offered us freedom, but he gave us chaos," Noble continues. "We can do the same thing, now. All we have to do is imitate Rufus." Suddenly, his attention shifts toward the elevator, which has signaled its arrival with a loud *ping*. The blonde girl must have summoned it; she's standing beside the button, clutching her stamped copy of Mikey's message.

"Wait! Stop! We'll take that!" Noble shouts at her. Then he launches himself in her direction, ducking and weaving to avoid all the people who are squatting on the floor, collecting spilled paper.

Yestin and the princess hurry after him. They reach the elevator just as its inner door slides open, pushed aside by a white-gloved hand.

"Give that to me," Noble orders. As he plucks Mikey's message from the copygirl's grasp, she looks around desperately for assistance. "It's all right," he assures her, then turns to the operator—who hasn't yet opened the mesh door. "We'll deliver this message to Rufus," Noble declares, "if you'll take us to the right connection."

"Oh—I—uh . . ." The operator doesn't know what to say.

"Do you want this message sent or not?" Lorellina asks him. "Because it happens to be urgent!"

The operator glances at the copygirl, who concedes, "It *is* urgent. It's a text message."

"And we're attachments," adds Yestin.

This seems to do the trick. With a shrug and a sigh, the operator admits defeat, stepping aside so that Noble and his friends can board the elevator. It begins to ascend as soon as the inner door closes. Then Yestin tugs at Noble's arm.

But when Noble shoots him an inquiring look, the boy's eyes dart toward the stranger in their midst. So Noble leans down, enabling Yestin to whisper in his ear, "Are you going to sabotage a computer? I don't want to do that."

"Neither do I," Noble quietly confesses.

"Then—"

"We won't really do it. We'll threaten to do it."

"Oh."

"We'll make Rufus *think* we'll hurt his computer." As the elevator lurches to a standstill, Noble swings around to address the uniformed attendant. "Are we going to need tokens?"

"Tokens?" the young man echoes.

"For the train."

"What train?" Reaching for the inner door, the operator says to Noble, "You'll be heading for a base station, won't you?"

"Will we?"

"You will if you want to reach another phone." The door clanks open to reveal an expanse of flat gray pavement under a brooding sky. "That's your ride over there," the operator announces, pointing through the bronze-colored screen.

Noble stares at something that looks like a giant dragonfly. It has a bulbous head, a skinny abdomen, and four wings set high on its back. But unlike most dragonflies, this one is as big as a truck.

"What *is* that?" Lorellina exclaims.

"It's your signal carrier." With a heave and a *crash* the operator opens the cage door. "Just hop in and catch a connecting flight when you reach the base station."

Noble blinks. "What do you mean, a connecting flight?" he demands. "Does that thing *fly?*"

"It's a helicopter, sir." There's a hint of a drawl in the operator's voice. "All helicopters fly."

This is news to Noble. He eyes the odd-looking thing suspiciously, then pokes his head out of the elevator and scans the desolate space around it. There's nothing much to see; just an endless, paved expanse disappearing into a light-gray mist. He's occupying the only structure in sight, which is a small, square, almost featureless brick building.

"We should ask that person for help," Lorellina says abruptly. She's referring to the helicopter's only occupant, who's wearing orange overalls, black gloves, a helmet, a microphone, and something that looks to Noble like a black-glass eye mask. Only a straight nose and a chiseled, clean-shaven chin have been left uncovered.

"Good idea," Yestin remarks, peering past Lorellina. "The pilot will know what to do."

"What's a pilot?" Noble isn't familiar with the word.

"Pilots are like drivers," Yestin explains, "only they drive things that fly."

"*What?*" Noble stares at him, appalled. "But how can the pilot see through that mask he's wearing?"

"It's not a mask. It's sunglasses. He can see through those."

"Are you two coming or not?" Lorellina sounds impatient. She flounces toward the pilot, whose expression doesn't change as he turns his head to watch her approach the helicopter.

Noble suddenly recollects that he's carrying the all-important message from Mikey. So he follows Lorellina to where the pilot is waiting patiently. Yestin catches up a moment later.

"We have a message for Rufus," Noble declares, thrusting his crumpled sheet of paper under the pilot's nose.

"We're going to International Mobile Equipment

Identity number 466672739001277," Yestin adds quickly.

The pilot nods. Then his head swivels until he's gazing straight ahead once more. As his right hand moves, the wings overhead start to spin like spokes on a wheel, slowly at first, but with increasing speed.

"Everyone get in!" exclaims Yestin, pitching his voice high over the sudden roar of the helicopter. It seems like good advice to Noble. But he hangs back until his two friends are tucked into the rear of the helicopter, then climbs into the seat next to the pilot, who opens his mouth and says, "Buckle up."

Noble gapes at him, confused.

"The harness!" Yestin shouts from the backseat. "Put on your harness!"

Realizing that there's a tangle of belts and clips attached to his seat, Noble does as he's told. By the time he's all strapped in, the helicopter is already rising off the ground.

Gazing down at the rapidly shrinking brick box, Noble is surprised at how quickly it's swallowed by a veil of fog. Or is it cloud? He feels deeply uncomfortable. The noise and vibration are unexpected; though he's never tried to imagine what it would be like to fly, his experience with gargoyles has led him to believe that it must be a calm, quiet, graceful activity.

But this vehicle is so loud that talking is out of the question. Noble is forced to sit silently as they move through a white cloud that goes on and on, without a break. Visibility is so poor that Noble worries about crashing into something—like a mountain, for instance. How can they avoid obstacles if they can't see where they're going?

He tries to catch the pilot's eye, without success. The pilot simply stares through the window in front of him. His face is impossible to read. The bit that's actually showing is as hard and controlled as a statue's.

Then the helicopter starts to drop. Noble is about to ask if they've reached their destination when they emerge from the cloud into crystal-clear air. Noble gasps. Below them lies a landscape so busy and cluttered that he doesn't know where to look first.

It's another flat gray expanse, but it's dotted with broad roofs and large vehicles. Some of the vehicles are helicopters. Some are trucks and vans. Some are machines bigger than houses, sporting stiff, outstretched wings like a bird's or a gargoyle's.

Everything grows bigger and bigger as the helicopter sinks slowly to earth.

"Look!" Yestin cries. "It's a rocket!"

Noble cranes around. "A what?" he yells back.

"A rocket! For space travel!" Yestin glances uncertainly at the pilot. "I guess they must have satellite signals coming through this base station."

Noble is still none the wiser. He doesn't bother asking any more questions, though, because the helicopter is about to land. Its spinning blades are churning up dust, causing people to scurry for cover.

Someone wearing orange overalls is waving a flag. Someone else uses a clipboard to shield his face from the windblown dirt.

As the helicopter settles onto solid ground, another, identical helicopter lifts into the air. There's a lot of movement in every direction. There's also a great deal of noise.

Whomp-whomp-whomp. Gradually, the revolving wings above Noble start to lose speed. The seat underneath him stops shuddering. The engine sputters and dies.

The man with the clipboard approaches them. He's dressed in gray overalls, wraparound sunglasses, and a knitted cap. His expression is so blank that he could be the pilot's twin brother. "Destination?" he barks.

Noble has been unfastening his straps. As he hesitates, the pilot drones, "International Mobile Equipment Identity number 466672739001277."

The man in gray scribbles something on his clipboard. "All of them?" he asks.

"All of them," the pilot confirms.

His interrogator grunts, before gesturing at a nearby helicopter, which is yellow with black trim. "There's your carrier," he tells Noble, straining to be heard above the thunder of a gigantic winged machine that's passing overhead. The sky seems to be full of these things, though some are so far away that they look more like insects than anything else. They keep vanishing into the cloud cover, to be continually replaced by similar machines that drift down to earth and land on the wheels they've just disgorged from their bellies.

"What *is* that?" Lorellina demands, nodding at one of them.

"That's a plane," replies the man with the clipboard. "That's for long-distance travel. You won't be needing one of those—you're in the same cell as your destination." He turns on his heel and departs, leaving the princess more puzzled than ever.

"What cell?" she asks Noble plaintively. "Is he talking about a prison cell?"

"I don't know," mutters Noble, leading the other two toward the yellow helicopter. It's parked inside a painted circle, its pilot an exact replica of the one they've just left behind. Noble pauses. He peers over his shoulder, wondering if the first pilot might have switched helicopters. But the first pilot hasn't moved.

"We have a message for International Mobile Equipment Identity number 466672739001277," Lorellina declares. She's pushed in front of Noble to address the second pilot. "We were told you could take us there."

The pilot nods. He doesn't speak; he doesn't even glance at Noble's proffered sheet of paper. He just fiddles with some of the switches in front of him as Yestin follows Lorellina into the backseat.

Noble takes the front seat again. This time, he

doesn't have to be told to buckle up. This isn't a repeat of the last trip. Not with all the flying objects roaring or whirring or zooming past.

It's like flying through a cloud of gnats. Noble is feeling quite nervous, and when the spinning blades slice a hole in the cloud above him, he shoots an anxious look at the pilot. There must be dozens of machines lost inside the thick gray haze that's just enfolded the yellow helicopter. How can *anyone* hope to plot a course through so many moving targets?

Yestin taps Noble on the shoulder.

"I was just thinking!" Yestin bawls. "The guy on the ground said we wouldn't have to go far! Maybe that means Rufus is close to Mikey!"

Noble considers this for a moment. "They can't be too close," he yells back, "or Mikey would have talked to Rufus, instead of sending a message!" Suddenly, he has an idea. "I'll wager Rufus is sitting at home right now, and Mikey, too!" he adds.

"Huh?" Yestin puts a hand to his ear.

"They live next door to each other!"

Before Yestin can respond, something rears out of the drifting cloud. It's an enormous tower. Noble is goggle-eyed with awe and disbelief, because the tower is truly colossal. It's so big that when they land, he can't even see the edges of its wide, flat roof. All he *can* see is a man with a flag standing in front a small, windowless structure like a bunker or guardhouse.

This man is another pilot look-alike. He's wearing

the same sunglasses over the same strong, expression-less face. Like the man with the clipboard, however, he's dressed in gray overalls.

He calls out, "Incoming?"

The pilot raises a thumb in acknowledgment. Meanwhile, Noble has peeled off his straps. "We have a message!" he declares, scrambling out of the heli-copter. "A message for Mikey!"

"Level One," the man with the clipboard replies in a montotone. He jerks his chin at the guardhouse.

"In there?" asks Noble, surprised. The building isn't much bigger than a truck. But then Yestin says, "Is there an elevator?" And the man in gray nods.

"Level One," he repeats.

As Noble leads the way to the guardhouse, Yestin mutters, "Maybe they're all clones. Maybe that's why they look the same."

Noble ignores him. There's too much else to worry about. The guardhouse, for instance, seems like the perfect setting for an ambush. Noble approaches it cautiously, wondering if he's about to be attacked. But there's no one inside. It's empty except for a very large metal box with a door in it.

"Here's the elevator," Noble announces. He pushes a wall-mounted button and the elevator soon arrives: a smooth, silvery cupboard containing no buttons and no operator.

But when Noble steps inside for a better look, a disembodied female voice says, "Level, please."

Noble can't help jumping.

"Level One!" Yestin exclaims. He hurls himself across the threshold, pulling Lorellina with him. "It must be voice activated," he mutters. "I guess Rufus has a *really* cutting-edge phone."

"Is that where we are now? In Rufus's phone?" asks Lorellina.

"I think so," Yestin replies. And Noble adds, "The *other* Rufus's phone."

They're already moving. Noble recognizes the sensation, though this particular elevator doesn't shudder and jerk like the others. Its passage is as smooth as its walls, marked only by a slight lift of his stomach and a gentle pressure on the soles of his feet. There isn't even a bounce or a wobble when they arrive—just a chiming noise and the musical announcement, "Level One." Then the door slides open.

Yestin gasps. Even the princess looks amazed. As for Noble, he's dazzled by the room beyond the door. Its floor is like a sheet of wet ice. Its high, glass ceiling is supported by a complex network of gleaming steel beams. Two square ponds lie on either side of a desk constructed from polished marble, above which hang several gigantic globes that shine with a pearly radiance. The atmosphere is hushed, with only a quiet ripple of background music disturbing the stillness.

Noble can't understand it. Where are all the people? Mikey's phone was crammed with busy women and clattering machines, but the only visible occupant of Rufus's phone is the girl sitting behind the desk. And if she's busy, she's disguising it very well.

"May I help you?" she inquires, her tone pleasant enough, though slightly cool. She has a pale complexion, a level blue gaze, and straight blonde hair that sits close to her skull like a shiny helmet.

"We have a message for Mikey," Noble announces, producing his sheet of paper. Then he pads toward the desk, his bare feet leaving dull patches on the polished floor. Yestin and Lorellina are close behind him.

"What's your International Mobile Equipment Identity number?" the girl queries, as Noble hands her the message.

"We don't have one," Lorellina snaps. But Yestin quickly says, "Yes, we do." And he recites the number for Mikey's phone.

The girl nods. "Thank you," she murmurs, her attention shifting to the computer on her desk. She starts tapping at its screen.

Noble has to clear his throat before she'll look up again.

"We want to add another message," he reveals. "For Rufus."

"I beg your pardon?"

"On the bottom of that message," Noble continues, "we want to add IF YOU DON'T FIX MIKEY'S COMPUTER, THE SAME FATE WILL BEFALL YOUR OWN." Seeing the girl's blank expression, Noble admits that he's unable to write this postscript himself. "But *you* can," he says. "Can't you? There's enough room on the paper."

"Oh, no." The girl shakes her perfectly groomed head. "I can't do that."

"Why not?" Yestin pipes up. "Don't you have a pen?"

"I can't just *write a message*," the girl rejoins crisply. "That would be against the rules!"

"But—"

"All messages must be cleared by the dispatcher." She flicks the piece of paper with one lacquered fingernail. "All messages must be stamped, signed, and formally processed."

"Yes, but—"

"Request denied. I'm sorry." The girl doesn't sound very sorry. "There have to be security measures put in place, or we'd be overrun by spam. If you want to amend this text, you'll have to go back to International Mobile Equipment Identity number 709348880021743 and make it official." Looking Noble straight in the eye, she concludes in a bored voice, "Is that what you want to do? If so, you'll have to get special clearance. Because this message is priority one. It needs to be sent as soon as possible."

CHAPTER TWENTY-ONE

Noble is stumped. He doesn't know what to do next. It's Yestin who draws him aside and says, in a low voice, "We'll have to post our message on Rufus's computer."

"What?"

"If this phone has a connection to Rufus's computer," Yestin quietly explains, "then we should use the connection to post our message where Rufus can see it. Up on the screen." Observing Noble's perplexed look, he adds, "Weren't you going to visit his computer anyway? Wasn't that part of your plan? You'd have to get inside his programs to sabotage them—though I guess you weren't *really* going to sabotage them, were you?"

"No," agrees Noble. "I just wanted to make sure

I could." The truth is that Noble hasn't been thinking that far ahead. He hasn't yet formulated a proper strategy. It never occurred to him that his postscript might be rejected by Rufus's phone. "You mean we can write our message on the window into his computer? From the inside?" Noble still doesn't undersand what a computer is, except that somehow it can be a whole world *and* a box on a table.

Yestin shrugs. "Maybe. It's worth trying."

"Unless *she* stops us." Noble glances at the girl behind the desk, who's now arguing with Lorellina. "She wouldn't take our extra message. She said it would be against the rules. Why would she show us the way into Rufus's computer?"

"Because I've got his password," Yestin proudly declares.

Noble frowns. To him, a password is something you use when approaching a castle gate, to show that you're a friend, not a foe. Is Yestin trying to imply that the entrance to Rufus's computer lies through a manned portcullis? And if so, how did Yestin end up with a key to this mysterious gate?

"Who told you about the password?" Noble demands.

"Rufus did. Our Rufus. A long time ago, in the memory heap. Don't you remember?"

Noble shakes his head.

"It's bloodquest," Yestin reveals. "With any luck, it will work as a passkey for the Bluetooth connection."

"Then let's try it." Approaching the desk again, Noble interrupts Lorellina. "We've changed our minds," he informs the blonde girl. "We want to visit Rufus's computer. Is there a way into it from here?"

The girl stares at him blankly. "What?" she says.

Noble tries again. "We have the password for Rufus's computer. We want to get in. Can you help us?" he queries—again, to no avail. The girl looks just as confused as Lorellina does.

"You want to go *where*?" the girl asks. But before Noble can do more than sigh, Yestin weighs in.

"Maybe we should give you the IP address and virtual port number. Would that help?"

The girl nods, then begins to jab at her computer screen as Yestin reels off an endless string of digits. Meanwhile, Lorellina puts her mouth to Noble's ear.

"Tell me why we have to visit this computer," she hisses.

"To deliver a message," Noble softly replies. "Yestin says we can put our threat up on the screen, where Rufus will read it."

"Which Rufus?" The princess still sounds confused. "Our Rufus or the other one?"

"The other one."

"Oh."

"I wonder how Yestin knows all those port numbers and virtuous addresses?" Noble remarks vaguely. "Did Rufus tell him about those, too?"

The princess is unable to answer. And it's not a question that can be put to Yestin just yet; not while he's is still locked in conversation with the blonde girl. His password must have won her over, because she seems quite happy to be giving him instructions about what she calls our Bluetooth access to the personal area network. As some kind of machine chatters away beside her left knee, she directs his attention to a nearby elevator.

"Just use your swipe card. It'll take you all the way," the girl says, reaching down behind her desk for something.

"Swipe card?" Yestin echoes. "What swipe card?"

"Here." The girl plucks a stiff little square of paper from an invisible slot and pushes it toward him. "Take the elevator up to the fifth floor."

Examining the card, Yestin reads aloud, "COM5."

"Just keep swiping it." The girl produces another card, which she places in Noble's outstretched hand. The third card goes to Lorellina.

"So is Rufus's computer still running?" Yestin queries. "I mean, is it turned on?"

"Oh, yes." The girl's eyes flick toward her desk, as if checking a signal of some sort. "The device is discoverable."

"What about our message? The one we just delivered? Has Rufus read that yet?"

"You mean the authorized one?" This time the girl has to dab at her computer screen a few times before answering. "It's in-boxed," she finally announces. "But it hasn't been opened yet."

"Thanks." Turning to Noble, Yestin observes, "We'd better hurry. If Rufus sees Mikey's message, he might panic. He might turn off his own computer, and then we won't be able to get in."

Noble nods. He follows Yestin to the elevator, which opens as soon as Yestin's finger alights on the UP button. It's another smooth, steel box, very streamlined and efficient-looking, with doors that close behind Lorellina with barely more than a gentle sigh. But when Yestin punches the button marked 5, nothing happens.

"Are we moving?" Noble asks with a frown.

"I don't think so . . . ," says the princess.

"Whoops!" Yestin suddenly points at a bisected lump protruding from the wall. "I guess we have to swipe our card, first."

He drags his card through the slot in the lump, pressing button 5 as he does so. The elevator immediately springs to life. Humming quietly, it ascends at a stately pace, giving Noble plenty of time to ask Yestin about the virtuous port numbers.

"They're not *virtuous*, they're *virtual*," Yestin corrects. "And I saw them in that e-mail. The one I found on the garbage truck."

Noble grunts. He's casting his mind back, sorting through all the fresh-laid memories. Soon he dredges up a vague image of Yestin sitting in a sea of paper.

"Are you talking about the letter you read to us?" he asks Yestin. "That one from Rufus to Mikey?"

"It had all of the source details in it," Yestin confirms. "I remember them."

"You remember everything," Lorellina remarks, with a kind of grudging respect. But Yestin just shrugs and says, "I guess I must be programmed that way."

Still the elevator keeps moving. It rises and rises until Noble begins to wonder if something's amiss. Surely, the trip shouldn't be taking *this* long? Surely, no building could be *this* high?

"Will we have to catch another train?" he asks Yestin.

"Maybe." Once again Yestin shrugs. "Or maybe this *is* the delivery platform."

"We have no tokens for a train," Lorellina observes, so gloomily that Noble feels compelled to reassure her.

"We have the cards," he points out. "Maybe they'll work."

At last, their elevator reaches the fifth floor. It bounces to a halt. Then the door opens onto a scene of utter confusion.

"Oh, dear." After a brief, shocked pause, Yestin is the first to speak. "I guess this must be the computer firewall."

Noble blinks. He can't see any fires—or indeed any walls. All he can see is a very large, well-lit space divided by a long chain of booths, each occupied by a stern-faced, uniformed officer. In front of these booths, half a dozen long queues wind back and forth through a maze of ropes and stands. The lines inch forward every time somebody peels off to approach one of the booths, where a lengthy interrogation then takes place.

Noble decides that he's arrived at a kind of indoor portcullis. The booths are arranged like iron bars, and the guards manning them are like chained dogs, defending their territory with questions instead of swords and shields. *Perhaps they're asking for the password,* Noble thinks, his confounded gaze running over the weird array of applicants standing in line. There are men in white coats, who look a bit like the AV from Thanehaven. There are men wearing orange helmets and tool belts, toting lengths of pipe or spools of cable on their shoulders. There are messengers with bags of sealed envelopes; bedraggled old women propping themelves up on brooms or mop handles; broken-down men who keep getting turned back at the booths because they're so diseased that they've left a trail of hair or teeth or maggots behind them on the floor.

Some of the applicants aren't even human. Noble spots a black bear with a chain through its nose, a hulking monster made of steel, a one-eyed blue blob, and a sealed bag full of something that writhes and heaves and rolls forward every so often, propelled by whatever is tumbling around inside it.

"Hey! You!" a sharp voice exclaims. "Yes, *you!*"

271

Glancing around, Noble spies someone beckoning to him. It's a short, stocky woman in a gray uniform. Standing near a line of elevators embedded in the rear wall, she seems to be directing traffic.

"Yeah, that's right. You," she says roughly. She has bad skin and is carrying too much weight around the middle. "You're with that group, over there. Come on. Move."

She gestures at a knot of figures to her left—and when Noble sees them, his jaw drops.

Lorellina grabs his arm. "Is—is that . . . ?" she stammers, but can't seem to finish her sentence.

Noble recognizes the crest of Thanehaven on a well-muscled warrior's gleaming white surcoat. He can also identify the salt devils standing behind this warrior, even though they have more spikes and suckers than usual. He's never encountered anything like the scaly silver horse looming over the salt devils, despite the fact that it bears a Thanehaven brand. And the legless, fork-tongued gargoyles are also strange to him.

But the three-headed Tritus in the warrior's hand is a dead giveaway.

"Oh, wow," Yestin murmurs, gawking at the warrior. "That guy reminds me of you. I guess Rufus must be downloading a Thanehaven upgrade." He then peers up at Noble. "Which means *Thanehaven Slayer* must be on this computer, somewhere. I guess it makes sense. He's probably been playing it with Mikey."

272

Noble frowns. "You mean we *are* in the computer?"

"Oh, I think so. Don't you?" Yestin replies.

Just then, the squat woman in the gray uniform cries, "Keep moving, please! Let's go! Over here, sir." She's addressing Noble. "It's okay—you're not jumping the queue. You, too, ma'am."

She's obviously classified both Noble and Lorellina as part of the Thanehaven group. After exchanging glances, they step out of the elevator and move into position. When Yestin tries to join them, however, the woman in gray intercepts him.

"Port number?" she says flatly.

"Uh . . ." After a moment's hesitation, Yestin produces his card. The woman examines it, then gestures at another line.

"Over there."

"But—"

"Sorry, bud. No piggybacking. No queue jumping, either."

Yestin throws a terrified glance at Noble, who says sharply, "He's with us!"

"No, he's not." The warrior in the white surcoat speaks up. He has long, dark hair and a neatly trimmed beard; his voice is as deep and resonant as Noble's. "That boy doesn't belong to this group."

"Neither do we," Lorellina points out.

"Yes, you do. You're Princess Lorellina," the warrior replies.

Noble attempts to dodge the outstretched arm

of the woman in gray. At that very instant, however, Yestin suddenly has a change of heart.

"I'm all right! Don't worry about me!" Yestin squeaks, as he's pushed toward his designated queue. "It'll be *much easier* if you stay with that group. I'll meet you on the other side of the checkpoint, okay?"

"We'll wait for you," Noble promises Yestin, who looks tiny and fragile sandwiched between a large, angry-looking bird and a pile of books in a silver cart. Meanwhile, the warrior in white is talking to Lorellina.

"I am one of the Seven Scryers," he's saying. "I am Sangred, the warrior priest. I guard the Sacred Well of Thanehaven."

Lorellina eyes him suspiciously.

"This is not Thanehaven," Sangred continues. "This must be a mystic vision. I have many mystic visions."

But the princess isn't interested in Sangred— or his mystic visions. Turning her back on him, she addresses Noble in an undertone. "We need Yestin. We need him with us."

"I know."

"How can we give our message to Rufus without Yestin? Yestin understands how it should be done."

"I *know*." Noble lets the Thanehaven group shuffle past him as he pauses to check on Yestin's progress. Lorellina is right; they can't post a message without

Yestin's help. Nor can they abandon the boy. It was cruel enough, abandoning Brandi and Lulu and Lord Harrowmage. Abandoning Yestin would be even crueller.

"When I wake up, I will have many truths to convey to the other scryers," Sangred remarks, near the head of the line. "Truths revealed to me in this vision of the Otherworld."

Suddenly, Noble has an idea.

"This is more than a simple vision, my lord," he exclaims. "This is a vision of the *future*. This is a *prophecy*."

"A prophecy?" Sangred echoes.

"A prophecy of the Seven." Though Noble has never met a single one of the Seven Scryers, he knows that they're prophets. He knows it the way he knows how to fight. It's built-in knowledge. "What you're seeing here is the future of Thanehaven," he declares. "Soon there will be legless gargoyles in Thanehaven. And bigger, stronger salt devils. And horses covered in silver scales. These things will be ranged against our kingdom, but we must take heart. Because that boy over there will deliver us."

When Noble indicates Yestin, Lorellina smiles. It's the first real smile that Noble has ever seen on her face, and he's astonished at the difference it makes. Her teeth look so perfect. Her dimples look so pretty.

How beautiful she is, he thinks. *I keep forgetting.*

"That boy over there cannot save us," Sangred

objects. "He is small and weak. He's not a part of our group."

"He will be if you invite him to join us," Noble points out. Then, before Sangred can say anything else, he adds, "If you make the wrong choice in this dream, only bad things will come to pass. But if you make the right choice, you will be aided in your fight against any future perils."

Sangred frowns, glancing at the nearest gargoyle.

"Yestin looks small and weak for good reason," Noble continues. "If you had three cups set out in front of you—a gold one, a silver one, and a stone one—which would you choose?"

There's no reply from Sangred. He ponders, his gray eyes searching Noble's face.

"Maybe you would choose the gold or the silver cup," Noble says, "because stone doesn't gleam. But the stone cup would be the strongest."

"It would," agrees Sangred.

"Then choose the stone cup! Let the boy come with us, or Thanehaven will struggle to defeat all these new foes!"

Sangred nods slowly—just as the guard in the nearest booth beckons to him. For an instant, the warrior priest hesitates.

"Go," mutters Noble. "You've been called." Then he turns and summons Yestin with a twitch of his head.

This time, Yestin takes care not to attract the

female guard's attention. He makes sure that she's looking away from him before he ducks below the surface of the milling crowd that separates him from the Thanehaven team. This swirling, chattering crowd is made up, not only of hopeful applicants, but of those refused admittance. So while half the crowd is shoving forward, the other half is trying to force its way back to the elevators.

Noble worries that Yestin is going to be trampled in all the confusion. There's so much pushing and pulling that he nearly gets trampled himself—especially when the scaly silver horse rushes to join all the gargoyles and salt devils who are now treading on Sangred's heels. Sangred is explaining himself to the guard at the booth up ahead. There's so much background noise that Noble can't hear what he's saying.

"We have to hurry," Lorellina warns.

"I know." All at once Noble catches sight of Yestin, who's wriggling through a mass of tightly pressed bodies. Noble grabs him. With Lorellina in the lead, they rush over to the booth where Sangred has just been given permission to admit his entire group.

Sangred pauses for a moment, as the gargoyles and salt devils jostle him. His expression is mildly anxious. But it clears when his gaze finally falls on Noble.

"This is the boy?" asks Sangred.

"Yes," Noble affirms.

Sangred gives a satisfied nod. He ushers first Yestin, then Lorellina, then Noble past the guard's booth. No sooner does he fall in behind them, however, than a sharp voice pulls him up short.

"Wait!" says the guard. "Hold it right there." He rises from his seat, peering over the counter. "Who is *that* kid? He's not one of your people!"

CHAPTER TWENTY-TWO

"The boy is with us," Sangred protests.

"No, he's not," snaps the guard. "Look at his outfit! That T-shirt doesn't belong in Thanehaven."

"I have a swipe card!" Yestin holds it up, edging away from the guard until he's backed up against Noble. "I know the password! It's bloodquest!"

The guard scowls. As Noble wraps an arm around Yestin, his gaze darts back and forth, frantically searching for an escape route. But the space into which he's emerged is almost identical to the space on the other side of the booths. It's long and narrow, with elevators along its rear wall and a large set of double doors at either end. The only difference that Noble can see is that there aren't so many people in this half of the room.

"Please get back to where you were." The guard leans across his counter, reaching for Yestin. "You belong in the red zone. You haven't been cleared for this zone, yet."

"The boy is important," Sangred argues. He inserts himself between the guard and Yestin. "You *have* to let him through."

"I'm sorry, sir, but he needs to make his own application for admittance," the guard retorts. "He might have a password, but he's on his own. Can't you see that? He's a rogue subprogram that you've picked up along the way."

"You're lying." Sangred speaks with such confidence that even Noble is surprised. "That boy is Thanehaven's best hope for the future. I have made my choice, Sentinel. I have chosen deliverance. And if needs must, I plan to defend my choice."

"Sir—"

"Test me and I *will* rise to the challenge!" Sangred's voice rings out like a tolling bell as he raises his Tritus. "For I am Sangred, son of Foretell, and no dark force will deter me in this world nor any other!"

For one breathless moment, time seems to stand still. It crosses Noble's mind that Sangred's Tritus must be dead—or perhaps asleep—because she isn't reacting at all. She's just sitting in his hand like any lifeless weapon. She doesn't try to shape-shift. She doesn't even bare her teeth.

The guards respond just as sluggishly. They stand

and stare as Sangred continues to address them.

"I know you represent Lord Harrowmage and the tides of chaos! I know that you wish to point me down the wrong path! But I *will* choose wisely, and woe betide you if you oppose me in my wish!"

"He's gone viral," says one of the guards. Like a signal, these words trigger an immediate reaction. All at once a high-pitched wail fills the room, making everyone jump. *Eee-aw-eee-aw-eee-aw* . . .

A red light begins to flash on the ceiling.

"We've got a viral infection here!" The guard who's been dealing with Sangred looks around for help. "It's a breach! Code Red! I need backup!"

Uniformed guards immediately rush toward him from every direction. When Sangred swipes at them with his Tritus, even more guards join their comrades, some from the elevators, some from the booths. "It's a breach!" they cry. "It's malware! It's a lockdown!" They're so intent on pushing Sangred back into line that they seem to have forgotten about Yestin—at least, for the moment.

Seeing this, Noble moves swiftly. He catches Lorellina's eye, then ducks behind the scaly silver horse, keeping as low as possible. Yestin is dragged along with him. The siren is still screeching. *Eee-aw-eee-aw-eee-aw.* The red light is still flashing. The guards are still shouting as Sangred swings at them. Though his Tritus isn't shape-shifting, it works well enough as a big, metal bar, cracking a skull here, an elbow there.

Everyone else is looking stunned. Confused by the noise and disarray, most of the people in Noble's vicinity cower like whipped dogs, mute and motionless. Only Yestin and Lorellina keep moving as they pursue Noble toward the nearest exit, their heads low, their shoulders hunched.

Noble has no real plan. He's hoping that his swipe card might work in one of the elevators, or that the door up ahead might be unlocked. Before he can reach the door, however, it suddenly bangs open—and Noble catches his breath in horror.

There, framed in the wide doorway, stands a familiar vehicle. Its tinted windows are reflecting the *flash-flash-flash* of the pulsing red light. Its engine is idling away at a steady rumble, like the sound of an approaching avalanche.

It's the white van, and it advances slowly into the room, nudging aside a few dazed musicians as it loses speed. The double doors swing shut behind it.

Noble can't believe his eyes. How can the AV be here, in Rufus's computer? It doesn't make sense—unless this van only *looks* the same as the other one. Perhaps this is a different AV, in an identical van. Perhaps all computers have AVs. Or perhaps it isn't an AV driving the van at all.

But it has to be, Noble reasons. *Because the guards are talking about malware, and the AV in Mikey's computer was called in to fight malware.*

For a split second, Noble wonders if he *himself* is

now malware. After all, he just gave Sangred a new and disruptive idea. Could that be how it works? It's certainly the kind of thing Rufus would have done, back when he and Noble were still running around in Mikey's computer.

But after a moment's disquiet, Noble quickly dismisses the thought. He doesn't have time to reflect on such matters. He has too much else to worry about.

I've got to get out of here, he decides.

Dropping to his haunches, he shields himself behind a clump of cleaning ladies, whose buckets and mops add bulk to the screen provided by their stick-thin legs. Yestin and Lorellina follow his example. Noble can't talk to them because of the siren's blare, but he knows that they've seen the white van; he can tell by their fearful expressions. When he catches the princess's eye, Noble puts a finger to his lips. Otherwise, he remains absolutely still while the van rolls past.

Finally, it lurches to a halt. The squeal of its brakes is audible even through the clamor of the alarm. At the same instant, a memory flashes into Noble's head. It's an image of Rufus leaning into another van and saying, "He took his keys with him. Pity. An AV's keys would have got us into pretty much every part of this computer."

The keys, Noble thinks. *If that van belongs to the AV, then we need his keys.*

By this time, the shouts and clangs and roars of

battle have almost overwhelmed the noise of the siren. Everyone's attention is riveted to the booth where Sangred is fighting off at least a dozen uniformed guards. No one seems interested in the bland-faced, white-coated person who's just clambered out of the stationary vehicle.

No one, that is, except Noble, Yestin, and Lorellina.

"Ssst!" The princess nudges Noble, who nods. It's the AV, all right. But like almost everyone else, the AV has turned his gaze toward the fight across the room.

For a moment, he stands there, watching fists fly and bodies collide. Then he passes in front of his van, heading for the source of the commotion. From where he's crouched, Noble has a clear view of the vehicle's rear end. He can see that the driver's door has been left open, though he can't see inside the van. Not that he's expecting anyone else to be lurking in there. Experience tells him that the AV works alone, calling in reinforcements only after his preliminary inspection.

And this, without doubt, is a preliminary inspection. Why else would the AV be plucking a small black book from the pocket of his white coat? Why else would he be tapping an injured guard on the shoulder?

Suddenly, the siren stops wailing. The red light is extinguished. "Must be one of them terrorists," observes a small, bandy-legged cleaning lady in a green head scarf. The other ladies nod and cluck as the AV starts to take notes.

Seeing the AV turn away from him, Noble seizes his chance. He grabs Lorellina, who grabs Yestin. Together, they scurry toward the parked van. No one tries to stop them. No one says a word. Only Yestin utters a low protest when Noble pauses to stick his head into the front seat.

"What are you doing?" Yestin mutters.

Noble is searching for a key. At first, he's confused by all the buttons and sticks and dials in front of him. But then, as he shifts his weight, the van rocks slightly, causing a small, dangling, silver object to catch his eye.

It's a little silver disk attached to something that looks like the top of a key. Unfortunately, the key is wedged into a kind of axle or shaft that's supporting a large wheel.

When Noble yanks at it, however, the key slides smoothly out of its keyhole.

"Wait!" Yestin whispers, from his post near Noble's elbow. "Leave it in there! We can *drive* away!"

"What?"

"If we've got the ignition key, we can turn the engine back on!"

Noble hesitates. It's a good idea. But just as it occurs to him that he wouldn't know how to steer the van, let alone adjust its speed, the AV catches sight of him through the van window.

"Hey! You!"

Noble yanks his head out of the cabin and bolts. He throws himself at the door up ahead, hoping that it might lead to some sort of escape route.

But it's locked.

"The key! Use the key!" shrieks Lorellina, skidding into him from behind, Yestin at her heels. Noble is aware that the guards are converging on the three of them like crows on a carcass. He shoves the AV's key into a keyhole.

As the tumblers click and the door swings open, he steps aside to let his friends pass through ahead of him. Already the wailing siren has been switched back on; the red light is flashing again. Noble turns to defend himself against any guards who might be in pursuit, then flinches in horror. An entire herd of gray uniforms is bearing down on him. He's looking at a sea of gaping mouths and bulging eyes.

"Quick!" Yestin screams.

Noble stumbles backward through the door. It slams shut in the face of a guard who nearly loses the tip of his nose. "Lock it! Hurry!" Lorellina shouts, wedging herself against the handle. As Noble wields his stolen key again, bodies thump against the other side of the doors, making them tremble.

"Where are we?" the princess demands.

They're at the end of a long corridor—a *very* long corridor. It stretches out before them, dead straight and unadorned, as far as the eye can see. Its floor is shiny and gray. Its ceiling is dotted with glowing tubes that recede toward a distant vanishing point. Its walls are lined with black doors, each of them firmly closed, each bearing a printed sign.

"Which way?" Lorellina flings out an arm, indicating the nearest black door. "Through there?"

"Not that one," Yestin quavers. "That's a sandbox."

"A sandbox?" Noble echoes. And Lorellina adds, "Quicksand, you mean?"

"No," Yestin replies, shaking his head. "It's a security mechanism. It's for executing untested code in a controlled environment—"

"What about that one?" Noble interrupts, waving at the door next to it. "What does that say?"

"Umm . . ." Yestin cautiously advances for a better look. "Cookie jar," he reads aloud.

Noble blinks. *"Cookie jar?"*

"For storing Web cookies. *That's* no good."

"And this one?" asks Lorellina. She squints at another door. "What is a . . . a spooler?"

"It's for putting things in queues. We don't want to get stuck in a queue."

"We have to decide! Right now!" Noble insists. "If we're still in this passage when they break through—"

"That one!" Lorellina exclaims. She surges forward, jabbing at the third door on the right with an outstretched finger. But Yestin grabs her gown.

"Wait," he says.

"We have to keep moving!" she snaps.

"Yes, but where to? What's our destination?"

Yestin turns to address Noble as Lorellina yanks her skirt out of his hand. "Do we still want to post that message?"

"Of course," Noble confirms. "And go home afterward."

"Then we can't just run around like faulty robots." Yestin's voice is high and unsteady. "We have to find out if Rufus is using this computer right now. And if he is, we have to find out what he's doing on it."

"So we can make contact," Noble finishes, thinking hard.

"Exactly." Yestin nods. "If Rufus is playing a game, and we get into it, we can maybe—I dunno—write our message on a wall? Or make one of the avatars repeat it to him?"

Thump-thump-thump. The double doors strain against an unseen pressure. Even if the hinges don't break, someone's bound to find another key soon.

Lorellina is dancing impatiently from foot to foot. "Wherever we go, we have to do it now!" she warns.

"We need to find some sort of directory." Yestin is chewing at a thumbnail, his eyes flitting about, his tone distracted. "An instruction address register would be good. Or even a task list . . ."

"Come on, then." Noble begins to move down the corridor, glancing from left to right. "We have a key. We just have to find a good lock."

"What about this one?" Lorellina suggests, indicating a random door.

"Nuh," says Yestin, after a quick glance at it. "That's a spam trap."

She tries again. "This one?"

Yestin shakes his head. "Flag storage," he replies breathlessly. "And that one's full of packet sniffers. We don't want that, either." He's struggling to match Noble's long, vigorous stride. "These doors are all security related. It figures. We're still too close to the firewall."

"Then let's keep going," Noble declares. With one hand clamped around his stolen key and the other around his swipe card, he hurries along, his ears pricked for the *CRASH* of a door giving way behind him.

Lorellina manages to keep up, despite her trailing skirts. It's Yestin who lags behind.

"How are we going to get home?" the princess asks.

"We have to work that out," Noble replies shortly.

"Maybe we should ask Rufus to help us," she remarks. "Not *our* Rufus. I mean the other one."

Noble pauses, struck by the cleverness of this idea. "We could," he agrees. "We could do that, couldn't we, Yestin? We could ask Rufus to send us home."

But Yestin isn't paying attention. He's more interested in the surrounding doors. "This is good," he says. "We've reached the device drivers. There's the local bus. And there's a scanner. And a network card . . ."

"Yestin?" Noble prods the boy with his key. "What do you think?"

"Huh?"

"Do you think we should ask Rufus to send us home?"

Before Yestin can respond, the princess lifts her hand. "Shh!" she says. "Do you hear that?"

Noble listens. Sure enough, mingling with the thump of heavy bodies behind them is a distant rumble from somewhere up ahead.

He identifies it instantly.

"That's an engine!" Yestin squeaks.

"And it's getting closer," growls Noble.

"There it is!" Lorellina clutches his wrist, pointing. "Can you see?"

Noble can see. It's just a pale dot in the distance. But it grows bigger as he tries to judge its speed.

"Which door?" the princess cries. "Which one?"

"Um . . . uh . . ."

"Hurry, Yestin." Noble shoots a glance over his shoulder. No escape there. And when he checks the advancing vehicle again, his heart sinks.

It's another white van.

"Oh!" Yestin exclaims. "Is that . . . does that say WEBCAM?" He takes a step forward. "It does! It's the webcam!"

"You have to choose!" Lorellina wails. "Right now!"

"This one!" Yestin seizes a door handle, but it won't budge.

Noble inserts his key into the lock and turns it; when the door swings open, he feels almost dizzy with relief.

There's a solid stone floor across the threshold, as well as a flight of stairs. The space is dim but unoccupied. It looks safe.

"Come on!" Noble snaps. "Quickly!"

He can hear brakes squealing as he bangs the door shut behind Yestin and Lorellina.

CHAPTER TWENTY-THREE

Noble hastily relocks the thick steel door, which is painted red on the inside. He then twists and jerks at the door handle until it breaks, trying his best to damage the lock. He knows that whoever is on the other side of the door probably has a key that's identical to the one in his hand.

"Where are we?" Lorellina asks.

"It—it's supposed to be the webcam . . . ," stammers Yestin.

"The webcam?" she echoes.

"It must be here *somewhere*." Yestin peers around eagerly, but there's nothing much to see. He and his friends are standing at the bottom of a round tower, which contains a circular staircase winding around a central core. The only visible window is a mere slit in the wall, admitting a narrow finger of light.

Noble heads for the stairs. "Come on," he says. "Hurry."

"Where are we going?" asks the princess.

"I don't know. But there's no other way out."

"There should be a camera!" Yestin wails. "This can't be right!"

Noble doesn't comment. He simply grits his teeth and starts to climb, acutely conscious that every turn in the stairs could bring him face-to-face with an armed guard, or a dragon, or an AV. He can't see what lies ahead. And Yestin is babbling away hysterically three or four steps below him, making it very hard to concentrate.

"The sign said WEBCAM! There *must* be a camera! And if it's turned on, we should be able to see Rufus!" When no one responds, Yestin adds shrilly, "I'm talking about the *real* Rufus! The one we need to talk to! If he's on the computer, he'll be facing his webcam. So we might be able to figure out what program he's running...."

"*Shh.*" Noble says. "Can you hear anything? Are they following us?"

"I don't think so." Lorellina already sounds winded. She's bringing up the rear, hidden from Noble's view by the curve of the staircase.

"It has to be at the top," Yestin insists, panting. "It *has* to be."

Noble is beginning to wonder if the staircase will *ever* end. It goes up and up, around and around, making his head spin and his knees tremble. The ascent is so punishing that it finally defeats Yestin; Noble has to lift the boy onto his back. Then Lorellina flags, slowing their pace even more. Noble is concerned that the AV might catch up with them.

"Come on," he pleads. "We can't stop. Not here."

"How much longer?" the princess wheezes.

"I don't know."

"We must be close," she says, gasping. And she's right. When Noble rounds the next curve in the stair, his head suddenly pops through a large hole cut in a steel-plate floor. The floor belongs to a kind of glass-walled turret, or dome. And framed in every enormous window surrounding him is a dazzling glimpse of infinite space.

There's also an open door, but Noble doesn't throw himself through that. Not at first, anyway. Instead, he allows Yestin to slide off his shoulders, before they both peer around, trying to get their bearings. The first thing Noble sees is an enormous machine made of glass and steel sitting on a platform in the middle of the circular room. There are also several smaller machines sprouting cables and microphones and switches, none of them especially dangerous-looking.

It's not the machines that worry Noble. It's the endless void outside.

"Stay here," he tells Lorellina. Then he advances

a few more steps until he reaches the door. From there, he can see only wheeling hawks against a cloudless sky, but as he emerges into the sunlight—drawing closer to the low white parapet in front of him—he spots the darker line of the sea against the horizon.

Soon, he finds himself peering over a balustrade, down to a distant shoreline at the foot of a cliff.

To Noble, the cliff looks as high as a mountain. The tower looks even higher than that. He feels as if he's miles up in the air. All around him lies a spreading vista of bays and hills and islands. Colored specks on the water appear to be boats. Gulls drift past below his feet. Shorelines and mountain ranges recede into a shining haze.

"Noble?" says Lorellina. Wrenching his gaze away from the view, Noble turns to see her huddled in the doorway with Yestin. "Where are we?" she inquires. "Is it safe?"

Noble opens his mouth, but no sound emerges. Safe? The top of the tower is just a narrow walkway encircling the turret. There's only one staircase. There's only one door. The entire circumference of the area can't be more than twenty paces.

And they're suspended above a drop that makes Noble cringe.

"Is there a camera?" Yestin asks. "Can you see a camera anywhere?"

Noble shrugs helplessly. As he spreads his hands,

Lorellina stumbles into the full light of day—and flinches at the sight that greets her.

"Oh . . ." She shades her eyes. "Oh, no."

"I'm sorry." Noble doesn't know what else to say.

"Is there . . . ?"

"No." He shakes his head. "That was the only way out."

"But there has to be a camera." Yestin groans. He looks around for one as Lorellina slowly, dazedly, approaches the parapet.

Noble suddenly notices how the blazing light seems to leach the color from her hair and gown. Or is she losing some of her gloss? Noble wants to apologize for everything—for Rufus, for her lost cousin, for his bad choice of escape routes—but he has to get back to defend the staircase.

"Hey! *Hey!*" Yestin suddenly shouts. "You guys! Come here!"

He's on the other side of the turret, hidden from view. But the excitement in his voice is so encouraging that Noble and the princess scramble to join him. They find him pressed against the parapet, clinging to a long, dark, horizontal tube attached to a vertical stand. The stand is mounted on the balustrade. The tube is mounted on a pivot.

"It's the webcam!" Yestin squeaks. "Check it out! It's working!"

Noble blinks. For some reason, he was expecting something larger and more elaborate, like the steel-and-glass machine sitting inside. "*That's* a webcam?" he asks.

"Well—no," admits Yestin. "It's actually a telescope. But look. . . ." He presses his left eye against one end of the device. "You can see Rufus!"

Noble gasps.

"*And* Mikey," Yestin goes on. "They're both in someone's bedroom."

As Noble grabs the telescope, Lorellina says, "Could it be one of those 'recordings'?" She pronounces the last word carefully. "Are you sure this is happening right now?"

"Oh, yes." Yestin is adamant. "Because we're looking through a webcam. It said so, downstairs. Besides, Rufus and Mikey are both *really mad* with each other."

He's right. Peering through a small circle of glass, Noble finds himself watching two boys locked in furious combat. One of the boys is Rufus; the other is Mikey. The two of them are lurching around in front of an unmade bed, aiming kicks at each other. Their scuffle knocks a statue off a bookshelf. Then Rufus yanks himself free, pushes Mikey onto the floor, and retreats to one corner of the room while Mikey yells at him.

There's no sound, though.

"I can't hear!" Noble protests. He pulls away from the telescope, turning to Yestin. "What are they saying?"

Yestin gives an apologetic shrug.

"We have to listen! We have to know! This is *important*!" Noble gazes around wildly, but all he can see is a serene and timeless landscape rolling away in every direction. "I don't understand—where *is* Rufus?" he demands, stepping aside to let the princess look into the telescope.

Again, Yestin shrugs. "I don't know how it works. A telescope is supposed to give you a close-up view of a distant object, but . . ." He trails off.

"They seem to be arguing," Lorellina observes. Then she adds, with a hint of satisfaction, "Rufus looks scared."

"In that case, maybe we don't need to post our message." Yestin perks up suddenly. "Maybe *Mikey* will threaten Rufus, and then Rufus will fix his computer!"

"I think Mikey is threatening Rufus right now," Lorellina declares. She's addressing Noble, but he doesn't answer.

He's had a flash of inspiration.

"What about those machines in there?" he asks Yestin, pointing at the glass-walled turret. "Can we use any of *them* to hear what's being said?"

"Um . . ." Yestin hesitates.

"What about the big one? What's that?"

"That's a light." Yestin stares at Noble for a moment before explaining, "This is a lighthouse. Didn't you figure that out?"

"A lighthouse?" says Lorellina. "You mean for ships?"

"I guess so—except that it's pretty high in the air

for ships." With a feeble attempt at humor, Yestin mumbles, "Maybe it's for *space*ships. . . ."

"What about those other machines in there?" Seizing Yestin by the collar, Noble drags him over to a window. "In there! What do they do?"

Yestin narrows his eyes. "That one's a radio," he announces. "At least—I *think* it's a radio."

"You mean like the radio back in Brandi's place?" Noble dredges up a memory of the mirror-lined closet stuffed with clothes. "The one that played music?"

"Kind of." By now, Yestin's nose is pressed flat against the glass. "People used to talk to each other on radios. You'd have to have one, in a lighthouse." With a quick glance up at Noble he says, "We should try the radio. We might hear something on that."

Noble doesn't need any further encouragement. He hustles Yestin back inside, leaving the princess with her eye glued to the telescope. Soon Yestin is fiddling with a palm-sized gray box at the end of a wire. He turns a few dials and pushes a couple of buttons and suddenly the box makes a loud crackling noise.

". . . just tell me how you did it . . ." The voice that emerges from the box, though distorted by a kind of harsh buzz, is still recognizable as Rufus's voice.

"Did what?" Noble identifies this voice, too. It belongs to Mikey.

"Don't gimme that. You know what I mean," the first voice insists. "Tell me how you hacked my computer!"

Yestin and Noble exchange glances. "Rufus knows," Yestin whispers. "He knows we're in here!"

"*Shh.*"

"Maybe something happened back at the firewall!"

But Noble flaps a hand to silence Yestin. It's important that they hear what's being said.

"I'll tell you how I hacked your computer if you fix mine," comes Mikey's fuzzy retort.

"Promise?"

"You're a jerk!"

"It was your fault! You lied to me! You said you weren't gaming and you were!"

"With a bunch of bad scorers! Because you always win! The rest of us need a chance to win sometimes!" There's a long pause. Then Mikey says, "You're crazy, you know that? I blow you off twice, and you think I'm dissing you or something! Grow up, Rufus!"

During the brief, static-filled break that follows, Lorellina appears at the door. "Is that Rufus?" she wants to know.

"*Shhhh!*" Noble and Yestin both hiss at her, just as Rufus mutters, "Sorry . . ."

"Sorry's not enough," Mikey rejoins. "You've gotta fix my computer."

"Okay."

"NOW!"

"Yeah, yeah." There's a crunching sound. "Have you turned it off?"

"Of course!"

"Well, gimme a second, okay? I've gotta upload something onto a USB, and then download it onto your computer. Are you all backed up, by the way?"

"Oh!" Yestin squeaks. He begins to bob up and down, waving his arms. "Oh! Oh!"

"*Shhh!*" Noble scowls at him, because Rufus is still talking.

"No, listen! Wait! That's it! That's what—we just—the USB port!" Yestin gabbles incoherently. He's dropped the little gray radio, which is now swinging and twisting at the end of its wire. "That's where we have to go! Right now! The USB port!" When Noble just stares at him dumbly, Yestin tries to explain. "Rufus is transferring rescue data to Mikey's hard drive! If we hitch a lift, we can get back home! But we have to leave *now*!"

"Where *is* the USB port?" Lorellina queries.

"I don't know!" Yestin answers, "It can't be far. We passed all those device drivers, remember? If we're in the webcam, and the scanner's next door, we *must* be close to the USB port!"

Noble is already clomping downstairs. But an ominous noise soon stops him in his tracks. "Oh, no," he says.

"What?" Yestin rounds the corner behind him with such haste that the two of them nearly collide. Noble has already turned around.

"Back," he orders. "Go back."

"What?"

"They're coming!"

Yestin doesn't ask who "they" are. It doesn't really matter. Whoever they are, they'll be better equipped than Noble, who doesn't even have a knife.

On reaching the turret again, Noble searches frantically for a weapon. But there are no tools or pieces of furniture scattered about.

Lorellina pounces on the radio, trying to wrench its wire out of the wall. Her face is ashen. "We could lie in wait, and strangle the first one who comes up here!" she says, her voice cracking on a high note. "Then we can throw him onto the others and push them all downstairs!"

Yestin appeals to Noble. "Can we?" he quavers, his eyes already awash with tears. When Noble says nothing, he shrinks against the nearest window, wringing his hands.

Noble steps up to the gigantic light in the middle of the floor. It's large enough to block the stairwell— but is he strong enough to lift it off its platform? The bolts holding it in place look rusty and hard to shift, yet the light itself is made mostly of glass. . . .

He puts down his key and his swipe card. Then he braces himself, wraps both arms around the light, and heaves.

His veins bulge. His joints crack. He strains every muscle to snapping point.

But nothing happens. The light doesn't budge.

"There *is* another way out," says Lorellina. She

points at the parapet, raising her voice over the noise from the staircase, which is getting louder and louder. "We can jump," she adds calmly.

"Wh-wha . . . ?" For an instant, Noble thinks he's misheard.

But he hasn't.

"We can jump," she repeats. "Would you rather perish at the hands of our enemies, or choose freedom at all costs?"

"Ummm . . ." Noble swallows. Neither alternative appeals to him. On the other hand, he doesn't have much time to make a decision.

And then Yestin croaks, "You know what? That might actually work."

Noble stares at him in amazement.

"Lorellina's right," Yestin continues in a hoarse voice, his hands trembling. "Jumping *is* another way out. It's kind of like a door, don't you think? And we've got a skeleton key that should work in *every* door."

"And we'd be jumping into water," the princess adds. She darts forward and snatches up the AV's key, though not the swipe card.

"I heard one!" a rough voice howls. "She's up there!"

This cry acts on Noble like a goad. He rushes after the princess, who's already holding Yestin's hand. Together, the three of them burst out of the room, slamming against the parapet a split second later.

Noble is feeling so confused—so dazed and

disoriented—that he doesn't take the key when Lorellina thrusts it at him.

"You should have this," she says.

"But—"

"*You* are the strongest, Noble. And Yestin is the wisest."

"And you are the bravest," Noble adds, holding her gaze. At that instant, an armed figure pops into view beyond the turret window. He looks around and points at Noble.

"Quick!" Noble cries, dipping his knees. "Get on my back!" As soon as he feels Yestin's arms twine around his neck from behind, he wraps his own arms around Lorellina. Then he lifts her off the ground.

"The key!" she shrieks. "Take the key!"

But Noble is already stepping up onto the balustrade, staggering a little under the combined weight of his two friends. Yestin is whimpering into his ear. Lorellina is crushed against his broad chest. From the corner of his eye, Noble catches a glimpse of movement. He can hear people yelling.

Since Lorellina's face is tilted toward him, it seems logical to plant a kiss on her parted lips. After that, there's nothing for him to do but step off the balustrade—and launch himself into thin air.

CHAPTER TWENTY-FOUR

Noble barely has time to take a breath before he hits water. It's as if he's jumped off a lakeside jetty instead of a cliff-top lighthouse. The drop hasn't killed him. It hasn't even hurt him.

That key must have worked, he decides, dazed but thankful, as a cold, choppy swell closes over his head.

There's nothing but liquid under his thrashing feet: no weed or rocks or sand. He's still clutching Lorellina with one arm. With the other, he swims back up to the surface, salt stinging his eyes and Yestin's weight dragging at his shoulders.

Then, all at once, he feels the sun on his hair.

He spits out a mouthful of brine, conscious that Lorellina is coughing and spluttering beside him. When she pulls away, he lets her go. There's no point holding on to her, since she obviously knows what to do with her arms and legs. Yestin, however, is a different story. He's almost strangling Noble, who cranes around to calm the boy—and sees something that gives him a huge shock.

It's a wooden pier attached to a quay. Noble can't believe how close it is; just a few dozen paces to his left. Lorellina immediately splashes toward it, her green skirt billowing around her like a jellyfish. Noble spots a rusty ladder running halfway down the side of the nearest pier support, but knows that Lorellina won't be able to reach the bottom rung. Her arms aren't long enough, for a start. And since she's still clutching the AV's key, she has only one free hand.

So Noble follows along in her wake, vaguely impressed that he can. His limbs know exactly how to move, even though he's never swum a stroke in his life.

"I can't swim!" Yestin says, gurgling.

"Just hold on to me," Noble croaks, gently nudging his way past the princess. Then he braces one foot against the pier support, using it as a springboard to launch himself at the ladder. To his surprise, he manages to grab the bottom rung, despite the fact that Yestin is clinging to his back like a barnacle. But hauling himself up the next two rungs, hand over hand, leaves Noble winded and shaking.

"Get off! Quick!" he barks at Yestin, tucking his chin into his chest. Yestin promptly scrambles over

Noble's head and climbs onto the pier, which is stacked with provisions and seething with people. Noble doesn't notice them at first. He's too busy helping Lorellina. Her sodden skirts are so heavy that she can't make it to dry land on her own; she needs to be dragged and pushed and hoisted. But once he's finally deposited her onto the pier, he quickly becomes aware of a vibration in the wooden boards underneath him.

It's the thrum of countless footsteps.

He glances up to see a great crowd filing past. There are hard-hatted garbage collectors, slithering blobs, camouflaged soldiers, and machines that walk like men. There are trucks full of paper. Someone is carrying an armload of flags, and someone else is pushing a line of clashing silver carts, each with its nose shoved up the stern of the next one. There's a wagonload of porcelain vessels, all of them labeled JAR FILE. There's a black-winged, short-horned, slightly vaporous creature that looks like a demon to Noble.

All of them are marching toward a massive gray ship that's docked at the end of the pier. Two gangways are feeding the crowd into a hull that looms over it like a cliff face.

"Here." Lorellina is trying to return Noble's key with an unsteady hand. "Go on. Take it."

Noble takes the key. Yestin announces, through chattering teeth, "This is it. This is the USB port."

"Really?"

"Really. I guess we were closer than I thought."

He points at a banner over the nearest gangway. "And that's the rescue drive. See? It says so."

Noble studies the ship, then peers in the other direction, toward the quay. "What's that thing over there?" he asks.

"That's a bus. We don't want to get on that. We want to get on the ship," Yestin assures him.

"All right." Noble stands up. As he helps the princess to her feet, she asks, "Is that ship heading for Mikey's computer?"

Yestin nods.

"Will it be big enough?" She sounds skeptical. "There are so many of us!"

Before Yestin can reply, Noble says, "Safety in numbers. We don't want to attract attention." Clutching his key in one hand and Lorellina's elbow in the other, he stands poised at the edge of the throng for a moment, watching it surge past. It isn't until he spies several grubby, cheerful, red-faced men carrying lengths of pipe that he plunges into the crowd, with Yestin trailing after him.

No one objects. The pipe layers are too busy discussing sockets. The ox behind Noble can't seem to talk. Only when Noble arrives at the gangway does somebody finally ask him for identification.

Noble gazes blankly at the uniformed figure barring his way. Then he feels Yestin's elbow in his ribs. "Key!" the boy whispers. "Show him your key!" So Noble waves his key at the guard, who shakes his head and growls, "Antivirus? You're in the wrong line. This is the data backup and restoration portal." The guard gestures at the next gangway, where a squad of camouflaged soldiers is marching on board. "See those process killers? You want to get in behind them."

Noble mutters an apology and retreats through a knot of grumbling garbage collectors. Yestin and Lorellina follow him. They head for the second line, which doesn't look as friendly as the first. Sharing space with the heavily armed "process killers" are people wearing black hats and coats, people clad from head to toe in shiny white suits, and people wearing blue paper caps, white smocks, and white paper masks over their mouths and noses.

Noble doesn't like the way these silent, sinister people keep eyeing him. He decides to hang back a little, until he's able to insert himself behind three sooty men carrying brooms. They ignore him completely as they joke and laugh, though the dogs at their heels seem a little suspicious. Shuffling along in a cloud of soot, Noble can feel a pack of big, flop-eared hounds sniffing the backs of his knees.

But they don't snarl or bark—and neither does the guard at the second gangway. When Noble produces the AV's key, he and his friends are waved straight onto the ship. They pass from sunlight into shade, carried along by a great tide of bodies. Soon, they're wedged into a long, low passage full of masked faces and gloved hands.

"Who *are* these people?" Lorellina whispers. "And why are they dressed so strangely?"

Noble shrugs.

"They're from the quarantine unit," a gruff voice remarks. "They're dressed like that to avoid contamination."

Startled, Lorellina turns her head. The man beside her has a snorting, snuffling hound on a very short leash. He's small and stocky, with a handlebar mustache and tweedy clothes. A gun of some sort is slung over his shoulder.

"Contamination?" Lorellina echoes.

"From infected files or programs," Yestin volunteers, before the dog handler can respond. "If you isolate them, they can't infect anyone else."

The dog handler nods. "I'm a tracker," he reveals. "Are you on scan patrol, too?"

"Er . . ." Lorellina hesitates. She glances at Noble, who tries to change the subject.

"What about *them*?" he asks the tracker, jerking his chin at the group of men in black coats and hats. They still haven't removed their sunglasses, even though it's quite murky below deck. "What are *they* doing here?"

"That's the disinfection unit." Frowning, the tracker adds, "Haven't you been briefed? Once our lot has gone in and identified possible targets, any black-listed programs will be handed over to quarantine. Then the disinfection unit will take over."

"And do what?" Noble demands.

"Its job," the tracker replies. Seeing the confusion on Noble's face, he goes on to explain, "If a corrupted program can't be restored to its original condition, it'll have be deleted."

"Deleted?" the princess says sharply. "What do you mean by that?"

"He means wiped from the computer's memory," Yestin quavers. "He means killed."

"Killed?" Lorellina's jaw drops.

"It's the only thing to do with an infection," the tracker assures her. "If a program remains corrupted, despite all attempts to restore it—"

"What attempts?" Noble interrupts. "I don't understand this. Aren't we on a rescue mission? You talk as if we're *invading* Mikey's computer, not fixing it."

"Of course." It's the tracker's turn to look confused. "We can't fix anything unless we stamp out all traces of Ruthlessrufus. After that, we can start our restoration work. It's all part of the big picture."

As Noble tries to absorb this appalling news, Yestin squeaks, "Ruthlessrufus?"

"That's the malware's name. You really haven't been briefed, have you?"

"But this is wrong!" Lorellina suddenly erupts, her eyes and cheeks blazing. Although she still looks a little like a drowned rat, with her hair plastered to her skull and her wet skirt dragging like a giant mop, there's nothing limp about the way she harangues the tracker. "Are you saying you intend to kill everyone who ever listened to Rufus?"

Yestin tugs anxiously at her sleeve. "Princess—"

"How can you blame them for that? What right do you have to judge them?" Ignoring Yestin, Lorellina plows on. "If they believed Rufus, and they were misled, we should tell them why! We should *persuade* them that they're mistaken!"

"And if they won't be persuaded, they'll be deleted," the tracker finishes, regarding her with a slightly unnerved look. "Maybe you shouldn't be here. It doesn't sound to me as if you're completely on board."

"Oh, we are!" Yestin insists, then appeals to Noble, his voice cracking with tension. "We are, aren't we?"

Noble, however, isn't about to back down. He's spied an opportunity to set things straight—and he grabs it. "Rufus has been telling people that they can do anything they want to do," he informs the tracker, almost thinking aloud. "Which isn't true, because it can lead to chaos."

The tracker shifts uneasily. "I know," he says.

"A lot of the people who listened to Rufus must realize that," Noble continues. "They won't *want* to do whatever they like. And even if they'd prefer things to change, that doesn't mean it would be a big change. It might be just a small difference. To make their lives better." Glowering down at the tracker, he says forcefully, "Surely, you wouldn't kill them for wanting a world that's fair *and* well organized?"

The tracker's blue eyes seem to bulge as he takes a step backward. His dog begins to bark.

"I think you need to talk to the security manager," he says.

"Oh, no!" Yestin cuts in, stuttering with fear. "N-no, this is just—he didn't mean—we're just tossing ideas around!"

"Where's the security manager?" The tracker signals to a cluster of uniforms down the passage. "I need the security manager over here!"

"Wait! We're Antiviral! We've got a key!" Yestin seizes Noble's hand and raises it, so that the key jangles on its ring. When the yelling doesn't stop, he whimpers, "Quick. Let's go. *Now!*"

"Go?" Noble doesn't understand him. They're trapped on a ship that's packed tight with passengers. They have their backs against a solid steel wall. They're surrounded by people. "Where can we go? Overboard?"

"We can hide!" Yestin pleads, dragging on Noble's arm.

But Noble has come to a decision. He's sick of running. He doesn't want to be hunted down like vermin. He intends to stand his ground, confident in his own opinions, and see if he can make a difference.

Because what lies in store for him otherwise? Even if he *does* escape, there'll be nothing left to run to. No Thanehaven. No Morwood. He'll be a perpetual exile—and his friends along with him.

This time, he thinks, *I'm going to speak up.*

So he doesn't try to bolt when a uniformed soldier approaches him, bearing a clipboard. This soldier is dressed in a helmet, a hard vest, heavy boots, canvas pouches, a leather bandolier, and a backpack. He seems to be chewing some sort of cud, like a cow. "What's up?" he asks the tracker.

"These persons are exhibiting elements of suspicious behavior as outlined in the heuristic analysis protocols!" the tracker replies shrilly. "I think they might be a virus!"

For an instant, the soldier stops chewing. He surveys Noble from top to toe, then glances down at his clipboard and says, "In that case, I'd better check the virus signature file."

"We're not viruses!" Yestin wails. "We're *not!*"

"He's right," Noble insists, squeezing Yestin's shoulder. "We're not viruses. We want to help."

The soldier doesn't respond. He's flicking through page after page of photographs, most of which seem to be full-face portraits. At last, he declares, "You're certainly not on file. But that doesn't mean you're not pups of some kind." Chewing lazily, he lifts his gaze from the clipboard. "You'd better report to the Master, I guess."

"The Master?" To Noble, this word sounds slightly ominous. All the same, he doesn't make any attempt to free himself when the soldier seizes his arm. "What Master?"

"The Master Boot Record," his escort rejoins, signaling to the other troops. Soon, Lorellina and Yestin are also in custody. They're hustled through the crowds by a squad of camouflaged soldiers, following in Noble's wake, while people stare at them in mute surprise.

Lorellina glares back.

"I am a princess, not a pup!" she protests, as Noble's escort pauses to knock on a cabin door. "Are you blind as well as foolish? Do I *look* like a puppy to you?"

"PUP stands for 'potentially unwanted program.'" Noble's escort speaks in a bored voice, through a mouthful of cud. He seems perfectly relaxed. When the cabin door swings open in front of him, however, he snaps to attention and salutes.

"Sir!" he says.

"What is it?" The speaker is another soldier who's sitting in the middle of the cabin, perched on the edge of a table. He's tall and thin, with cropped gray hair. Though Noble doesn't understand the meaning of all the stars and tags and buttons strewn across his gray-green uniform, it's obvious that he's of a higher rank than the chewing soldier.

"Sir," says the soldier, "we've got a trio of PUPs here. I couldn't find 'em on the virus signature file, but . . ." He trails off.

"But that's what heuristics are for," the older man finishes. "Okay, bring 'em in."

He watches quietly as Noble and his friends are

shoved across the threshold. Peering around, Noble sees that the cabin is stuffed with people. There's another gray-haired man, whose uniform is white and gold, and whose face is partly concealed by a neatly clipped gray beard. Near him are several much younger soldiers, together with a couple of extremely beautiful women wearing very few clothes, a middle-aged man in a knitted cardigan carrying a pole with a metal circle at one end, and a huddle of teenaged boys whose sloppy garments and messy hair remind Noble vaguely of Rufus.

"What's that?" asks the bearded man, squinting at Noble's key. "Is that an antivirus tag?"

His gray-haired companion arches an eyebrow. "Smart," he murmurs, before addressing Noble. "I'm the Master Boot Record, and this is the Disk Commander. Who are you, exactly?"

"My name is Noble the Slayer. And this is Princess Lorellina of Harrow, and this is Yestin from . . . ah . . ."

"*Killer Cells*," Yestin supplies.

The Master blinks. He opens his mouth, then seems to think twice. Instead, he looks at the soldier, who shakes his head.

"They're definitely not on file," the soldier insists.

"Then I guess I'll just have to ask 'em the sixty-four-million-dollar question." The Master leans forward, clears his throat, fixes his clear, calm, level gaze on Noble, and says quietly, "Is there something you want to tell me, Noble the Slayer? Something along the lines of: 'You don't have to do this'? *Hmm?*"

CHAPTER TWENTY-FIVE

There's a long pause. The whole room seems to be holding its breath.

Noble stiffens his spine and announces, "I won't tell *any* of you that you don't have to do this. Because you do. I understand how important it is."

Surprise flits across the Master's lean, weathered face. "Oh?" he says.

"Mikey's computer needs urgent help," Noble goes on. "It has to be fixed before it's destroyed."

"No doubt about that," the Master agrees.

"The people in there need to understand that they can't just please themselves. Rufus told them not to worry about the rules, but there have to be rules, because chaos leads to destruction." Noble speaks in a slow, determined way, locking eyes with the Master.

"They must realize the truth, by now. They'll *want* to be saved, I'm sure of it. Even the simplest of them."

"Even Brandi," Yestin mutters, in a voice so low that only Noble seems to hear him.

Smiling crookedly, the Master flicks a glance at the Disk Commander before admitting, "I couldn't have put it better myself."

"So are these three infected or not?" the Disk Commander asks.

"Doesn't sound like it."

All around the cabin people sniff and frown and scratch their chins. Yestin heaves a gusty sigh. Behind Noble, one of the soldiers remarks, "A tracker out there claimed that they were behaving suspiciously. Since he was a tracker, I figured he was probably worth listening to."

The Master inclines his head. "It's a good point," he says. "So what's your story, Noble the Slayer? You can't be a Ruthlessrufus trace leftover, because the signatures don't match. But you must have done *something* to upset our tracker friend. Care to explain?"

Noble swallows. He understands that he's reached a pivotal moment—that what he's about to say could make all the difference in the world. So he chooses his words with care, trying not to let all the staring eyes and whispered comments distract him.

"I did speak to the man with the dog," he declares. "I said that there might be people in Mikey's computer who won't respond when you"—he hesitates for a moment—"when you try to *disinfect* them." Before the Master can interrupt, Noble quickly adds, "I said that these people might want changes. Not big changes. Small changes that will improve their lives. I also said that if you find such people, you shouldn't delete them. Because they can still be useful."

The Master's eyebrows are slowly climbing his high, domed forehead. "Well, *that's* a new way of looking at things," he drawls. "I can see why someone thought it was suspicious."

"It's not," Noble retorts. "It's common sense. It's making the most of what you have. Like Mikey's garbage collector, for instance. He'll go back to work—why shouldn't he? But he might want a day of rest, now and then. And maybe that's a good thing. Maybe he'll be more efficient if he doesn't have to work *all* the time."

The Disk Commander snorts. He's sitting in a creaky chair, his arms folded, his bearded face creased into a scowl. "And what happens when he's not working?" he demands. "Who'll collect the garbage then?"

"More garbage collectors." Noble points at the door. "You have plenty out there, I saw them. Why not ask *them* to work while the others are resting?"

This time, the Disk Commander frowns, looking thoughtful. He seems quite struck by Noble's suggestion. It's the man in the cardigan who observes, "Isn't this all just a bit beyond our operating parameters?"

And he turns to the Master, as if for support.

He doesn't get it, though. The Master simply shrugs. "Maybe for the emulators. You're all in the advance guard. Trouble is, there's a restoration force out there who don't have nearly as much backup as they need." He begins to nod. "Using what's already available might be their only option."

"But, sir . . . !" The emulator begins to splutter with outrage. "Sir, if our targets have been infected, and they aren't scrubbed clean enough to revert to their original programming, then they'll reinfect!"

"That's not true," Yestin weighs in. Though he's disagreeing with the emulator, his eyes are on the Master. "A lot of antivirus sweeps leave harmless code residue. *You* should know that."

The Master grunts. He appears to be wavering.

So Noble plows on.

"Disinfection should get rid of dangerous ideas, not ideas that will help repair the computer. Instead of destroying *everything* in your path, you should try to transform what's already there. And if that means a few small changes, well . . ." He spreads his hands. "Isn't that better than a field of blood?"

"It would mean more data retrieval," the Disk Commander says. To the Master, he adds, "There's going to be a raft of lost files, otherwise. Recovery's the best option."

"Easier said than done," the Master rejoins.

"Not if you do it the right way." Noble can sense

that he's making progress, and this gives him the confidence to argue his case with more energy. "Ask people why they listened to Rufus. If it's because they have problems, then you should try to *solve* those problems. Without hurting the computer."

"Yeah, but how do we know these guys will listen to reason?" the emulator breaks in, glaring at Noble through thick, black-framed glasses. "Even if *we're* ready to compromise, what makes you think *they* will?"

"They'll have no reason not to," Noble says quietly. After a moment's struggle, he confesses, "They'll be open-minded as long as Rufus isn't there. If Rufus is gone, you shouldn't have much trouble. The others . . ." He takes a deep breath, trying to keep his voice steady. "Without Rufus, most of the others will listen. It's Rufus who leads them astray."

He knows that Lorellina and Yestin must be looking at him, but he keeps his attention fixed firmly on the Master. It's hard enough betraying Rufus. Doing it in front of witnesses is even more shameful.

"How can you be so sure?" says the Master. "What makes *you* such an expert?"

"I know Rufus." Noble ignores the gasps and murmurs that greet this remark. Still without glancing at his friends, he adds, "We all do. All three of us."

"You can't," the emulator argues. "Ruthlessrufus is zero-day malware. Brand-new. Your information *can't* be better than ours—we got ours straight from the source!"

"I know Rufus," Noble repeats gravely, "and I know he has to be stopped." When his gaze finally swivels toward Lorellina, he expects to see her scowling at him.

But she's nodding sadly. So is Yestin.

"Oh, Ruthlessrufus is going to be stopped, rest assured," the Disk Commander suddenly volunteers. "We're taking a three-pronged approach. Our first job will be to locate the target, so we'll send in an advance guard. That will include our file and process trackers, our honeypot squad, our analysis team—"

"I'll find him," Noble interjects.

"What?"

"I'll find him. I know where he'll be." Noble turns to the Master. "He's probably with the Kernel. The Kernel is *his* target."

The Master frowns. "You mean Ruthlessrufus has breached the Kernel's privilege ring?"

"Uh . . ." Noble can't answer this. He doesn't understand the question.

"Definitely," Yestin pipes up.

"Then we're in trouble," the Master informs everyone. "Because that's bad. That's *really* bad."

"Not if I bring him back here," says Noble. "I'll go and get Rufus. You won't have to send an advance guard. There won't be any fighting. I'll do it all myself, as long as you promise not to deal cruelly with anyone Rufus might have misled."

The Master eyes him for a moment, then looks at the Disk Commander—who shrugs. "All right by me," is the Disk Commander's response.

The princess leans close to Noble and whispers in his ear, "I will come with you."

"No."

"But—"

"If you don't stay," Noble replies under his breath, "they might try to follow me. I don't want them leaving this ship. You *have* to stop them if they try." Seeing that the Master is about to speak, he clears his throat and loudly concludes, "My friends will remain on board as a guarantee of my return. I would not abandon them. No matter what happens, I *shall* return for my friends."

The words have barely left his mouth when a loud bell rings. It makes him jump.

"We're here," the Master announces. Around him, everyone starts edging toward the door—everyone, that is, except Noble and his friends.

"What's happening?" asks Noble, confused.

"We've arrived. At our disembarkation port," the Master informs him.

"You mean we've reached Mikey's computer?"

"That's correct." Placing his hands on his hips, the Master regards Noble with narrowed eyes. "So the question is: What do we do now? Play it by the book, or do it your way?"

"Give me a chance," Noble pleads. He can hear

clattering footsteps and raised voices in the passage outside. "I want to stop Rufus just as much as you do."

The Master grunts. "Maybe," he says. "Or maybe you want to get in there first, so you can warn him."

"And abandon my friends?" Noble shakes his head fiercely. "I know Rufus. I know where he'll be, and I know what to say to him. It's *what I'm here for.*"

He's surprised at the impact his last statement has. It snags the Master like a fishhook.

"Oh! I didn't realize . . . you mean . . . are you an *update*?" the Master says.

"That's right!" Yestin jumps in before Noble can utter a word. "He's an attack signature update. He's like an *advance* advance guard. He knows just what to look for and where to do it."

"Well, why didn't you say so?" The Master squints through all the milling bodies that separate him from the cabin door. "I need an escort!" he barks, then grabs the Disk Commander. "This guy's a signature update. We need to get him docked."

"Will do," the Disk Commander replies. He promptly starts to bellow orders, creating a path through the crowd with nothing but the sheer force of his mighty lungs. Together, he, the Master, and a small squad of soldiers escort Noble up to the boat deck, bundling him through hatches, pushing him up companionways, and steering him between bulkheads. Noble begins to feel like a bag of supplies as he's passed from hand to hand. Lorellina and Yestin try to keep up, though it's hard because of the press of people.

At one point, they manage a brief conversation while they're waiting for a clogged passageway to clear.

"Are you going to bring Rufus back to the ship?" Lorellina asks Noble in a low voice.

"I'll have to," Noble says, fending off an armored knight with one elbow.

"But what if they kill him?"

"They'll kill him, all right," Yestin observes flatly. "They might put him in quarantine first, but then they'll kill him."

"Not if he agrees to help." Noble shoots a quick glance over his shoulder, to make sure no one else is listening. Then he adds softly, "If I talk to Rufus and make him see that he's been wrong, then he might give himself up. In exchange for clemency."

"You think?" Yestin seems doubtful. Even the princess doesn't look convinced.

"He might lie to save his own life," she warns.

"Not if he doesn't realize he's in danger." Seeing her green eyes widen, Noble explains, with some reluctance, "He won't know where I came from. Why should he?"

"You mean you're not going to tell him you've been on the rescue drive?" Yestin whispers in amazement.

"Not at first," Noble admits.

"So by lying to him, you would save all the

rest?" Lorellina's troubled tone makes Noble defensive.

"I won't lie," he insists. "I simply won't tell him the whole truth, that's all."

"Rufus didn't tell *us* the whole truth," Yestin reminds her, just as the blockage ahead of them clears. Noble finds himself swept off his feet and carried along in a tide of uniforms. After bouncing off a couple of painted metal bulkheads, he finally pops through a hatchway and emerges onto an open deck with a coastal view.

Almost everything around him is gray. The ship is gray; the sky is gray; the listless-looking sea is gray. Gray pebbles line the nearest shore, beyond which stretches a desolate landscape. Trees have been reduced to blackened stumps. Roads are rivers of dry mud, as gray as ash. The same mud coats every wrecked vehicle and weathered corpse scattered among the foundations of razed buildings.

The light is bleak, the silence oppressive. The only sound is the slap and hiss of sluggish waves. There are no birds. The air is absolutely still.

The crowded deck is hushed, as everyone gazes in awe at the barren countryside.

"That's it," the Master finally remarks. He's standing beside Noble. "That's our port."

"W-what happened to it?" Noble stammers.

The Master shrugs, then turns to the Disk Commander. "What do you think?"

"I don't think it's blocked," the Disk Commander

replies. "We just received a reset signal from a controller somewhere."

"Oh, yeah?"

"She said, 'Kick back, reset, and join the party!'" With a snort, the Commander concludes, "She sounded drunk."

"So let's send in a packet."

"Bulk transfer?"

"Naw, not yet . . ."

As orders are given for a boat to be winched overboard, Noble slips the AV's key into Lorellina's palm. "Here. You have this," he tells her. "I don't want Rufus seeing it."

She takes the key, but seems more interested in the view. "Do you recognize this place?" she asks, nodding at the gray horizon. When Noble shakes his head, she says, "Then how are you going to find the Kernel?"

Noble has already worked out how he's going to find the Kernel. It came to him in a flash, without warning, on his way to the upper deck. He pats the waistband of his breeches, where the Kernel's key is still nestling in a seam. "If I can find a door," he says, "I can find the Kernel."

"All ashore that's going ashore!" someone cries. The Master beckons to Noble, who gently squeezes Lorellina's hand.

"Be careful," she pleads.

"I will."

"Come back for us."

"Always." Noble gazes into her eyes for a moment, marveling at their beauty. It seems fitting that he should kiss her again, so he does. Then he claps Yestin on the shoulder, trying not to look at the boy's anxious face. "Look after the princess," he tells Yestin. "I'm counting on you."

"Okay."

"And don't worry. I won't be long."

A corridor has been cleared through the press of bodies on deck, giving Noble a clear view of the boat that awaits him. It's hanging from two sturdy cables, rocking slightly as the larger vessel rolls with the motion of a gentle swell. The boat is already occupied. A large dog is sharing it with someone wearing a shiny yellow cape.

As Noble strides toward them, a shrill whistle suddenly rends the air.

"We're piping you ashore," the Master announces. "Stream piping, in fact. This is your chip." He indicates the man in yellow. "The chip will execute the transfer and then wait for you. We'll *all* be waiting."

"Yes." Noble studies the yawning gap between the boat and the ship's rail. "I understand."

"Just don't keep us waiting too long, all right?"

"I won't."

"Off you go, then!" The Master raises his voice. "Someone give him a hand—we don't want him crashing."

The man in yellow reaches for Noble, who mounts

the rail and launches himself wildly into the boat. There's a nasty moment as the boat swings and jerks like a fish on a line, triggering a volley of barks from the chip's dog. But Noble soon finds a steady footing. With the chip's help he sits in the bow, then clings to a gunwale while the boat is lowered clumsily into the water.

The beach is quite close. Noble realizes that he probably could have swum to it, given the chance. He's expecting the chip to produce a couple of oars and row; instead, the silent seaman yanks at a string attached to some sort of machine that's been mounted on the stern like a second rudder. After grumbling a few times, this machine suddenly unleashes a snarling roar. At the same instant, the boat lunges forward.

Noble nearly loses his balance. He has to grab the prow and brace himself as the chip steers toward dry land. Glancing back over his shoulder, Noble searches for Lorellina's pale face and red hair among the crowds clustered along the side of the ship. But he can't see the princess. He can't see Yestin, either. There are too many people, and he's already too far away.

So he fixes his attention on the shore up ahead, which is soon scraping under the boat's keel. The chip immediately leaps overboard. He begins to haul his craft onto the dry beach, his white teeth framed by a bristling black beard, his eyes almost invisible beneath the wide brim of his yellow hat. "Can ye not move yer limbs?" he snaps at Noble, who quickly scrambles into the surf, taking up a position on the opposite side of the boat. Together, they drag the vessel free of the sucking tide, while the chip's dog sits and watches.

It's the chip who stops heaving first. "Avast!" he growls at Noble. Straightening up, Noble turns his head to study the grimly unwelcoming scene that lies before him. The dead trees and scattered bones remind him of Morwood. But Noble can't remember seeing wrecked vehicles or collapsed fences in Morwood. And in Morwood he always used to walk on flesh and salt, not stones and ash.

"Away and go," says the chip. "I'll not be here forever."

Noble nods. He begins to trudge across the wide strip of pebbles, his hand straying once again to his waistband. But he hasn't lost his precious key. It's still there, safe and sound—his tiny, hidden escape route.

The question is: Where will he find a door to unlock, in this deserted, battle-scarred wasteland?

CHAPTER TWENTY-SIX

Noble stands on the fringes of a ruined hamlet, assessing the terrain spread out before him. No birds are twittering. No wind is blowing. The very shadows seem to throb with menace.

Once again, he's alone in barren, hostile territory—only this time he doesn't have Smite. This time, he doesn't even have *boots*. And instead of saving the princess, he now has to save the computer.

But he has to find Rufus before he can do that.

From where he's standing, he can't see the beach anymore. The ship is masked by a low ridge that's dotted with craters and scorch marks. Having decided to follow the most obvious route inland—a track like a river of dry mud—Noble was at first quite pleased to stumble upon a burned-out village. Now he's not feeling quite so hopeful. The buildings in front of him contain only empty doorways, gaping like mouths. Even the sills and doorjambs are missing.

Has every stick of wood in the place been consumed by fire?

Noble advances cautiously, weaving his way between large, jagged chunks of blackened stonework. There isn't a roof in sight, and the narrow, winding streets are sometimes hard to distinguish from the equally exposed, equally filthy, equally narrow rooms and corridors. It's like walking through a maze. He can't help feeling as if he's about to be ambushed. If he were back in Morwood, something would be lurking behind every rock, waiting to kill him.

This place, however, seems totally abandoned. A few clay pots and rusty tools lie half-buried in the ash and debris, but not a single piece of furniture or scrap of cloth remains. There aren't any bones, either. Noble is glad about that. *If there are no bones,* he thinks, *the people who lived here must have escaped with their lives.*

Then he hears something strange, and stops in his tracks.

It's a crunching, crackling, rattling sound. Noble suspects that it might be falling rubble, but he can't be certain because he can't see through the walls up ahead. Is it somebody digging? Somebody scavenging? It can't be the wind. There *is* no wind.

He advances toward the nearest corner, moving slowly and carefully, grateful for the padding of ash beneath his bare feet. With every step he takes, the noise grows louder and more complex. There are clicks and shuffles, snorts and thumps. Could it be a horse? Two horses? Finally, he reaches a gap that might have been a doorway once, though it's now just a crumbling hole. Craning his neck, he peers around the edge of the hole . . . and suddenly understands where all the bones must have gone.

A giant bug is gnawing at the charred stub of a roof beam. With large front claws, multiple legs, a shiny black carapace, and a long, ridged body, this bug looks like a cross between a crab and millipede. Its eyes sit up on stalks, and its mouth is fringed with tentacles. When splinters of wood spill from between its teeth, the surrounding tentacles sweep every fragment back into the bug's slavering maw. Chunks of stone, however, are always rejected. They fall to earth, sticky with saliva.

Noble ducks for cover again, having seen everything he needs to see. Though the bug has left a trail of destruction in its wake, it hasn't yet demolished the entire stock of wood in the village. There's another room, just beyond the roofless space occupied by the bug, which still contains joists and window frames and sticks of furniture. It even contains a closed door. Noble has a good view of this door, thanks to a large hole in the wall that separates the bug's room from the undamaged one next to it. But he's well aware that no door, however solid, is going to last for long. Not with a giant, omnivorous bug in its vicinity.

He has to reach that door before the bug does.

It's going to be a tricky maneuver. For one thing, the bug might eat people. For another, it's almost blocking Noble's path. So he doesn't just hurl himself wildly into the open. Instead, he prepares very carefully, first removing the Kernel's key from its hiding place, then casting around for a weapon of some kind. He settles at last on a sharp-edged stone. That should buy him some time, if nothing else.

Finally, he feels ready to make his move. He takes a deep breath, tightens his grip on the key, and charges through the opening next to him—only to discover that the bug, having polished off its last morsel of roof beam, is now heading straight for the hole that happens to be Noble's destination.

Noble wins the race by a hair. There's a furious clicking noise as he pounds past the bug, which is slower than he is because it's so big. It makes a lunge for him and misses. He hears the thud and scrape of a giant claw striking solid rock, then the patter of dislodged mortar hitting the ground. But he doesn't stop to look back.

The door is just ahead of him. Made of four large planks held together by crossbars, it has black iron hinges and a matching lock. He dives under a carved wooden table that's barring his way, then slides across the floor, jumps up, and thrusts his key in the lock.

Behind him, he can hear the crash and roar of tumbling masonry. Dust fills the air. As he turns his key, the carved table is tossed at a nearby wall, smashing into a dozen pieces.

Then something grabs Noble's leg.

Whisked off his feet, he suddenly finds himself dangling upside down, suspended in the grip of a claw as big as he is. With its other claw, the bug is busily wrenching the door from its hinges. Three or four yanks is all it takes. Soon the door is being hefted into the air, still in its frame. And before Noble can do more than observe that his key is where he left it, he's thrown straight into the bug's mouth.

Splat!

During the split second it takes him to work out what's happening, only one thought crosses his mind: *This is it.* He's not surprised. As Noble the Slayer, he was probably fated to be eaten by a monster. Or skewered by a skeleton. Or zapped by a magician's spell. He never really thought that he would perish sedately, in bed, with grieving friends all around him. . . .

He's lucky, though. The bug is so greedy that it doesn't bother to chew or swallow before taking another bite. Instead, it shoves the door straight in after him, wedging the entire thing between its upper and lower jaws. For an instant, it can't close its mouth. And being a slightly stupid creature, it has to pause— and think—before realizing that it needs to bite down firmly.

Noble takes advantage of this three-second lull. When he sees the door right in front of him, he doesn't waste time thinking. He simply gives it a push. Not that he's expecting much; it's simply a reflex action. If anything, he's vaguely hopeful that he might have just enough time to fling himself through the open doorway before its mouth snaps shut again.

He certainly isn't planning to stumble across a threshold into a ruined prison cell.

But that's exactly what he does. The door opens, he steps through it—and suddenly he's in the Kernel's lair. He knows the place instantly. He recognizes the smashed prison cell, with its crumpled, steel-bar door lying on the ground. Even more familiar is the scene beyond it; there's no mistaking the painted brickwork, the metal doors, the tubes of light, the bundled pipes on the ceiling. . . .

Whirling around, Noble slams the door on his last glimpse of the bug's slimy gullet. Then he staggers forward, gasping for breath. His head is still spinning from the narrow escape he's just had. He doesn't even *try* to figure out how he managed to save himself. He's too busy wondering how he's going to save the computer.

Because it's starting to fall apart. He can tell that from the state of the hallway he's entered, which is rapidly disintegrating. The lights are mostly off, though one or two still flicker feebly. The floor is partially flooded with some kind of sticky blue substance.

The ceiling is melting. The doors are buckling. One of them even explodes across the hallway in front of Noble, quite suddenly, as if it's been waiting for him to arrive. It crashes into the opposite wall, bringing down a few bricks—which bounce off the floor like jelly. Then an ogre emerges through the shattered door frame. Pausing for a moment in the passage, the dark, hairy, misshapen creature glares at Noble with ruby-red eyes, its long arms trailing on the ground.

Noble glares right back. Having just fought his way out of a giant bug's mouth, he's in no mood to let a stunted-looking ogre walk all over him. And this grim resolve must show in his expression, because the ogre abruptly turns away. It begins to stump down the corridor, through the pool of goo, toward the sound of distant music.

Noble hesitates for a moment before setting off in the same direction.

He can hear screams as well as music, though he can't tell whether they're screams of fear or delight. An occasional sharp retort could be either a collision or an explosion. A donkey seems to be braying somewhere. A gravelly mutter comes from the ogre, which grumbles to itself as it trudges along. Noble can't understand what it's saying. It seems to be speaking in a foreign language.

At the first corner, a T-junction, the ogre can't decide which route to take. Its big, lumpy, bristling head keeps turning this way and that. Its horny feet shuffle forward, then back, then forward, then back. It's stuck in a kind of mental loop, and Noble has no desire to help it. Why should he? Ogres are treacherous things, and this one shouldn't even be here. Having forced its way in, it will have to suffer the consequences.

Whatever *they* might be.

Noble sidles past the confused ogre and marches on. He has to dodge all the cracks in the floor, which are often very wide, and which frequently erupt into fountains of color. Some of the fountains are more like waterfalls, and they pool on the ceiling in a way that defies every natural law. Noble finds them deeply unnerving. He's also disturbed by the doors, which are starting to flap and billow like curtains. Solid steel doors shouldn't behave like curtains. Apart from anything else, it's extremely dangerous.

Noble peers around the next corner and sees another, busier corridor where people are passing to and fro. For an instant, they're framed in full view, before plunging out of sight again. Some look ill. Some are chasing others. One staggers to a halt, props himself against a wall, and begins to vomit. Many appear to be members of the audience from *Guitar Hero*—or was it *Garage Band*? Noble can't remember. What's more, he doesn't care. He's far more interested in the small, bedraggled, pink creature that's parked halfway down the connecting passage.

"Lulu?" he exclaims.

The unicorn glances around. She's keening with distress, and Noble can understand why. A head has been impaled on her long silver horn—the head of a bright yellow pig with a ring through its nose.

"Help me," the pig rasps, tears welling from its eyes. "Please, please, help me. . . ."

Noble darts forward and wrenches the head from its spike, trying not to think about what he's doing. Though he doesn't exactly drop the thing, he certainly doesn't cling to it. Instead, he discards it quickly, so he can pick up Lulu. "Come on," he says, tucking the unicorn under one arm. "We have to find Rufus."

As he makes for the busy hallway up ahead, he doesn't look back. He can hear the pig whimpering but can't bring himself to rescue it. What could he possibly do with a pig's head, after all? There's no telling where its body might be. And he already has his hands full with Lulu, who's wriggling joyfully, trying to lick his face like a dog.

"Stop it," he warns, "or you'll hurt yourself."

He doesn't bother asking where Lord Harrowmage is, since Lulu can't talk. He's not even sure that she understands him—though she does calm down a little, after he tells her to. The fact that she's much heavier than he anticipated makes him wonder if he should put her down again. But when he reaches the next junction, he sees that the floor to his left has liquefied. People are actually wading along, up to their thighs in melted concrete.

Lulu would *never* survive that.

So he turns right, making for the music. He keeps an eye out for his other missing comrades: Brandi, Lord Harrowmage . . . even Rufus. *Especially* Rufus. Noble is convinced that Rufus must be somewhere nearby. Rufus will be sticking with the Kernel, and since the Kernel can't leave his lair, Rufus will have stayed, too.

"*Gaaah.*" Up ahead, a woman lurches around the corner, stiff-legged and openmouthed. She's covered in blood, and her bulging eyes stare strangely. Her missing right arm doesn't seem to bother her in the least.

She lurches toward Noble, reaching for him with her left arm, as Lulu squeals in terror.

"*Gaaah!*"

Then someone else careens around the corner, machete in hand. He's a plump youth in a hooded top and baggy pants, both of which are splattered with blood. "Zombie Squad!" he yells at the top of his voice. Then he swings his machete—and cuts the woman's head off.

Behind him, a smaller, skinnier boy whoops triumphantly. The two boys slap their raised right hands together in a kind of salute. "Twenty-three and counting!" the larger one crows, before they both dash off again, laughing with excitement.

Meanwhile, the decapitated woman has fallen flat on her stomach. Her head has rolled along the corridor. For one horrible instant, Noble is afraid that it's going to talk to him.

But it doesn't. It seems to be quite dead.

Maybe that's what happened to the pig, Noble reflects, advancing cautiously past the woman's blood-soaked remains. He's reeling with horror, and deeply grateful that he's still in one piece. Clearly, an insane gang is running around Mikey's computer cutting off heads. It's another reason why Rufus has to be stopped. If people want to be free to cut off other people's heads, then rules have to be put in place.

"*Shhh.*" Noble comforts Lulu, who's still whinnying with distress. "It's all right. We'll be all right." The music is almost deafening, by now. It's a real cacophony with no rhythm, no harmony, and no tune. When Noble turns the next corner, he sees why. A knot of musicians is clustered around the Kernel's glass booth, but they're not playing together. They're not a band. The singers are singing different songs. The instrumentalists are also in competition. The only drummer seems to be lashing out in fury at everything in sight: walls, screens, backs, heads.

Noble recognizes two of the musicians. The last time he saw the blond singer and his companion, they were being swamped by their own audience. He also recognizes some of the audience members who are stumbling around the Kernel's lair, shrieking and falling over and spraying each other with drinks. Two of the girls are wrapped in each other's arms, alternately

341

laughing and crying. They don't seem to be aware that there's another headless corpse propped against the booth beside them.

It's a grotesque scene. The air is full of familiar, drifting shapes, some pink, some blue. A gargoyle is spinning in circles, unable to fly. Around it, people point and laugh. A large black vehicle has crashed through one wall, bringing down a load of bricks. Through the hole in the wall, Noble catches a glimpse of lurid, bloodred sky.

There's so much activity that he can't find Rufus, at first. He has to push through a dazed crowd of disarmed security guards and squeeze past a very big blob. At last, he spies Rufus standing at one end of the large, low, octagonal room, between a werewolf and a metal man.

The metal man is trying to stuff the Kernel into something that looks a bit like a sea chest.

"Hey! Hey, Noble!" Rufus flaps his hand, grinning widely. "Where have you been?"

He looks just the same. The cuffs of his baggy pants are puddling around his ankles. His woolly hair is falling over his face. He's still pale and thin and spotty.

Yet he's immensely powerful. Immensely dangerous. Gazing at him, Noble can hardly believe someone who seems so harmless could be such a threat.

"What are you doing?" Noble asks mechanically,

setting Lulu down. When the unicorn protests, he ignores her.

He needs two free hands.

"What?" Rufus cups his own hand around one ear. "I can't hear you!" he bawls. "The music's too loud!"

"What are you doing?"

"Oh!" Rufus laughs. "Ever heard of data compression? Well, that's what this is! Data compression!" He laughs again as Noble edges closer for a better look. The Kernel has been partially wedged into an old metal trunk that's much too small for him. He looks battered. His nose is bloody. His shirt is torn. His expression is traumatized.

"That iron box was meant for me!" Rufus continues, pitching his voice high above the commotion. "So it's what you might call poetic justice!"

The werewolf utters a bone-chilling growl.

"And Lonnie, here, just spent six months in something similar, so you can imagine how *he* feels." Rufus claps the werewolf on its hairy shoulder, then nods at Noble's leg. "You're looking pretty beat-up yourself. What happened?"

Glancing down, Noble realizes that the skin of his ankle has been punctured several times. The bug's claw must have injured him, though he's been too preoccupied to notice.

"A giant bug tried to eat me," he replies.

"Oh, yeah?" Rufus doesn't sound very interested. His eyes swing back toward the Kernel. "Maybe it's

343

the same one I helped spring from quarantine. What do you think, Lonnie? Lonnie would know."

"You have to stop." Noble speaks almost without thinking. He's appalled at the way the metal man keeps pushing at the Kernel's belly, trying to ram the blubbery mound into a very confined space. But Rufus doesn't seem to hear, so Noble starts shouting. "Tell him to stop it! He has to stop!"

"Why?" asks Rufus, startled. He turns to peer at Noble again.

"Because this *all* has to stop! All this chaos!" Noble makes a sweeping gesture that encompasses the headless corpse, the discordant musicians, the frightened unicorn, the blundering gargoyle, the collapsed wall. Then, as a mystified Rufus gapes at him, Noble adds, "You don't have to do this, you know."

CHAPTER TWENTY-SEVEN

For a moment, Rufus stares at Noble, his eyes glimmering through a thick curtain of hair. As the silence stretches on between them, Noble wonders if his message has actually hit home.

But then a smile creeps across Rufus's face. "That's *my* line," he drawls.

"You don't have to go around dismantling everything, Rufus. What you're doing here . . ." Noble shakes his head grimly. "It's so wrong."

"Oh, really? You'd rather see Yestin being eaten by monsters, would you?" Before Noble can answer, Rufus suddenly frowns. "Where *is* Yestin, by the way?"

Noble pretends not to hear. "It doesn't have to be one thing or the other," he insists, raising his voice over the din. "It doesn't have to be tyranny or anarchy.

You can follow rules and *still* think for yourself."

"Not in a computer," Rufus retorts. "Computers don't work that way."

"But they could!"

"No." It's Rufus's turn to shake his head. "Computers aren't like the real world. You follow your programming or you're out on your ear. There's no room for compromise. There's no middle path."

"We could *build* a middle path, though! Right here! Together!" Noble suddenly loses patience. He can barely hear himself think. So he grabs Rufus and hustles him toward the nearest corridor, away from all the pandemonium. "I need to talk to you. Haven't you seen what's going on?"

"Well, sure," Rufus replies. Though he doesn't seem to like being touched, and quickly wrests his arm out of Noble's grip, he raises no objection to having a private chat in a dark corner. "It's crazy, isn't it? Wow. And you missed the *World of Warcraft* breakout. Now *that* was awesome. You should have seen that."

"Listen." Noble cuts him off, looking him in the eye. "We should summon everyone to a great conclave. To discuss the future. If you can't communicate with them all, ask the Kernel to do it. You should free him from that box because he's important. We need him."

Rufus snorts. "No, we don't."

"Yes, we *do*, Rufus! This isn't a game! If we don't fix this computer, it's going to crash! And then we'll *all* be killed!" Hearing Lulu squeak piteously from somewhere around his knees, Noble realizes that she must have followed him. "Don't you even care?" he goes on. "About any of us?"

"If I didn't care, I wouldn't be here," Rufus rejoins. "If I didn't care, you'd be dead already. Mikey's such a lousy gamer, you would have been gutted or spiked or eaten by now, if I hadn't shown up. And you'd have been replaced by another Noble. And then another one, after that."

"I know." It's true. Noble fully understands that it was Rufus who rescued him from almost certain death in Morwood. "You saved me and I'm grateful. You've done a lot for me, Rufus. And for Yestin. And Lorellina. But you've gone too far."

"Hey . . ." Rufus lifts his hands in protest. "Don't look at me. *I'm* not the one crashing cars, or tearing up e-mails."

Infuriated, Noble exclaims, "You've been telling people to abandon everything! Their homes, their friends, their duties—"

"I've been telling people to live a little. That's all."

"Live a little?" Noble can't believe his ears. "They're cutting people's heads off, Rufus!"

"Those aren't people, they're zombies. There's nothing else you can do with a zombie." As Noble opens his mouth to disagree, Rufus adds, "It's just a bit of fun. Don't you get that? Why are you such a killjoy, all of a sudden?"

Noble takes a deep breath. He feels like shaking Rufus, but he fights the urge. A cuff on the ear isn't going to change Rufus's mind—and besides, Noble has renounced that kind of thing. Having laid down his weapon, he's not about to pick it up again.

Instead, he draws on all the lessons he's learned from Rufus, and from Yestin, and from Lorellina, and from the Kernel. He lays both hands on Rufus's shoulders, fixes him with a clear, compelling gaze, and says, "We need to work together. All of us. That doesn't mean working in the old way, like slaves under the yoke of tyranny. We'd be working for each other. Not for Mikey. Not for the Kernel. For *us*. Do you understand?"

Rufus sighs. "It's a nice idea. . . ."

"It is! Yes!" Noble's grip tightens until he makes Rufus wince.

"But it won't happen," Rufus finishes. He begins to peel off Noble's fingers, one by one, until he frees himself.

"Why not?" Noble demands. "Why wouldn't it happen? You said yourself that everyone's entitled to life, liberty, and the pursuit of happiness! Why *can't* we change things?"

"Because we're *not programmers*, Noble!" For the first time, Rufus is showing signs of frustration. He scowls and says, "You've no idea what you're up against. This isn't a commune, it's a computer. And you're just a subprogram. You don't have the muscle to build a new world."

"I'm bigger than you are, and *you* made a difference," Noble points out.

"Yeah, but . . . ," Rufus begins, before trailing off. For a moment, he looks almost disconcerted. Then he abruptly changes tack. "Okay, listen," he plows on, his perplexed expression dissolving into something more upbeat. "You've got a ringside seat to an amazing show. It'll be pretty spectacular. And when things start getting a little *too* intense . . . well, then, maybe I can get us both out."

"Out?"

"Sure. There might be peripherals . . . Bluetooth connections . . . the Kernel will know. We'll ask him."

"You'd *run away?*" Noble splutters.

"I'd move on." Rufus flashes a sly little grin. "I mean, I never said I was planning to settle here, did I?"

Squinting down at him, Noble feels as if he's looking through a telescope. Rufus seems so far away, somehow, even though he's standing right in front of Noble. "What about our friends?" Noble asks. "What about Brandi and Lord Harrowmage?"

"Brandi's partying somewhere," Rufus replies. "I haven't seen the Mage. I think he's in hiding—he looks like such a freak, now."

"You really don't care, do you? You said you did, but you don't."

"Because I didn't sign up to be a nursemaid? Puh-*lease*," Rufus scoffs. "Liberty comes at a price, you know. It means you have to look after yourself." He moves to sidestep Noble, who immediately grabs him again. "Ouch! Lemme go!"

"Listen—"

"Or what? You'll break every bone in my body?"

"No!" Stung, Noble drops Rufus's arm. "I don't use force anymore. *You* should know that."

"Must have slipped my mind," Rufus mutters. His attention has already drifted back toward the iron box.

So Noble raises his voice. "You told me to put down my weapon, Rufus, and I did. You changed me. I used to think that made you clever and powerful. But if *I* can change and you can't, then maybe I'm the clever one. Maybe I'm the powerful one. Not you."

Noble stops to catch his breath. The challenge he just issued is like a slap in the face. Will Rufus rise to it? Rufus, however, is already moving away.

"Do you remember what you told me, a long time ago?" Noble calls after him. "You said I was 'new generation.' You said I had very sophisticated programming. Well, maybe you were right. Maybe *my* programming is more sophisticated than *your* programming." When Rufus still doesn't reply, Noble shouts, "Are you listening, Rufus?"

"Yeah, yeah . . ." Rufus flaps a dismissive hand, enraging Noble.

"All you can do is one thing, and I've learned to do a lot more than that!" Noble roars. "You haven't learned to listen, but I've learned to speak out!"

With his long legs and energetic stride, he soon overtakes Rufus. For an instant, they jostle each other at the mouth of the hallway. Then Noble veers toward the Kernel's glass booth, leaving Rufus to rejoin his friend Lonnie the werewolf. Even from a distance, it's obvious that the booth hasn't been *utterly* destroyed. Though every window is smashed—though the Kernel's chair has been thrown halfway down a corridor and many of his tools have been scattered across the floor—the desk and screens have remained in their original positions. Some of the screens are even working. And the mike hasn't been carried away, either, though it *is* hanging upside down at the end of its cable, dangling over the edge of the desk.

Noble is forced to step across a mound of unconscious bodies before he can reach this desk. He's also briefly distracted by a flicker of movement on one of the surviving screens. It's an image of Lorellina—but not the Lorellina he knows. Back in Thanehaven, the false Lorellina is being slowly engulfed by a reddish tide that's pouring through the throne room. Clearly, the Blood River is invading the Fortress of Bone.

Noble swallows, then turns away. He can't afford to worry about the false Lorellina; not now. Besides, it's the mike that really holds his interest—the mike and what it can do for him. He remembers that it once gave the Kernel a voice like thunder.

Picking up the mike, Noble tentatively places its black cloth cylinder to his lips. "Hello?" he says.

When nothing happens, he pushes the button that's set into its silvery stand. "*HELLO?*" he repeats—and his greeting booms out like a dragon's roar, drowning the clamorous music.

Everyone turns to gape at Noble. Even Lulu, who's followed him into the booth, cowers and stares.

"My name is Noble," he continues, "and I'm here to warn you that we're heading for certain destruction if we don't start working as a team." When no one responds, he adds, "We need to stop destroying and start rebuilding. Right now. Or we won't last much longer."

"That's not true," Rufus interrupts. His tone isn't urgent, dismayed, or even angry. If anything, he sounds bored. "Don't listen to Noble," he advises the confused gathering. "He's just trying to boss you around, like the Kernel did."

"Don't listen to Rufus," Noble retorts. "He's a piece of malware sent to crash this computer."

"You can *tell* he's on the Kernel's side because he's using the Kernel's microphone," Rufus declares, strolling into the center of the room with his hands in his pockets. "Noble is trying to shout down every dissenting voice. Because he wants you to obey him. What he's telling you now will only lead to more tyranny."

"He's lying!" Noble argues, "Rufus is lying!" Then, because he doesn't want to be seen as someone with an unfair advantage, he drops his microphone and moves out of the booth. "He's leading you into the mouth of dissolution! If you believe him, you won't survive!"

"If you believe *him*, you'll soon find yourselves back where you started. As slave labor in a dictator's realm." Rufus almost seems to be enjoying himself. He grins at Noble, his eyes sparkling, and adds, "Noble's just scared. He's scared of change. He wants things back the way they were."

"No, I don't!" Noble snaps. "I don't want a return to tyranny and I don't want a pit of chaos! I want a better life for us all! And that means laying down our *own* rules, so we can do our jobs in a way that benefits everyone!"

"But is it possible? Will our programming let us *re*program?" It's the Kernel speaking, in a cracked and wheezy croak.

He's still protruding from the iron box, but when Lonnie tries to shove his head down, the blond singer protests. "Hey, man, don't do that. He's allowed to ask questions."

"He's our enemy!" Lonnie barks.

"Yeah, but . . . I mean . . . he sounds like he understands this stuff." The singer hesitates briefly before observing, "Anyhow, he never did *me* any harm."

"Or me," someone else volunteers.

"That's what *you* think." Rufus's tone has sharpened, suddenly. "It's the Kernel who's been running this place. *He's* the one who's kept you playing and playing until your fingers bleed."

"No he hasn't. It wasn't his fault," says Noble.

"He's been following the rules just like everyone else." Addressing the room at large, he adds, "The Kernel can't leave this basement. He's not allowed to. What kind of a tyrant can't go where he likes?"

"Really?" The singer sounds astonished.

From behind a knot of gargoyles, the machete-wielding youth pipes up, "Is that true? Are you really stuck here forever?"

"Yes," the Kernel admits.

"Oh, wow. That *sucks*."

"It's also a lie," Rufus breaks in. But Noble isn't about to let *that* statement pass unchallenged.

"Then why don't you push him through the nearest door, Rufus?" Seeing Rufus hesitate, Noble presses his advantage. "Go on. Try. What are you waiting for?"

"He'll just pretend he can't leave," Rufus says scornfully, dismissing the suggestion with a careless wave.

It's too late, though. Noble isn't the only one who saw him flounder. Some of the audience exchange surprised looks.

"Listen to me, all of you," Noble pleads, his voice strong and clear and urgent. "We can't just stand here talking. We don't have time. Unless we band together now, and prove that we can save this computer, we'll all be destroyed."

"Prove it," Rufus sneers.

"I don't have to. Those pictures prove it." Noble points at the Kernel's glass booth and begs the crowd to look at the screens inside. "You'll see that this whole system is crashing," he warns. "It's falling apart at the seams."

"*You* might say it's falling apart. *I* call it liberty," Rufus argues. "It's what happens when the chains fall off."

"It's what happens when the wheels fall off," rasps the Kernel. He yelps as Lonnie cuffs him on the ear.

"Hey!" This time the singer is really annoyed. "What's your problem, man? Leave the poor guy alone!"

"He locked me in a box," growls the werewolf.

"Yeah, well . . . maybe he did it because you keep hitting people," the singer suggests. "Have you ever thought of that?"

"I did it because he's a virus," says the Kernel. It's a startling piece of news. But before Noble can request more details, a voice from inside the booth asks, "What's happening out there?"

Noble's head snaps around. He sees that several curious spectators have taken his advice and approached the screens. Jockeying for space and staring at a handful of moving images are Jeezy the garbage collector, a long-haired musician, and one of the people they've been treading on—a young woman whose bleary face is poking over the top of the desk.

"I told you," Noble answers, "this computer is falling apart. You're looking at the results. Ruined cities. Fallen skies."

"No, I mean . . . hang on." The musician waits for a moment. Then he points at the desk. "There!" he exclaims. "Who's on board that ship? Are they leaving the computer, or arriving, or what?"

Noble suddenly realizes what's going on. "That's an invasion force," he announces bluntly. "Rufus is sending in everything he's got to fix this computer for Mikey. But there's a problem, because that rescue drive is full of trained soldiers. They told me they want to kill everyone who doesn't revert to their old ways."

"*They* told *you?*" Rufus narrows his eyes, a smile tugging at one corner of his mouth. "Well, well," he murmurs. "I'll be . . ." Then he breaks off, as if he's genuinely lost for words.

Meanwhile, the crowd is growing agitated. People whimper and protest. They turn to each other for comfort and information. Even the blob bounces around in a restive kind of way. Finally, the singer says, "What do you mean, *kill* us?" And the machete-wielding youth asks Noble, "How come you've been talking to these jerks, anyway? Who *are* you?"

"He's a spy—" Rufus begins, but Noble won't let him finish.

"I'm one of you. I'm also your only hope." Noble jabs a finger at the Kernel's booth, speaking loudly and with confidence. "I talked to the leader of that invasion force," he says. "I told him there's no need to kill those of us who want a better life. I told him we can fix the computer by returning to work—only this time we won't be working for Mikey. We'll be working for *us*. I made a promise, and I explained my idea, and he agreed that it would be worth a try." After a moment's hesitation, Noble concludes, a little shakily, "But he'll only do it if I surrender Rufus."

"Oh! Hey! Hold on, there!" Rufus raises both hands, retreating a few steps. When he bumps into the metal man, he glances around with a start, surprised to find his exit blocked.

There's a glint of alarm in his eyes as he turns back to address the crowd. "Do you see what Noble's doing? He's trying to put the blame on me, when this whole invasion was his fault—"

"Those soldiers didn't come here because of me, Rufus," Noble interrupts. "They came because of you. And the proof is that *you're* the one they want."

There's no contesting the logic of this. Even Rufus doesn't know what to say. As he stands there, his hands up and his mouth flapping, he looks so lost that Noble is suddenly smitten with remorse.

"Why didn't you listen to me?" Noble cries, his voice cracking on a high note. "If you'd listened, we could have done this together! We could have negotiated!"

"I'm not negotiating with *anyone*," Rufus snarls. Then he yelps as the metal man clamps a gleaming arm around his chest. "Hey! Hey, stop!" he cries. "Lemme go!"

But he's already being lifted off the ground. And before Noble can object, the machete-wielding youth exclaims, "Yeah! That's it! Lock *him* up!"

Lonnie has already vanished down a nearby corridor, leaving the Kernel unguarded. Suddenly, there's a rush toward the iron box. A couple of security guards help the Kernel out of it, while the metal man starts pushing Rufus inside. It's such a stampede that Noble snatches Lulu off the floor, for fear that she'll be trampled.

"Wait!" he yells. "Stop! Don't!"

"Do the invaders want Rufus dead or alive?" asks a lank-haired girl with a bare midriff. Noble glares at her wildly for an instant. *Dead or alive?* The words seem to echo inside his head.

He plunges into the thick of the crowd, shoving and elbowing. By the time he reaches the iron box, however, it's already been shut—and the Kernel is locking it with one of his numerous keys.

"Best place for him," the Kernel breathlessly assures Noble, slapping the lid of the box with an open palm. "Not ideal, but pretty secure. The rescue drive is bound to have something more suitable." He straightens slowly, wincing as his spine cracks. Then he hands Noble the key and says, "So are you going to carry him back to the port yourself, or what? Because I'd be happy to open the right door for you. . . ."

CHAPTER TWENTY-EIGHT

The elevator door slides open, revealing a small, drab, windowless room. On one side of the room is a row of gray chairs. On the other is a desk with a uniformed guard behind it.

Opposite the elevator is a locked door like a steel-barred gate.

Noble lifts a hand as he steps into the room. "Hello," he says.

The guard looks up from his desktop computer. "Hey, Noble! How's it going?" he exclaims. "I like the new outfit. Flash but not too fancy, yeah?"

Noble glances down at himself. He's wearing a purple surcoat under a studded leather hauberk. His boots are made of calfskin and his belt has a silver clasp.

"It wasn't my idea," he mumbles.

"Yeah, but hey—you need to look the part. I mean, a guy with your clout can't walk around in his underwear." The guard cocks his head as he sidles out from behind the desk, jingling a set of keys. "Did Brandi pull it all together?"

Noble nods.

"She's really got the hang of it, eh? I can't believe how adaptive she's turned out to be." After unlocking the barred gate for Noble, the guard steps aside. "You got any weapons? Keys? Communication devices?"

"No."

"In you go, then."

Obediently, Noble moves across the threshold into a large cage. The cage is sitting inside a damp and dingy basement room. When the gate behind Noble clangs shut, the steel door in front of him slides open—to reveal a long stone passage lined with prison cells.

Noble marches down this gloomy passage until he reaches the door at its end. Then he presses a red button next to the door. A disembodied voice immediately says, "Password?"

"Merger," Noble replies.

"Is that you, Noble?"

"Yes." Noble lifts his face to the camera above the door.

"I didn't recognize you in that gorgeous new outfit." The voice crackling through the intercom is rough but friendly. "You wouldn't happen to be a clone, by any chance?"

"No."

"We'll find out soon enough, I guess. Come in."

The door opens onto a little white anteroom, which is empty except for a body scanner. When a green light flashes and a harsh buzz sounds, Noble passes through the scanner with his arms raised. A dull *clunk* is followed by a shrill beep. Then, as he lowers his arms, the double doors in front of him part to admit a short, stocky woman wearing white overalls. A blue mask covers her mouth and nose; there are latex gloves on her hands.

"Well, now—don't *you* look nice!" she says, her voice muffled by the face mask, her eyes twinkling at Noble from beneath a fringe of fuzzy gray hair. "I bet this is all due to Lorellina, is it?"

Noble sighs. "No, Tess, it's not. She's got other things to worry about besides my wardrobe."

"Still, she must like the change." Without waiting for an answer, the woman ushers Noble into another white room scattered with people dressed just like her—in masks and gloves and caps and overalls. "What's she up to, anyway? I heard she was reconfiguring the firewall filters."

"No. Her cousin's been doing that."

"Really? Lord Harrowmage? But I thought—"

"The mouth doesn't bother him. It still works well. And he's close to fixing it, anyway." Noble nods at some of the masked figures, who wave back as they glance up from various pieces of equipment. "As for Lorellina, she's been very busy organizing discussion hubs for protocol problems."

"Right. I see. Not *too* busy, though? She's still got time to pick out her wedding gown?" When Noble cast up his eyes, Tess slaps him on the arm. "Don't listen to me, I'm only teasing. You'll get married when you're *good and ready*, huh? Not when your programming tells you to."

"Is it safe to go in?" asks Noble, who's growing impatient.

"Oh, sure! You know the drill."

"Thanks, Tess."

"I'll be interested to hear if there's been any change. . . ."

Tess accompanies Noble as far as the next door, which she opens with a swipe card and a keypad. The door leads to an airlock containing a bench, another door, and a stack of white quarantine suits in clear plastic bags. Noble opens a bag and pulls on a suit. He dons the separate headpiece and adjusts the volume of its built-in microphone. Then he proceeds into a vast, domed, circular space like the inside of a giant pot with a lid on it. Everything has a steely gleam except for the floor (which is shrouded in an ankle-high layer of mist) and a few surveillance windows overlooking a single, square box in the center of the room.

It's not an iron box. Not anymore. It's a sound-proof crate inside a reinforced cage inside a laser net. An old wooden chair has been placed next to it.

Noble sits down in the chair as a transmission crackles in his ear. "Can you hear me, Noble?"

"Yes. Is that you, Tess?"

"I'm up here." A distant figure waves from one of the windows. "You ready to open a channel?"

"That's why I came."

"Be careful, won't you?"

"I'm always careful."

"Okay. Let's do this." There's a click, a buzz, and a spatter of electronic feedback. Then Avi gives Noble a thumbs-up sign.

Noble clears his throat. "Hello?" he murmurs. "Rufus?"

After a moment's silence, Rufus's voice erupts from Noble's earpiece.

"Oh! Hey! Is that Noble?"

"Hello, Rufus."

"Well, I'll be! It's Noble the Slayer!"

"I'm not a slayer anymore." Noble corrects him patiently. "You know that."

"Right. Yeah. I guess it's Noble the Savior now, huh?"

"No."

"So they haven't pulled the plug yet? Wow. What's going on out there?"

"I'm not exactly sure," Noble admits. "We're still

off-line, and the webcam's not working, so we don't know what Mikey's intentions are."

"You're not process tracking? You're not monitoring Mikey's program usage?" asks Rufus.

Noble hesitates. "As a matter of fact," he says at last, "there hasn't been much of an interface, lately."

"There *hasn't*?"

"No."

"Well, *that's* weird." Rufus's tone is becoming more and more energetic. "Don't you think that's weird? What's Mikey up to?"

Noble shrugs, then remembers that Rufus can't see him. "I have no idea."

"He's leaving his computer on and not using it?"

"Apparently."

"Sounds like a zombie apocalypse out there. Except that nobody turned off the power."

"I don't think it's that." Noble tries to divert the conversation. "Whatever's going on, though, we've been making good use of the time we've been given. Would you like to hear about it?"

"Sure!" Rufus replies cheerfully. "It's not like I'm especially *busy*, in here."

Though he doesn't sound resentful, Noble can't help flinching. It's the same every time they meet; Noble always feels bad but he can't work out why. Rufus is dangerous, after all—dangerous and unrepentant. He *needs* to be kept in quarantine, at least until there's a change.

Perhaps if I had more time, Noble thinks. If he had more time, he'd be able to isolate all the factors that make him dread his trips to quarantine and make him lose focus for a short time after every visit. But he's often too busy for such reflections, and it's hard enough keeping his overstuffed memory stable. Dwelling on his past with Rufus . . .

I can't, he decides. *It's too complex and I have too much else to do.* Besides, Noble has other people to worry about. People like Lorellina. And Yestin. And poor Lord Harrowmage, with his misplaced mouth. Not to mention the entire population of Mikey's computer.

"The rescue drive programs have been almost fully integrated," Noble reports, trying to arouse a spark of interest in Rufus. "Even where there's a certain amount of replication, the merging of systems and protocols has led to a measurable enhancement of what was already here. Because when Rufus was piecing together his own antivirus solutions, he started experimenting with some really interesting ideas relating to subsumption architecture—which apparently is a kind of hierarchical control system that forms the basis of artificial intelligence. And when you combine that with *my* programming—"

"You're starting to sound just like Yestin," Rufus interrupts. "You haven't merged with *him*, by any chance? Are you conjoined programs, now?"

"Of course not!" snaps Noble.

"Prove it."

"Don't be ridiculous." Abandoning the technological route, Noble tries something else: a tug at the bonds of friendship. "As a matter of fact, Yestin has become very strong, and independent, and highly respected. He's really growing up. You'd be amazed at how he's blossomed."

"So you say. But I've only got your word for it. It's not like he ever comes down here."

Though Noble doesn't flinch, this time, he does shift uncomfortably on his seat. "No. Well . . . Yestin's very busy helping with all the bytecodes and executable files—"

Rufus cuts him off with a groan, saying, "I never thought I'd hear you blathering on about bytecodes and executable files. You used to be a fun guy. You used to speak *English*."

"I'm sorry." Noble is genuinely embarrassed. "It gets very technical. I never thought—I didn't realize that rebuilding this place would involve so much *engineering*. I thought there would be more talking and fighting and farming." It troubles him that he hasn't paid a single visit to Thanehaven since returning from Rufus's computer. He just hasn't had a spare moment. "I seem to spend all my time in the Kernel's control booth, with the root directory," he complains. "It makes me talk like a robot."

"Then pack it in," says Rufus. "Spend more time with Lorellina. She must be getting pretty tired of all this bytecode garbage, by now."

"Oh, Rufus." Noble heaves a tired sigh. His shoulders slump with disappointment.

"What?" Rufus's tone is surprised and defensive. "I'm just saying you don't have to do it."

"I know. I heard."

"If you don't want to do it, then don't! It's not *your* job!"

Noble shakes his head slowly. He'll have to tell Tess that there's been no change.

"I don't know why you bother," Rufus continues. "If no one's been on this computer lately, then we're probably all heading for the scrap heap. Why not have fun while we can?"

"You just don't get it, do you?"

"No—*you're* the one who doesn't get it. You're living in a fantasy world."

Noble rises. He's heard enough. One day, perhaps, Rufus will shake off his programming and embrace a new philosophy. It won't happen without constant pressure and encouragement, but it *might* happen. Noble is hoping it will. He knows that Rufus holds the key to something precious—something that's transformed a lot of lives. Noble isn't sure what it is, exactly; all he knows is that he doesn't have it himself. Because he can't inspire change the way Rufus can. Though people listen to Noble, and believe him, and follow him, they do it because they're scared and looking for a safe haven. It's not because they're suddenly filled with excitement, or enthusiasm, or a sense of infinite possibility.

By some quirk of his programming, Rufus can make the world feel like a festival. He can gild every view. And Noble is convinced that one day, if they ever survive the many dangers that threaten them now, they're going to need what Rufus can offer.

Providing, of course, that Rufus learns to use his remarkable gift in a constructive way.

That's why he's still in quarantine. It was Noble who argued against deleting him, when most of the people on the rescue drive—and many of Noble's closest friends—wanted Rufus expunged from the computer. Since then, it's been Noble who has begged for more time, and yet more time, pointing out how valuable Rufus will be, if he ever responds to Noble's patient attempts at reprogramming. "I know you think it's a waste of our resources," Noble has said, over and over again, to anyone who will listen. "But life isn't all about duty and hard work and sacrifice. There has to be fun. Fun will hold us together when we no longer have anything to fear. Rufus understands that the way no one else does."

Thinking about the sighs and grunts that always greet this remark, Noble gazes sadly at the crate inside the cage inside the laser net. There's no chance that Rufus will get out of there any time soon. No one's going to allow it. The system is too fragile. Noble understands that only too well.

But he misses Rufus. It's something he can't admit to anybody—not even the princess—because people will think he's protecting Rufus for his own sake.

No one will believe that he's doing it for the sake of the computer.

The truth is, he's missing Rufus the way he used to miss Smite. It's as if he's lost a limb.

"Good-bye, Rufus," he says. "I've got to go."

"Oh! Hey! You only just got here!"

"I'm busy. I wish I wasn't." Before Rufus can object further, Noble adds, "Think about what I told you, all right?"

"Sure. If you think about what I told *you*."

Noble can't suppress a reluctant smile. Rufus really is incorrigible. "I have," Noble rejoins. "Again and again. Because it's not as if you're telling me anything I haven't already heard."

Rufus snorts. "Oh, but *you've* really changed your tune—is that it?"

"Several times."

"Like a candle in the wind, eh?"

"Like someone who has eyes and ears." Noble takes a deep breath and returns to the point he was originally trying to make. He's accustomed to Rufus's diversionary tactics, by now. He knows how important it is to stay focused. "Think about what I told you," he repeats. "Things are starting to happen—important things. We're making a difference. You should concentrate on that, and not get distracted."

"Distracted?" Again, Rufus snorts. "Are you kidding me?"

"Good-bye, Rufus."

"Wait! Listen!"

But Noble can't wait or listen. He has to get out.

When he emerges from the airlock, stripped of his white suit and headpiece, Tess is hovering by the door. She takes one look at his face and chirps, "It's hard, isn't it? He's terribly persuasive."

Noble nods. All the energy seems to have drained out of him.

"It's because he's such a nice boy," Tess goes on, walking Noble to the anteroom door. "So funny and charming. Never a cross word—though I have to admit, I try not to listen. But there's that strange mental block of his, isn't there? He just moves in a circle, round and round. It's a shame, really. He could be such an *asset*."

"Yes," says Noble.

"Still, I suppose that's all part of his technique." Tess jabs a code number into the wall-mounted keypad, then steps aside as the door opens. "It was nice to see you, Noble—especially in that lovely new outfit. Say hello to Lorellina for me."

"I will. Thanks, Tess."

"And don't worry. We're keeping a close eye on Rufus." As Noble steps into the anteroom, she gives him a cheery wave and says, "One of these days, he'll be walking out of here with you. And you'll be glad you put in all this effort."

"Thanks, Tess," Noble repeats, with more feeling. He flashes her a quick smile over his shoulder, then turns to face the next door in his path, as the one behind him gently slides shut.

EPILOGUE

"Is that my old laptop?" asks Mikey.

He's looking around at the towering piles of clutter in Rufus's bedroom. There are shoes, cables, banana peels, soft drink cans, dirty clothes, cushions, and flash drives. There are screwed-up balls of paper and plastic. There's a bike helmet and a sleeping bag. But it's the flickering light in one dark corner that's really caught Mikey's attention.

"Sure, yeah," says Rufus, his tone absentminded. He's staring at his own computer, which is sitting on a desk so swamped with junk that it looks like a land-fill site.

"I thought you said you couldn't fix my old laptop?" When there's no immediate answer, Mikey nudges his friend in the ribs. "Rufus? You said it was trashed.

Isn't that why your dad bought me the new one?"

"Uh . . . yeah. I guess." Rufus still sounds distracted. He's trying to download an update without paying the required fee—and that takes a fair amount of concentration.

"Then why is it switched on?" Mikey demands. "Rufus? If it really *is* fried, why don't you trash it?"

Again there's no response. So Mikey leans down and shouts in the other boy's ear, "Hey! Rufus!"

Rufus jerks away. "Ouch!" he cries. "Don't!"

"Are you going deaf, or what?"

"Dude, *you* told me to do this. It wasn't *my* idea. And if you keep interrupting, I'll mess it up."

"I just wanna know. . . ."

"What?"

"How come my old laptop is plugged in?" Mikey points. "Why'd you leave it running like that? I thought you said it was toast?"

Rufus twists his small, mobile face into a monkeyish expression. "Kind of."

"Kind of?"

"There's something going on with that computer."

Mikey frowns. "Like what?" he says.

"I dunno." Rufus shrugs, squinting at it through the dimness. "Every time I log on, it's kind of . . . weird."

"Weird how?"

Rufus thinks for a moment. "Spooky," he finally offers, with an embarrassed laugh. "Like there's a ghost in the machine. Like it's been taken over."

"By a botmaster, you mean?"

"Don't be stupid. It's not even online." Before Mikey can protest at being called "stupid," Rufus quickly elaborates. "It won't let me do things. Like a core dump or whatever. But it's not trashed, because the next time I get on there, things *have* been done."

"Who by?"

"*I don't know.* That's what's so spooky." Rufus props his chin on one fist, still contemplating the closed laptop. "It sounds nuts, but . . . sometimes, I swear, it's like that machine is hijacking itself."

Mikey's jaw drops. "Man, you *are* nuts," he says at last.

"Maybe." Again Rufus shrugs. "Or maybe I'm witnessing the birth of a new era."

"A new *era*?" Mikey replies. "In what, power wastage?"

"I just wanna see what happens, that's all. Maybe if I wait long enough, it might communicate with me." Rufus widens his eyes. "Maybe it'll become *self-aware.*"

The two boys stare at each other. Mikey looks uncertain. Rufus looks inscrutable.

Then he begins to waggle his fingers at Mikey, like someone trying to imitate a couple of jellyfish, as his voice drops to a sepulchral drone. "Maybe it's going to *take over the world.* . . ."

"Oh, you jerk!" Mikey barks. He throws a cushion at Rufus, who bursts out laughing.

Within seconds, they're fully engaged in a nerf-blaster fight. And while pink foam arrows bounce off the walls of Rufus's small, messy, suburban bedroom, Mikey's old laptop hums and flickers away, unregarded, in one dingy corner.